AiA
DoN

D0198873

Sixteen

Also by Megan McCafferty

Sloppy Firsts
Second Helpings

Edited by
Megan McCafferty

SIXTEEN

Stories About That Sweet and Bitter Birthday

 THREE RIVERS PRESS · NEW YORK

Published by Three Rivers Press, New York, New York.
Member of the Crown Publishing Group, a division of Random House, Inc.www.crownpublishing.com

THREE RIVERS PRESS and the Tugboat design are registered trademarks of Random House, Inc.

Printed in the United States of America

DESIGN BY ELINA D. NUDELMAN

Library of Congress Cataloging-in-Publication Data
Sixteen : stories about that sweet and bitter birthday / edited by Megan McCafferty.—1st ed.
1. Adolescence—Fiction. 2. Maturation (Psychology)—Fiction.
3. Short stories, American. 4. Birthdays—Fiction. 5. Teenagers—Fiction. I. McCafferty, Megan.
PS648.A34S595 2004
813'.0108354—dc22   2003027919

ISBN 1-4000-5270-X

10 9 8 7 6 5 4 3 2 1

First Edition

For T.J., my best friend
(and first writing partner) at sixteen

contents

16

foreword

Megan McCafferty

Many readers have asked me why I wrote my debut novel about a sixteen-year-old girl rather than a character closer to my own age. There are a lot of answers to that question, from my obsession with books, movies, music, and TV targeted at audiences half my age, to the distinct possibility that I might have some (ahem!) unresolved issues about my high-school years.

Since I spend so much energy mining my teen years for material, I've come to realize that sixteen was *the* make-or-break age for me. It's when I first started to believe that I would one day successfully escape the social stranglehold of my high school. I had big dreams about going to a great college somewhere far, far away—culturally and intellectually if not geographically—and doing something important with my life. Maybe I would write for the *New York Times*! Maybe I would star on Broadway! I was hopeful, knowing that there was more in this world than football games, proms, pep rallies, and other trivialities that dominate adolescent consciousness. Of course, the downside to my epiphany was that I had two more years of high school to get through before my "real life" could begin. At sixteen, I still hadn't recognized that my "real life" could begin at any time.

While not every sixteen-year-old has shared my suburban New Jersey angst, fans' fervent reactions to Jessica Darling's cringe-worthy coming of age indicated that I certainly wasn't alone. So one morning, after reading an e-mail thanking me for my unflinching depiction of the so-called sweetest birthday, it hit me: *What about a book of stories about being sixteen years old?* It seemed too simple, too obvious not to have been done before. Then I started to worry. Maybe the reason this anthology didn't already exist was because turning sixteen is a big deal only for people who lack the maturity to *just get over* their high-school traumas already. Hmm.

To find out whether this was source material for a book, or fodder for a therapist, I sent out an e-mail to my fan list, asking the following question: What does being sixteen mean to you?

The inquiry clearly struck a nerve because the response was immediate and overwhelming. Within ten minutes, I had thirty-eight e-mails. Within twenty-four hours, I had just over 250. In all, I got more than 500 hilarious and heartfelt takes on what I'm now convinced is a universally tumultuous age. Younger respondents used dreamy language to describe what a magical, transformative year it would be for them. Older writers expressed the often disappointing reality. Twenty- and thirty-somethings described an inexplicable sense of nostalgia for a time that they know is more fondly *remembered* than actually lived. Together, the responses were funny, profound, and often contradictory—much like the age itself.

In their own (slightly edited) words, sixteen means you . . . *are an acceptable age to go to second base . . . don't have to lie about your age anymore when all the sketchy guys on the boardwalk come up to you and your friends . . . can go out on dates without your parents getting psycho paranoid about it . . . get into more than enough harmless trouble in backseats . . . are tempted by sex, sex, sex, drugs . . . fit the cliché: sweet sixteen and never been kissed . . . feel strange in your own body . . . hope you'll be transformed into this beautiful, popular person and that this new school year will be a fresh start . . . pray your face will clear and your bra size will increase . . . are the same as you were at thirteen, only an inch taller . . . have your license and are finally free! free! free! . . . are still too young to vote, buy cigarettes, or get into R-rated movies, but too old to jump into the ball pit at Chuck E. Cheese . . . can do anything, like running through an empty field screaming "I love Jelly Bellys" without anyone to stop you . . . can go into Sharper Image without adult supervision . . . still look up to Ariel the Little Mermaid . . . only get as much freedom as you earn from your parents . . . are young enough to goof off and old enough to have an opinion . . . are wondering, I'm sixteen, dammit, when does the fun start? . . . are stressed because college really matters and your grades really matter and everyone is on your freaking nerves . . . are halfway through high school and don't know if that makes you happy or sad or both . . . learn that everything in life is not fun . . . hope people will start taking you and your views seriously . . . are legally allowed to work past seven P.M. and your employers take total advantage of it . . . are full of stupid emotions . . . have no clue what path you're taking, but can decide what shoes to wear on the journey . . . still have to deal with your strict Italian father, who thinks he's the law and can't deal with the fact that you're growing up . . . learn that people change and grow apart and aren't always who you think they are and won't do what you expect them to do . . . spend a lot of time expecting something great to happen, like meeting your soul mate or becoming rich . . . wonder if you'll reflect on this part of your life and regret that you didn't conform just to make things easier . . . don't feel sweet at all . . . feel so girlie, in a good way . . . look back on life and realize it is time to look forward . . . know what's out there and all the things you can do but you can't do them or aren't sure if you even want to . . . are getting older, and fast, and unfortunately your life still doesn't have much direction . . . are in charge of things, or at least it seems that way . . . can finally say you've arrived—almost.*

I wish I had room for all the responses. (Actually, that might make an interesting book of its own!) In essence, sixteen is a singular age—you have enough experience behind you to feel grown up, yet are all too often reminded of just how little you know. *Sixteen* captures this paradox through the distinctive voices of some of the most gifted authors writing for and about teens today.

Part of the reason I was so excited about this project was because I was eager to read others' interpretations of the theme. Even though I asked for contributions only from authors whose work I admire, I must admit, I had no idea how this book would turn out. But I'm thrilled (and relieved!) that their stories are all smart, strange, and surprising.

The first two stories I acquired for the collection were Sarah Dessen's take on virginity and driving and Steve Almond's meditation on a teen love affair gone wrong. I was immediately awed not only by the gorgeous prose, but also by how different the stories were from one another. "Infinity" perfectly captures the high-pressure importance placed on hitting certain milestones—or not. "The Day I Turned Chickenhearted" is steeped in the kind of melancholy wisdom that—unfortunately—comes only after the fact.

Emma Forrest's "The Grief Diet" is striking in its dark depiction of a friendship between two sixteen-year-old girls who are both wildly precocious yet naive. At its end, I was deeply worried about them both. Likewise, I finished Jacqueline Woodson's "Nebraska 99" wanting to know why? why? why? this bright young narrator would take such risks with her life, knowing only too well that so many real-life girls make similar errors in judgment. On the flip side, I was thrilled for the title character in Julianna Baggott's "The Future Lives of Emily Milty," a seemingly shy girl who emerges out of the shadow of her dynamic older sister. I was confident that she would find her way in the world.

"Cowgirls & Indie Boys" by Tanuja Desai Hidier is part of a much larger novel-in-progress about sexuality, language, and communication between cultures. I felt guilty as I cut it down to short-story length, and relaxed only when I realized that it would one day be available to read in its hypnotic entirety. With the story-in-verse "Cat Got Your Tongue?" I was amazed by Sonya Sones's ability to capture so much—sibling love/hate, lust at first sight, the thrill and fear of that first time behind the wheel—in so few words.

Joseph Weisberg's clever stories-within-a-story format in "Kissing Lessons" brilliantly reflects how there isn't one monumental coming-of-age event in our lives, but a culmination of smaller moments that makes us who we grow up to be. Cat Bauer's "Venetian Fan" portrays that common first-kiss-in-a-foreign-land fantasy more vividly and beautifully than any bad straight-to-video flick starring the Olsen twins. And Sarah Mlynowski's tale of love, betrayal, and mononucleosis puts a deliciously entertaining twist on "The Perfect Kiss."

Several stories hit me on a very personal level—I don't doubt that they will do the same for you, only in different ways. "Relent/Persist" by Zoe Trope is the first story I've ever read that brought me back to the letters my husband and I wrote to each other as we hesitantly fell in love, when we wanted to tell each other everything but were afraid as to how the other would react to the revelations. In "Mona Lisa, Jesus, Chad, and Me," Carolyn Mackler tackles sex, religion, and fading friendships in a totally honest, nonjudgmental way that made me sad about the friends I've lost along the way to adulthood. And though it deals with the budding love between two boys, "The Alumni Interview" reminded me of just how common it is at sixteen—or any age, really—to try to be someone you're not. Fortunately, David Levithan's story also drives home how liberating it can be to put an end to all the lies.

All the stories are unique, but two in particular defy convention. When Ned Vizzini first told me that his story, "Rutford Becomes a Man," was going to be about sweet sixteen in the Wild, Wild West, I was like, "The hell?!" But Ned, through Rutford, proves just how timeless teen angst truly is. Rutford—like many tortured teens—is hilarious precisely because he's trying so hard to be serious. And "The Mud and Fever Dialogues" by M. T. Anderson is a brilliant story inspired by the teachings of ancient philosophers. It deals with questions that contemporary teenagers still find themselves pondering late at night with friends: Who am I? What's the point of anything? Furthermore, its antihero's suicidal pursuit of truth is certainly relatable to anyone who has tried to stop a friend or a loved one from self-destruction. Anderson's story pulverizes the boundary between "teen" and "adult" fiction in the spirit that defines this collection as a whole.

Finally, there is my story. "Fifteen Going On . . ." is a miniprequel to *Sloppy Firsts* about how Jessica and Hope spend— or rather, *don't* spend—their final moments together before Hope moves away. I find it very difficult to comment on my own writing, so just flip to the last story in the book and read it for yourself.

I like to think that the range and depth of these stories make *Sixteen* an ideal present for anyone on that landmark birthday. (Hey, that certainly wouldn't be bad for sales. . . .) But with its mix of insight and nostalgia, this book, I hope, will also be discovered by parents who are trying to understand their kids, and by those readers in between who, like me, watch *Sixteen Candles* every time it's on TNT and still wish that Jake Ryan would show up in his Porsche to sweep us off our awkward feet. Enjoy!

Sixteen

Infinity

Sarah Dessen

Lately I don't dream about Anthony. I dream about the rotary.

Now, Mr. Haskell, my psychology teacher, would say this has implications. That somehow my fear of the rotary is linked to my issues with Anthony, which are both many and complicated. Mr. Haskell has a certain way he says things like this, leaning over with both elbows balanced on his lectern. It's very unsettling, as if he can see deep into your soul. But the truth is, I was scared of the rotary before I even met Anthony.

Most people don't even know what rotaries are. That's because most towns have those most modern of inventions, stoplights, to deal with traffic. Not here. Instead, some genius decided however many years ago to put in this big circle, with all the main roads feeding into it, then sat back to watch people crash to their deaths as they attempted to negotiate it.

But I digress.

My first experience with the rotary was when I was about seven. We'd just moved to town so that my father could finally finish his dissertation. My mother and I were on our way to the grocery store when we suddenly came upon this big sign that said YIELD with an arrow pointing to the right. Cars were going around a big circle, off of which poked several different exits to different roads. The trick, apparently, was to kind of merge in, follow around until your exit, then merge out. Simple as that.

"Oh my God," my mother said, poking her glasses up the bridge of her nose, which she always does when she's really nervous. "What is this?"

The answer came in the form of a loud, impatient beep from behind us. My mother looked nervously to her left, then tentatively poked at the gas pedal, sending us inching out into oncoming traffic. Another beep.

"Mom," I said.

"I'm merging!" she shrieked, as if this were on the level of splitting atoms and I was distracting her on purpose. And we were merging, pretty well, slowly easing into traffic. In fact, we were almost relaxed when we had to try to get back out; no easy trick, as there were many cars merging in. We got stuck on the inside track for two more turns, watching our exit go by, before my mother panicked and just sort of jerked the wheel, sending us in its general direction. And that was when the station wagon hit us.

The scene ensued the way you would expect: dents all around, tears (my mother), angry muttering (the guy who owned the station wagon), plus everyone else driving past rubbernecking and jawing to one another while I sank down as far as I could in the passenger seat, wishing there was a way to meld permanently with the pleather beneath me. The entire episode ended with a ticket, our insurance rates rising, and my mother swearing to never do the rotary ever again, which seemed somewhat overdramatic, until we realized that she meant it.

What this means, essentially, is that she has spent nine years taking the longest possible route *everywhere*. Because the rotary is the hub of our town, avoiding it takes work. And maps. And no end of secret shortcuts, long detours, and general embarrassment. Even a trip to the Quik Zip, basically about four miles from our house, requires getting on the highway, cutting (illegally) through the senior citizen compound, and making three left turns against oncoming traffic.

My father calls this ridiculous. He is a rotary champ, folding easily in and out, even while chatting on his cell phone or fiddling with the CD player. He is also a mathematician, something that my mother always brings up whenever the Rotary Argument commences, as if his proficiency with numbers is somehow involved in his mastery of the traffic circle. What all this has meant to me is that when it comes to going anywhere, I'm usually hoping it's my dad who grabs the keys to the sedan off the hook by the door first. Which will soon be a moot point, now that I'm about to turn sixteen and get my own license.

My boyfriend, Anthony, is a year older than me. He's good at the rotary, too, but he understands my hesitation. In fact, since I got my permit, we've spent a lot of time going in circles together, practicing. We started late at night, when it was pretty much deserted.

"Okay, now the first thing you're gonna do is stop and look to the left here," he instructed me one night. "There's someone coming, so unless they merge off before they get here, we'll wait for them to pass."

We waited. It was a Cadillac, moving slowly. It had the whole rotary to itself.

"Okay now," Anthony said. "Just ease out."

I did. Just as my mother had, all those years earlier. But this time there was no one coming; it was dark. No problem. But still my heart was beating hard, thumping against my chest, even as I picked up speed.

"See?" Anthony said, reaching over to squeeze my leg. He left his hand there, warm on my skin, as we eased around the circle. "Piece of cake, right?"

"Right," I said. We passed all the exits once, then started

through again. Of course this was okay, I thought. Like a merry-go-round, only faster. But it was a trial run. And trial runs are always easier.

After a few more turns we were starting to get dizzy. Finally Anthony pointed toward the beach route exit, and I took it, following the bumpy road past subdivisions and marshes before finally hitting the turnoff to the shore parking lot. I slowed down, remembering the potholes, pulling up into a space right behind the lifeguard stand. Then I cut the engine.

"You did good tonight," Anthony said.

"Thanks," I said.

And then he leaned over and kissed me. I knew he would. I knew it just like I knew that after a few minutes he'd reach up and undo my shirt, then slide off my bra straps, easing me back against the seat behind me. He'd tell me he loved me, kiss my neck, run his hand down my back and into the waistband of my jeans, pressing his fingers there. I knew because we'd been practicing this, too, all this time, trial run after trial run. As with the rotary, what came next was obvious. And scary. And, it seemed, inevitable.

I'd been with Anthony for more than six months. We'd met at work: We both had jobs at Jumbo Smoothie. He worked the blenders, which was an advanced position, while I dumped sliced peaches and yogurt into cups, prepping. It wasn't a great job, but we got to play the radio and eat all the free smoothies we wanted, which was fun for the first week or so.

Anthony was tall, with a bony frame: He had big wrists, wild curly hair, and a sloping kind of walk that always made him look like he was taking his time. When he blended smoothies, he put his whole body into it, arms shaking, bouncing on the balls of his feet, as if the noise the blender made was music and he just couldn't help himself from dancing.

He wanted to sleep with me. He hadn't come out and said it, but he didn't really have to. He was a senior; we'd been together six months. Us having sex would be a natural progression, after kissing to letting him go up my shirt, then down my pants: Like moving from learner's permit to license, there's only one thing left. And so I have this choice. To either merge in or take the long way home.

"I'm so proud of you!"

That was my mother when I came out of the DMV office, holding my new license. It was still warm in my hand from where they'd laminated it, as if it were somehow alive.

"Let me see the picture," she said. She squinted down at it. "Very nice. You're not even blinking."

It was a decent shot. I'd even had a second to brush my hair while the guy was arguing with some woman over her picture—she'd blinked, I guess—which I figured was a bonus. And there, next to my face, was all my pertinent information. Height, weight, eye color. Birthday. And expiration date: 2007. Amazing. Where would I be in four years?

"McDonald's," my mother said when I asked her this. We were in the car. I was driving.

"What?" I said.

"I thought we should go to McDonald's," she said. She fiddled with her sun visor, up, then down. Although she'd never admit it, my mother was nervous riding with me. "To celebrate."

"Oh," I said. "Okay."

McDonald's was smack in the middle of the lunch rush, the noise of registers and commotion and the crackling of the drive-through speaker almost overpowering. My mother told me to go find a table, then stood in line clutching her purse. The people behind her were all public-works guys in orange jumpsuits, talking too loudly.

I found a table by the window and sat down. The surface was covered with salt, like a dusting of snow, too thin to see but you could feel it. I moved my finger through it, leaving a circle behind, until suddenly someone put his hands over my eyes.

"Guess who?" a voice said right next to my ear. It was Anthony. Without my sight, the McDonald's seemed to get quieter, as if you needed to see all the commotion for it to really be happening.

"I know it's you," I said softly, reaching up and putting my hands over his. I could feel the silver ring he wore on his index finger pressing gently against my eyelid, cool and smooth. He went to move his hands, the joke being over, but I kept them there for a second longer before he slipped loose and it was bright again.

"So, did you get it?" he asked, dropping one hand onto my neck and leaning over me. I reached into my pocket and pulled out my license, showing him. "Nice. Good picture, too. You're not even blinking or making a weird face."

"Nope," I said. Anthony's license picture was terrible. Just when the guy was about to pop the flash, someone slammed a door, and Anthony was startled: In the picture he looks surprised, as if his eyes are bugging out of his head. But it doesn't bother him. He says no one really looks like their license picture, anyway. "I'm lucky, I guess."

"Yes," he said, curving his hand around the back of my neck the way that always gave me chills. "You are."

"Well, hello there!" My mother set the tray down in front of me. Two chicken sandwiches with no mayo, two large fries, two Diet Cokes. We both always get the same thing. "Are you joining us?"

Anthony reached over, took one of my fries, and popped it into his mouth. "Nope," he said. "Some of us have to get back to school."

"Poor you," I said, taking my fries off the tray.

"I'll call you later," he said, bending down again and kissing my cheek in a very chaste, big-brother kind of way. Normally I would have at least gotten a kiss on the lips, but my mother was right there. Still, she ducked her head and pretended to be very busy opening ketchup packets until he walked away, waving once over his shoulder. "Get ready for that rotary!" he called out, and then the glass doors swung shut behind him.

My mother picked up her sandwich, adjusting the one piece of lettuce and one tomato: They never give you enough, and the distribution is always all wrong. "You know," she said finally, taking her first bite, "you don't have to do the rotary right away."

"I know," I said. We'd already discussed this during the weeks I'd had my permit, when she'd officially taught me all of her extended shortcuts. "But I think I should just go ahead and get it over with."

She took a sip of her drink and glanced out the window. We'd both known this day was coming, eventually. My mother and I were close, always had been. She didn't fall into any of the specific Mom types: She wasn't Nagging Mom, or Trying-to-Be-Young-and-Hip-Mom, or Superstrict Mom. My parents were rumpled academics. Books had been their greatest love, before me, and I just knew that when I had flown the nest and was long gone, they'd continue their set patterns, floating from the breakfast nook, which had the best morning light, to the big couch by the fireplace, where they could each take an armrest with their stacks of journals and novels between them. Sentences and paragraphs, themes and symbols—these were things my mother never feared. She had a Ph.D. and did the *New York Times* crossword every morning before she even had her first cup of coffee. Words didn't scare her, only shapes. Like circles.

She'd expected me to fall in with this. I knew it by the way she'd easily assumed I'd learn her shortcuts, memorizing them so that I, too, could take a four-mile circuitous route to the post office, which was, measured by the clean numbers of my odometer, a mere half mile away. My father had harrumphed at this, my mother's lessons in avoidance, and hinted broadly that maybe my induction into the driving public would be a good excuse for my mother to finally face this, the fear of all fears. But I, for one, doubted this would ever happen. My mother had gotten accustomed to taking the long way everywhere: It wasn't even a burden for her anymore. That's the thing about habits. And fears. At first they might seem like trouble, but eventually they just fold in, becoming part of the fabric, a jumped stitch you hardly notice except when someone else points it out.

Now, watching her sip her drink, I felt a tug of obligation. She was the lone rotary holdout, and wasn't it my duty, as her daughter, to stand with her in allegiance? On the other side was not only the rest of our town, but also, more important, my father, fearless warrior of traffic circles, and Anthony, who had crashed his parents' Volvo once on a rotary one town over and still not thought twice about going back for more. I longed for the simple, solid logic of traffic lights, no decisions necessary: Green means go, red means stop, yellow means slow down or run the light—make up your mind, though, because time's a-wasting. All straight lines, or variations thereof.

Out in the parking lot, my mother and I buckled up and I backed out slowly, careful of the cars lining up for the drive-through. "Good turning," she said, praising my slow but effective merging into traffic on the main road. She had her hands in her lap, fingers locked, and we didn't talk as we moved through three intersections, catching the green light at each. Up ahead I could see the signs for the rotary, warning us of its approach. My mother pulled her fingers tighter, like a Chinese puzzle, and looked out the window quickly, as if the office supply store on her right was suddenly fascinating.

I could do this. It wasn't any different from all those nights I'd merged and circled the rotary with Anthony or my father: The traffic was just a little heavier. I was not the bravest of girls, but I'd never been branded a coward, either. I told myself I wasn't just doing this for me, but for my mother as well. I pictured us breezing easily around the curves, the weight of this burden suddenly lifting, my achievement sparking something in her as well, just as my father had hinted. The traffic was picking up now, the last intersection coming up in front of us. The engine seemed to grind as I downshifted, the other drivers pressing in around me.

There was a honk a few cars back—not at us, but loud nonetheless—and I have to admit it threw me, sending a quick hot flush up the back of my neck. It didn't help, of course, that my mother gasped in a breath loud enough for me to hear over the wind whistling through my not-quite-shut window. And just like that, I lost my confidence, my hand reaching up to hit the right turn signal as if it had made the choice all by itself. As we took the turn onto Murphy's Chapel Road, my mother let loose of her fingers, pressing them against the fabric of her skirt. Puzzle solved.

"It's okay," she said as we breezed past a few neighborhoods, with only two left turns, one access road, and a shopping center parking lot to traverse before arriving home. "You'll do it when you're ready."

She was relieved. I could hear it in her voice, see it in the slow easing of her shoulders back against the headrest. But I was angry with myself for ducking out. It seemed a bad way to begin things, with a false start, a last-minute abort so close to takeoff. As if I'd come this far, right to the brink, and in pulling back set a precedent that would echo, like the sound of my mother's gasp, next time.

I avoided the rotary for a week and a half. There were several almosts, most of them with Anthony in the car, pep-talking me like a motivational coach.

"Be the road!" he urged me as we coasted up to the ROTARY AHEAD signs. He'd made mix CDs, full of bouncy, you-can-do-anything kinds of songs, which he blasted, thinking they were helping. Instead, they distracted me entirely, as if failing to complete the task meant letting down not only myself and Anthony but also several bands and singers from all over the world. "Visualize it! Breathe through it!"

But always, I took that last possible right turn. The music would play on, unaware of its ineffectiveness, while Anthony would just shake his head, easing an elbow out the window, and say nothing.

His urging was gentler, but no less insistent, when the car was off and we were alone together at the beach. There was music then, too, but it was softer, soothing, as was his voice, in my ear, or against my neck.

"I love you, I love you," he'd whisper, and I'd feel that same hot flush, traveling up from my feet, the adrenaline rush that was a mix of fear and longing. We'd gotten very close, but again, I pulled back. Scared. It seemed ludicrous that I was unable to follow through with anything, as if from sixteen on I was doomed to be ruled by indecision.

"I just don't understand why you don't want to," he asked me one night as we sat looking at the water, him now leaning against his door, as far away from me as possible, as if the fact that I didn't want him made it necessary to put the maximum amount of distance between us. There was no gray here, no compromise. We'd come up so quickly on all or nothing that it blindsided me, a mere glint out of the corner of my eye before full impact.

"I want it to be right," I told him.

"How can this not be right?" He sat up straighter, jutting a finger up at the windshield. "Moonlight? Check. Crashing waves? Check. I love you? Check. You love me? . . ."

It took me a second, just a second, to realize it was my turn to say something.

"Check," I said quickly, but he glared at me and let his finger drop, as if this explained everything.

As the days passed, and I found myself consistently taking the long way everywhere, I got frustrated with all these decisions. A part of me wanted to barrel into the rotary blind-folded, pushing the gas pedal hard, and let whatever was going to happen just happen, anything for it to be over. The same part sometimes was so close to giving into Anthony's pleadings, wanting to finally just relax against the seat and let him do what he wanted, let his fingers spread across my skin, trailing downward, just give it all up and finally ease myself of these burdens. Scenario number one, of course, was stupid: I'd cause a multicar pileup and kill myself. As far as number two, well, it was harder to say. What would change? Maybe there wouldn't be visible damage, dented bumpers or crumpled hoods. But something in me would be different, even if no one else could tell. Like a car that's been wrecked and fixed, but the frame stays bent, and only the most trained of eyes can feel it pull on curves, or nudge toward the right on straightaways. Just because you don't see it doesn't mean something isn't there. Or gone.

The fall carnival appeared in one afternoon, with rides and a midway and the huge Ferris wheel cropping up in a field by the shopping mall as if dropped from the sky itself. In daylight, as I took my shortcut to school, everything looked tired and rusted, the tarps covering equipment flapping, workers walking around with craggy faces, half asleep. But by that night, with the lights blazing and the sounds of the carnies rounding up business for the games, it was like a whole new world.

Anthony walked in, bought some cotton candy, and proceeded to lose twenty bucks in about five minutes playing a game that involved shooting water pistols at stuffed frogs. I just stood and watched him, silent after my first three tries to point out he was never, ever going to win.

"Tough luck, buddy," the guy running the game said in a monotone voice, his eyes on the crowd moving past, already looking for the next sucker.

"One more time," Anthony said, digging out some more bills. "I'm getting closer, I can feel it."

"How badly do you really need a frog, anyway?" I asked him. They looked like the typical carnival stuffed animals I remembered from my childhood, the kind with nubby fur that smelled faintly like paint stripper. They always looked better before you actually won them, as if the minute the carny handed them over they faded, or diminished somehow, the golden ring gone brass.

"It's not about the frog," Anthony snapped at me, bending down to better line up his shot. "It's about winning."

"Winning a frog," I grumbled, but he just ignored me, then slammed his fist down and stalked off when he lost. Again. He cheered up a little bit when I used my money to buy a funnel cake and tickets for the Ferris wheel, then stood in line with me, chewing loudly, the frog forgotten.

Behind us was a guy with his daughter, who looked to be about eight. She had a big stuffed lion under her arm and was gripping her dad's hand, staring up at the Ferris wheel as it moved lazily above us.

"Now, honey," the man said, squatting down beside her, "you don't have to go on it if you don't want to."

"I want to," she said firmly, switching the lion to the other arm.

"Because it might be scary."

"I want to," she repeated.

"Okay," he said, in the kind of voice that was usually accompanied by a shrug. As if he doubted this, her conviction. But as I watched her face, the careful way she studied the ride as it came to a stop, I envied her for knowing exactly what she wanted. But it was easy when you're little, I figured. Not so many choices.

We got on the ride, and as Anthony pulled the safety bar toward us, I craned my neck around, watching to see if the little girl would get into the next seat. She did, without hesitation, planting her lion next to her and laying her hands in her lap, as if she were only getting on a bus, or sitting in a chair, the world to remain always solid beneath her.

As we started moving, Anthony wrapped both his hands around mine and kissed my neck. I closed my eyes as we moved up, higher and higher, our seat rocking slightly. The Ferris wheel was higher than I'd thought, and as I stared down, everything seemed to shrink to a pinpoint. I could see the steeple from the church on my corner in the distance, beyond that the lights from the football fields. From up high, everything seemed closer together than it actually was, as if the farther away you got, the more the world you knew folded in to comfort itself.

Anthony was sliding his hands onto my stomach, moving one to the small of my back, one beneath my waistband, murmuring in my ear. We were still rising, higher and higher, and someone was screaming a few cars down, but I told myself it wasn't that little girl, not her. In my mind, I saw her solid face, her absolute determination, and refused to believe it would be so easy to sway her.

We were at the very top when I looked down and felt dizzy. Anthony was pressing against me, his fingers digging, hardly caring that this was not the place, not the time, so determined was he to win whatever it was he wanted so badly, that seemed so ideal, at least as long as it shrank back from his grasp. All those nights at the beach, when I'd pushed him away, I hadn't known exactly why, just that it hadn't felt right. But as my view from high up narrowed, I realized that my relationship with Anthony had done the same, going from a wide endless horizon of possibilities to one pinpoint of a destination. I wanted to have choices, to know that I could, at any moment, still take the long way home. Sure, there was a quick way to anywhere. But sometimes, when you took the shortcut, you missed the view.

"I love you," he whispered in my ear. "I want you."

But it wasn't enough, this time. Maybe later it would have been, but as I pushed him away, I knew that time would never come. Winning might not have been everything, but Anthony was tired of losing at this game. If he couldn't have me, he'd find an easier prize.

The ride hadn't even come to a full stop when he pushed the safety bar away from us. It rattled loudly and sent a ripple of force through my metal seat, an echo I felt in my bones. Then he stomped down the stairs to the midway, pushing past all the people lined up for the next ride while I climbed out slowly, taking my time, telling myself to pay attention to how the earth felt beneath me and not take it for granted anymore.

I'd driven, and Anthony was gone, lost in the crowd of sticky wrappers and screaming children and all the voices of the game workers, their coaxing and wheedling like a swarm of bees hovering. When I finally got to my car, it seemed as though everyone was leaving at once, a long snaky trail of brake lights leading out to the main road.

I pulled up behind a pickup truck and then sat there, moving forward in tiny increments, watching the stoplight up ahead drop from red to green, then climb to red again. Even though I'd only been driving for a couple of weeks, it already felt more natural. Things that before I'd had to think about consciously, like switching gears and working the clutch, now happened automatically, as if that part of my mind was handling it, making those decisions for me. Maybe all it took, in the end, was the time to let the new soak in. To stand in the face of change and size it up, acquaint yourself, before jumping in. It was all the pressure that was so hard, those little nudges forward, poke poke poke. If you just backed off and let it come to you, it would.

When I finally made it to the light, I hit my blinker, signaling the left turn that would lead me around the shopping mall and through two neighborhoods before depositing me neatly onto my own road. It was the way I'd always gone, up until now, but this time I didn't feel that burning burst of shame in it, knowing I was taking the easy way out. I just remembered the view from up high, the way all the roads led to one another eventually. It didn't matter which route you took, as long as you got home.

I was thinking this as I moved up to the solid green of the light. There was that burst of freedom in realizing that my choice was okay. But even so, at the last minute, I turned my wheel to the right, surprising even myself, and shifted into second as the rotary came up into my sight. It was crowded with carnival traffic, cars whizzing past: I could see it, as if I was still up high, the absolute geometry of that perfect circle. This was normally the moment I was dumb scared, hands shaking, but this time I only moved closer, pressing my shoulders back against the seat as if taking the scariest and most exhilarating of rides.

As I got closer, I glanced in my rearview and saw the Ferris wheel. It was far behind me, brightly lit, and looked small enough to slide on my finger and keep there. Another circle, representing a kind of infinity that I was only beginning to understand. So as I looked back at the road, easing myself closer to the rotary traffic, I sealed that image in my mind as I eased in, holding my breath, and felt myself fall into the rhythm of the cars around me. I turned the wheel, leaning into the first curve, feeling that rush of accomplishment and speed as we all moved away from the center, further and further out. It was happening so fast, but I was there, right there, alive, wanting this moment to be like brass rings and Ferris wheels and all the circulars of this life and others, never ending.

Relent/Persist

Zoe Trope

Dear Eliaphie,

How in the world do you pronounce your name? I'm sorry, you probably get that all the time. Ell-ee-aff-ee? I'm sure it's lovely, when said correctly.

That's really not the best way to begin a letter, is it?

I don't want to bore you with details. Where I live, my favorite food, my parents, my siblings, blah blah blah. That's boring, and from what I've heard, you'd probably crumple up my letter in a ball and throw it in the wastebasket if I squandered your time like that.

Not that I've heard anything bad about you. Just that you're tough to get ahold of sometimes. Elusive?

God, more accusations. This is getting less flattering all the time.

My name's Clarke. I saw your website and I was too scared to write you an e-mail, so I thought a letter might work best. I don't know how this is any easier than typing an e-mail, 'cause it's not. Just slower.

Do you really make a wish every night at 11:11 P.M.? What was the last thing you wished for?

Thanks,
Clarke
Portland, OR

clarke—

your letter rocked my socks, babe. i put my snail-mail address on my website thinking i might get some pervy letters from stalkers or whatever. yknow, then i could hang them up inside my locker or whatever. haha.

anyway, you're right about my name. elle-ee-ah-ffff-he. but don't bother with that, ok? i like to be called eli. as in eee-lie. got it? good. my name was just the first of many things that my parents couldn't agree on. dad wanted elliott for a boy, mom wanted sophie for a girl. it seems like they put the letters in a hat and tossed 'em around and pulled 'em out like a bad game of boggle or something

yes, i make a wish every night at 11:11 P.M. no, i can't tell you what i wish for. it's like your birthday cake, yknow? you blow out the candles and you make a wish and you can't tell a goddamn person otherwise it won't come true.

i wouldn't have crumpled up your letter, by the way. i'm not THAT mean.

it's so cold in seattle tonight. but it feels so good to sit outside in a t-shirt and just shiver and shiver and shiver. you should try it sometime, especially if you get a chance to sit on your roof.

take care & write soon.

oxox,

eli

p.s. im me sometime. xeliaphiex on AIM.

relentpersist: Hey, Eli. It's Clarke.

xeliaphiex: oh, hi!

relentpersist: I got your letter. Thanks for writing back.

xeliaphiex: my pleasure, babe.:>

relentpersist: Are you sick?

xeliaphiex: what?

relentpersist: Heh, I thought you might have a cold from sitting outside without a jacket.

xeliaphiex: you sound like my mother. jeezus.

relentpersist: Sorry. I didn't mean it that way.

xeliaphiex: haha. it's ok. no i'm not sick.

relentpersist: That's good.

xeliaphiex: can i ask you a weird question?

relentpersist: Please do.

xeliaphiex: what's yr gender? (if you have one that is.)

relentpersist: ...I'm a girl.

xeliaphiex: haha, rock. i thought so.

relentpersist: God, I bet you couldn't tell 'cause of my name, right?

xeliaphiex: that and yr handwriting. it's androgynous too.

relentpersist: Yeah, I got blessed with the Cushing Family chicken scrawl. It's awful.

xeliaphiex: don't worry about it. yr last name's cushing?

relentpersist: Yep.

xeliaphiex: that rocks. i wish i had a cool last name.

relentpersist: Your first name is pretty cool.

xeliaphiex: hah, thanks.

xeliaphiex: shit, i gotta go. parents are yelling at me.

xeliaphiex: catch you later, clarke.

relentpersist: Later.

To: xeliaphiex
From: relentpersist
Subj: Why does the rhythm get us every time?

Eli-

It was great to talk to you tonight. I'm working on another letter; I should have it mailed out by the end of the week.

Your website says you're 15, which would make you a sophomore, right?

Clarke

To: relentpersist
From: xeliaphiex
Subj: RE: Why does the rhythm get us every time?

c-

looking forward to yr letter.

i'm 15, but i'm actually a junior. i skipped the 2nd grade.

-e.

p.s. that's my favorite mates of state song, btw. i recognize the lyric in the subject line.

Dear Eli—

Procrastination should be my middle name, in addition to Quiet, Sarcastic, Broken, and, of course, Suzanne. It's 9:28 A.M. and I'm sitting in my first class of the day, pre-calculus. My teacher's giving a lecture on sine and cosine and I can feel my eyes roll like bowling balls down the long lanes of his dry erase board. This is not my best class, so logic dictates that I should be paying extra attention. But why bother? I just end up writing novellas in the margins of my notes anyway.

Speaking of which, I've read every word on your website in its entirety. I loved all of it. It made my teeth hurt. I'd say more, but I don't want to seem foolish or obsessed.

My teacher has a habit of holding the dry erase pen between his teeth and talking at the same time. I can hear his tongue lapping up against the end of the pen. It's horrible. I don't mean to seem like a germ phobe, 'cause I'm not, but this guy has a serious oral fixation. It's disturbing.

Okay, I should probably attempt to take some notes if I want to have any hope of doing the homework tonight. More later.

It's 10:44 P.M. and I've got a biology test tomorrow but I want to finish this letter first. It doesn't feel right, leaving you hanging there.

I have a close friend, Shaun, who talks with me in English class about plays and art and music. He is a homosexual. Well-read. Writes papers dripping with style and overflowing with sarcasm. He is the first gay boy I've ever known. He is brave; my school is fierce. I often wish he were my brother. He's one of the few people who will just listen to me without judging me or making some shitty remark. Do you have any gay friends?

I told you in my first letter that I wouldn't bore you with the details of my family. There aren't enough details to bore you with. I'm an only child, parents have been married for *nineteen years. Sickeningly suburban, right down to the dog and the SUV.*

I shaved my head last year. My mother cried.

This is getting disjointed so I should take off. Write when you can.

All the best,
Clarke

dear clarke—

you shaved your head? that is so hardcore. why'd you do it? what color is your hair? do you dye it? mine's cotton candy pink right now, but naturally it's this nasty pale blond that i can't stand. luckily, it takes really well to dye.

i suck at precal too, although my teacher doesn't give head to the pens. that'd be hilarious to watch, though, 'cause she's this totally prissy girlie girl who wears lots of makeup and curls her hair, like, every fucking day and wears a giant gold cross around her neck. 'cause, y'know, jesus will only save you if you've got raccoon eyes and a painted mouth. what the fuck ever. i don't get it.

i'm totally flattered that you read my website, thanks. most of the stuff on there is pretty old. i haven't been able to write in a while.

what else do you like besides mates of state? my favorite band right now is probably rainer maria or the postal service.

and i'm secretly envious of your suburban lifestyle. don't tell, tho.

gotta go. take care, babe.

oxox,

e.

p.s. my best friend's a fag, too. he lets me do his makeup every day before school.

From: xeliaphiex
To: relentpersist
Subj: something to note.

   i think i killed the moon.

      -e.

From: relentpersist
To: xeliaphiex
Subj: RE: something to note
>i think i killed the moon.

   How?

      Clarke

From: xeliaphiex
To: relentpersist
Subj: RE: RE: something to note

   i was just standing outside looking at it (you should go outside and try to find it if you can) and a big gray cloud stalked over and swallowed it up. it feels like my fault, like i had it and then i lost it to that stupid fucking cloud.

From: relentpersist
To: xeliaphiex
Subj: RE: RE: RE: something to note

It's not your fault, E. You are not a cloud and you did not swallow the moon. It will be there tomorrow night, too. I promise.

Clarke

From: xeliaphiex
To: relentpersist
Subj: RE: RE: RE: RE: something to note

thanks.

Dear Eli,

When you told me you killed the moon, I almost wanted to cry. I don't know why. I get very emotional about the strangest things sometimes.

I shaved my head because I felt like my hair was suffocating me. It's dark brown, almost black, and very straight.

Something in my neighborhood is burning tonight but I can't smell smoke. Do you ever feel that way, too?

God, I don't even know what I'm saying anymore.
Good night,
Clarke

From: xeliaphiex
To: relentpersist
Subj: heart stamp
babe,

what's up with your most recent letter? seems weird. are you ok?

eli

From: relentpersist
To: xeliaphiex
Subj: RE: heart stamp
Eli,

Sorry about that. I was just feeling kind of manic and...I don't know. Don't take it seriously, okay?

Talk to you later,

Clarke

dearest clarke,

i know things are burning all the time but no one listens to me. don't you ever just wanna get up on a chair or a desk and scream FIRE and watch everyone flood out just so you can have some space to yourself?

i do, i do, i do.

i spend a lot of time at school in the library. the teachers always let me go and i curl up on the couch with a book or

my notebook and i write. i was really sick last year and i
never wanted to be in class.
it's okay to be manic.
it's okay.
what do you want for christmas?
<3,
eli

relentpersist: I want a new heart for Christmas.

xeliaphiex: what's wrong with the one y've got?

relentpersist: Too battered, bruised, and torn.

xeliaphiex: from what? being emo?

relentpersist: No.

xeliaphiex: you sure? you totally seem like the argyle socks/rectangle
glasses/rivers cuomo type.

relentpersist: I'm sure. I'm not emo.

xeliaphiex: then what is it?

relentpersist: Everything.

relentpersist: Nothing.

relentpersist: You.

xeliaphiex: what?

relentpersist: I have to go. Bye.

From: xeliaphiex
To: relentpersist
Subj: xmas

get anything good?

e.

From: relentpersist
To: xeliaphiex
Subj: RE: xmas
>get anything good?

Nothing exciting, really. Clothes, CDs, jewelry, makeup. More boring consumeristic stuff that will break or be forgotten by Valentine's Day. God, I'm so fatalistic lately.

What's up with that?

What about you? Anything worthwhile?

C.

From: xeliaphiex
To: relentpersist
Subj: RE: RE: xmas

i got a new bike! it's totally sweet. i'm so stoked. it's a bright red old school huffy 1-speed. all i need to do is pick up a helmet and i'm off! i'm gonna bike to school every day, d00d. seriously.

e.

relentpersist: Congrats on the new bike.

xeliaphiex: thanks. it's so sweet.

xeliaphiex: i'm trying to think of a name for it.

relentpersist: A name?

xeliaphiex: yeah, i name everything.

xeliaphiex: my computer is morton the destroyer.

relentpersist: Like what else?

xeliaphiex: and my stereo is frida kahlo.

relentpersist: Oh.

xeliaphiex: what?

relentpersist: You should name your bike Clark Gable.

xeliaphiex: or maybe just clark for short.

dear clarke-

two square punches on each side of my jaw and a right-hook to my left eye. it happened 4 years ago and i can still feel the blows. the doctor said i was lucky that my jaw didn't fucking fall off. i think i swallowed a couple of my teeth. they felt like tic tacs with rough edges. 7th grade boys and their stupid fucking antics.

i just wanted you to know so if you think my smile is a little crooked, i'm not being sarcastic. my jaw's just fucked up.

oxoOo,

e.

Dearest Eli,

I was surprised about the envelope your last letter was in. How something so delicate could contain such a harsh story. Did you make it yourself? The envelope, I mean? It's awesome.

I'm sorry about those boys and their fists. How'd you get into such a fight? And how come no one was there to defend you, not even your fag-in-eyeliner?

I think imperfections are more beautiful than anything perfect. We've got machines and programs and technology to make everything just right down to the last chromosome, the last wrinkle, the last hair. I want something messy and imperfect and dangerous. Something like you.

heart,
Clarke

xeliaphiex: hey babe. got yr letter today.

relentpersist: Oh? Did you like the envelope?

xeliaphiex: yeah, it's really cool. did you make it out of a calendar page?

relentpersist: Yep. I had this awesome pin-up girl calendar last year and I saved it 'cause I liked the pictures so much.

relentpersist: I couldn't figure out what to do with it until I saw your envelope. You're so creative.

xeliaphiex: thx.

xeliaphiex: i wanted to tell you that i got into the fight 'cause 7th grade was the first year i cut my hair short and dyed it.

xeliaphiex: and i was sitting at a table outside reading a book and these boys just started screaming DYKE DYKE WHORE DYKE SLUT LESBIAN.

xeliaphiex: which in hindsight is pretty fucking amusing 'cause i was, like, 11 and i'd never even kissed anyone, but somehow i was a slutty lesbian.

xeliaphiex: anyway i tried to ignore them and they ripped my book out of my hands and pushed me to the ground.

xeliaphiex: then 3 good punches and they ran off when they heard a teacher yell at them.

xeliaphiex: pretty fucked up, i guess.

xeliaphiex: and daniel, my "fag-in-eyeliner," wasn't there cause i didn't meet him till freshman year.

relentpersist: Wow.

xeliaphiex: what?

relentpersist: Just…that's horrible.

relentpersist: What'd your parents say?

xeliaphiex: my mom was fucking pissed. she called the school and everything. we moved about a month later, so it was okay.

relentpersist: I'm sorry.

xeliaphiex: why? yr not the one who punched me.

relentpersist: I know, but I might as well have been. That whole control thing, y'know?

xeliaphiex: yeah i know but it really isn't yr fault, babe. i promise.

relentpersist: Thanks.

From: xeliaphiex
To: relentpersist
Subj: she called me up to tell me the color of the sky.

c-

    do you have a car? yr 16, right?

      -e

From: relentpersist
To: xeliaphiex
Subj: RE: she called me up to tell me the color of the sky

E.

    Yes, I have a car, and yes, I'll be 16 for 7 more months.

    I always get crushes on boys driving Volvos. Do you ever get a crush on anyone for the car they drive?

      C.

From: xeliaphiex
To: relentpersist
Subj: car crush

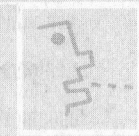

i get crushes on people who like well-done steaks and e. e. cummings. the combination of the 2 really says something about our society.

i get crushes on volvos, mini-coopers (the old ones, not the faggy new ones that all those CEOs drive), and really ugly cadillacs--just because no one else will love them. what kind of car do you drive?

From: relentpersist
To: xeliaphiex
Sub: RE: car crush

A 1988 Volvo. It's practically as old as I am, which is strange and disturbing to think about.

I saw a picture of e. e. cummings once. What an ugly man. But I couldn't help leaning down into my English textbook and pressing my lips against the black-and-white photograph. I didn't (and don't) want him to kiss me back, but I just want that moment in time. Me kissing e. e. cummings. That's all I need.

xeliaphiex: w00t, done with all my homework.

relentpersist: Congrats.

xeliaphiex: sound more bored and depressed.

relentpersist: All right. How about: Shoot me in the face. Now?

xeliaphiex: not today.

relentpersist: And why not?

xeliaphiex: you've got a future and a pretty face.

relentpersist: Thanks, I think.

xeliaphiex: well, yr depressing the hell outta me.

relentpersist: I'm sorry. School was shitty x 1000.

xeliaphiex: what happened?

relentpersist: Just … shit. I stayed up late studying for a chem test, fucked it up anyway, felt weird all day because I hadn't slept and my Spanish teacher is a complete retard.

xeliaphiex: what he'd do?

relentpersist: He made us copy pages out of the textbook all period. I finished early and took out a book to read and he gave me more pages to copy. I nearly screamed.

xeliaphiex: god, what a scrotum. put ex-lax in his coffee.

relentpersist: I think I should.

relentpersist: Anyway, I'm gonna go sleep.

relentpersist: Later.

xeliaphiex: gnight, clarke.

From: xeliaphiex
To: relentpersist
Subj: something like a remedy

hey babe. thought this story might cheer you up:

my aunt and i were watching the 2nd lotr movie, the 2 towers, right? and she's like, really confused about 20 minutes into the movie. "why are they jumping around so much?" and i'm like, "cause the characters aren't all in the same place, they're in three different places." and she says, "oh," but she still sounds pretty confused. and the next day we're talking about the movie and she's like, "god, yknow, elijah wood really grew up during the movie." i said, "what are you talking about?" and she says, "he looks really really different in some scenes, yknow, like older and skinnier." and i shrug and say, "maybe it was the lighting or something."

and here's the great part.

she screwed up her face and said, "but i don't understand--why did he start calling his sidekick merry?"

sigh.

moral of the story? life can always get worse. you could be so severely mentally damaged as not to realize that SAM and FRODO are different from MERRY and PIPPIN. cherish your mental capacities, clarke. someday they'll wander into greener and more coke-filled pastures.

oxox,

eli

From: relentpersist
To: xeliaphiex
Subj: Required

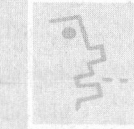

Eli-

The story about your aunt was great--it made me laugh. Thank you.

However, I think having weird aunts/uncles is kind of required. I also think that I can totally beat your LOTR/mistaken identity story.

I was staying with my aunt and uncle last summer for a couple weeks. They live a few miles outside of Seattle. I got back late from a concert 1 night to find both of them sprawled out on the living room couch, watching television.

"Hey," I said as I stepped through the door to their apartment. They didn't even lift their heads.

I stepped in front of the TV to get their attention. "I had a great time in Seattle," I said.

"That's good."

Silence.

"Well, don't you wanna know what I did, who I slept with, what kinds of drugs I scored?"

"Yeah, sure. Later. We're watching a documentary."

I turned around to see "Cheech & Chong: Up in Smoke" on the screen.

"That's Cheech & Chong, Dan."

He said, "I know. This is our youth, man. Seriously." He laughed and squeezed his wife's knee.

I guess that's what I get for staying with my dad's younger brother. He reminds me a lot of you, actually.

Smoke rings & apple seeds,

C.

xeliaphiex: i wonder if britney spears masturbates…

relentpersist: Only to pictures of herself.

xeliaphiex: she probably doesn't have to. but i just don't understand people who don't whack off.

relentpersist: Hah. Me neither.

xeliaphiex: they're like…aliens or something.

relentpersist: I have a friend who literally shudders at the thought of touching herself. But she's fucked her boyfriend in the school parking lot a dozen times.

xeliaphiex: ew.

relentpersist: My sentiments exactly.

relentpersist: She's pretty funny, tho. She calls that void between her legs her "poona" and, in return, I refer to it as her "tuna poona."

relentpersist: I'm so mature it kills me.

xeliaphiex: haha! that rocks so hard. yr hilarious.

relentpersist: I try.

xeliaphiex: i bet your friend has really horrible sex with her boyfriend.

xeliaphiex: 'cause she probably has no idea what she likes.

xeliaphiex: you know what i mean?

relentpersist: Yeah, definitely.

xeliaphiex: 'cause if you aren't the best fuck you've ever had, then who is?

relentpersist: Heh. Exactly.

relentpersist: You know how they have all those Christians who are against masturbation and they tell you to not give in to temptation and ruin your body and shame Christ and stuff?

relentpersist: You should totally give the opposite lecture about being pro-pork-pounding. You know, "Wank to freedom!" or something like that. You could make it sound really holy and appropriate, I'm sure.

xeliaphiex: yr such a fucking genius.

relentpersist: I try.

xeliaphiex: and pretty too on top of that.

relentpersist: You think so?

xeliaphiex: yeah totally.

xeliaphiex: i loved that picture you sent of you in yr car with your friends.

xeliaphiex: it's like i can hear you laughing in the picture.

relentpersist: That's a sign of schizophrenia, you know. Hearing things.

xeliaphiex: whatev. i think yr gorgeous.

relentpersist: Thank you. I think you're lovely as well.

xeliaphiex: in the immortal words of clarke cushing: "I try." hehheh.

From: relentpersist
To: xeliaphiex
Subj: wallet photograph

E-

   The black-and-white photographs on your web page are so beautiful. I love that white dress with the stripes…Are those self-portraits?

   -C

From: xeliaphiex
To: relentpersist
Subj: RE: wallet photograph

yep, those are self-portraits with a dress i found at a vintage store on capitol hill. i wore it to a dance last year. the other girl in the third photo with me is my best friend, hayley.

From: relentpersist
To: xeliaphiex
Subj: striped dress.

The photographs are really haunting and precious. The shadow of your collarbone is so delicate. I bet it would melt in my mouth.

From: xeliaphiex
To: relentpersist
Subj: an open invitation for general debauchery

Dear Ms. Clarke Cushing,

You are cordially invited to attend the Shins concert next Friday evening with Ms. Eliaphie Gray in Seattle, Washington. She thinks this event may be of particular interest to you based on your America Online Screen Name.

Please respond at your earliest convenience.

Much thanks,

the management

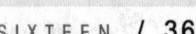

From: relentpersist
To: xeliaphiex
Subj: RE: an open invitation for general debauchery
yo mz. gray & co.-

    like, that clarke girl is totally excited to accept, yknow? so we be seein'
you in seattle on that friday, dawg.

    props to yr homies-

        the bitches of clarke c.

From: xeliaphiex
To: relentpersist
Subj: smiles are universal

    since when are you black? not that it makes much of a difference. i'll just
have to bring out more bling-bling for the concert.

        e.

From: relentpersist
To: xeliaphiex
Subj: necessities

    You don't have to bring anything to the concert. Just you.

        c.

relentpersist: So you like the Shins, too? You must, since you recognized my
  screen name.

xeliaphiex: yeah, i loved their last album.

xeliaphiex: i used to listen to it every morning while getting ready for school.

xeliaphiex: yummy stuff.

relentpersist: I also liked the formal invitation. Nice touch.

xeliaphiex: i like how you had your "bitches" reply for you.

relentpersist: Yeah, well, I'm busy.

xeliaphiex: i know.

relentpersist: Anyway, I'm really excited to hang out with you. It'll be great.

xeliaphiex: totally. wanna meet on capitol hill for dinner first?

relentpersist: Sure, where?

xeliaphiex: ever been to dick's?

relentpersist: Of course!

xeliaphiex: excellent. we can feast on delicious meats before the show.

relentpersist: And we can grab a burger from Dick's Drive-In.

xeliaphiex: haha. that too.

Dearest Eli,

*In a few short hours, I'll buckle my seat belt and push my
foot against the pedal and drive 187 miles to Seattle to see
you. And I'm hoping that we dance at the concert and I'm
hoping that we kiss softly in the dark. But this is a postcard
from the past being sent to your future, so who knows what
you'll think when you read this. Maybe a warm smile, maybe
nothing.*

xo, Clarke

dearest clarke,

you'll be here in nineteen hours and sixteen minutes, give or take a few seconds. i've got fingernails that disappear at the thought of your name. the shins concert is gonna rock so hard & all i want from you is a kiss goodnight. i hope you don't hate me when you get this, but that's forever away. and tomorrow is almost now and that's all i care about.

ox, eli

The Future Lives of Emily Milty

Julianna Baggott

Being Emily Milty is like being a wool coat, an old grandma type of wool coat with a horrible broach. Being Emily Milty is like being gray soup and SPAM and a yogurt dessert. Being Emily Milty is like being wall-to-wall Sears carpeting. It isn't fun. That's what I'm saying. And I should know because I am Emily Milty.

I've always thought of my life as a play. (I am currently in the chorus of my high-school performance of *Oklahoma!*; I've stolen four dust-bowl bonnets out of the costume closet.) But in the play of my life, there are only two possible roles, both leads: my own, Emily Milty, or my sister's, Miranda Milty. There were no auditions, of course, only a shifting down of my mother's eggs, like well-sifted flour, and an arsenal of my father's sperm shooting randomly. Not that I think of my father as a gunman; far from it. I hardly know the man. He lives in Pasadena with his new wife, Junie. But I do know that my family lineage consists of window-blind salesmen and Fotomat managers—no known gunmen. I'm only talking about my father's perfunctory anatomy. You know what I mean.

I'm only sixteen, but I'm not giggly about sex. My mother and my biology teacher, Miss Finch, have gone over the facts. And I like facts. They make me feel comfortable. So does Miss Finch, who is full of facts and smells forever tidy—a mix of breath mints and mothballs. Miss Finch is one of the possible futures for Emily Milty. My mother is another future for Emily Milty. Are these good futures? No. They're bleak, but highly likely, and so I try to embrace them.

I'll always live here in my same life. I was cast as sweet, passive Emily, and my sister as Miranda, my opposite. Miranda ran off with Tommy Eldridge when she was seventeen and pregnant with baby Marco. She would tell me about their nights out. We shared a bedroom, and she would come in late and wake me up and tell me where she and Tommy went and what it was like to have sex in his grandmother's basement or his parent's aboveground pool or on the greens of the par-three where he worked. This happened more than two years ago.

Early that fall, Miranda and Tommy disappeared but didn't get married. I was new to high school, still figuring out the maze of corridors, trying to go unnoticed while stealing things—a nervous habit. In those first few weeks, I swiped two padlocks, a sports bra, fourteen pens, two welcome banners, a lighter, a phone from the front office, and Miss Finch's hand-pump lotion, which sat on her desk. So now I smell like Miss Finch's hand lotion sometimes, on weekends, to prepare myself to become Miss Finch, nervously rubbing my hands together while thinking of the things Miss Finch thinks of— biology and whatnot.

Miranda vanished. I am left here forever.

I'm a virgin. Do I have to spell that out? I'm sixteen and a virgin, and I'm aware of the fact that no one would dare say something like this out loud. But I am, truthfully, Emily Milty, the virgin.

I have to admit it wasn't only eggs and sperm and the multiplication of DNA that made Miranda Miranda and me me. There was also nurture involved. Breath-minty, mothbally Miss Finch taught us about nature vs. nurture earlier this year. My meek mother always let Miranda have her way. Once upon a time, I think she let my father have his own way, too. So much so that he left us when I was two to drive across country with Junie in our old Chrysler LeBaron, which my mother had bought with her own money. From then on, my mother and I always shuffled behind Miranda's full head of steam, bowing and wilting. Miranda was the churning engine, the blowing whistle, and the two of us were only the clackity clackity of wheels: *pardon me, pardon me, pardon me.*

Yes, secretively, I've thought I could have played a wonderful Miranda, giving a memorable and heartaching performance. Miranda, in her body glitter and her berry lip gloss and her Get It Straight hair gel and her Gap perfume spray and her low-rise jeans. Sometimes, I picture myself running down the street as Miranda did that summer, her long blond hair swinging back and forth across her back. Sprinting under streetlight after streetlight like a row of moons, to the car at the intersection with the rusty, cancerous muffler, and the boy, Tommy Eldridge, waiting for her behind the wheel.

But I have taken up the role of Emily valiantly, because the audience is the most important thing after all is said and done. My audience consists of my mother, the adoring fan who always sits in the front row, hands clasped together, eyes shimmering with tears. My mother who needs me.

I don't think about Miranda too much. But sometimes lying awake on Saturday nights, listening to the drone of my mother's small bedroom TV, I try to imagine Miranda in a bar, flirting with big-armed men with flexing tattoos, then taking one of them back to her place, where Marco is already asleep, and what might happen next. And sometimes, in these imaginings, the guy turns out to be Justin Gunter, who stands beside me in the chorus, and sometimes Miranda turns out to be me, and then when I see Justin the next day, I feel hot and nauseous.

But things changed when Jean Pencher sidled up to my locker one day last week. Jean is shaped like a thirty-five-year-old mother of two. She's hippy and full-breasted with a saggy belly. She wears much too much makeup, penciled-in eyebrows that make her look suspicious, pinched and nearsighted. I only wear mascara, because you can't really mess it up.

Jean was just standing there, breathing.

"What is it?" I asked. It was just before last period, biology class with Miss Finch. I don't like to be late for Miss Finch, because she adores me. She sees in me a young Miss Finch, and she's invested a lot of sighing and warm, gentle smiling in my direction. Once she said, "What would I do without Emily Milty?" And she shook her head dreamily with this foggy smile and faraway gaze.

Another time, she took me aside and said, "I was a late bloomer, too, Emily." And I thought, My God, you once bloomed? I had no idea.

"I know something that you don't know," Jean said.

"What's that?" I assumed that this had to do with something that Jean had overheard while in a bathroom stall. Jean is a natural informant.

"Your sister, Miranda. My brother saw her at BJ's this weekend buying dog food."

The news made a little prickle of heat spread on my neck. People liked to talk about Miranda. Throughout my freshman year, I would get introduced as Miranda Milty's sister. Sometimes people would say things like "I heard she ran off with Tommy Eldridge. Is that true? Was she knocked up?" And I would be left to answer for her.

"I can't really talk about it," I'd tell them. "For legal reasons." As if there were some court battle somewhere and facts couldn't be released. I'd seen celebrities sidestep hard questions with an answer like that.

The other kids would nod knowingly. "Right, right . . ."

And as much as I hated being Miranda Milty's sister, I liked this feeling of respect. I was almost dangerous, by association. And because there is nothing really dangerous about being Emily Milty (or a wool coat, gray soup, or Sears carpeting), it felt good. (Almost as good as stealing a phone right out of the front office!)

"I'm sure it's a mistake," I told Jean with a firm voice. I wanted to add that there was no way my sister even had a dog, because the Miltys aren't dog people. My mother says so every time the subject of dogs comes up, in public or private. "We Miltys aren't dog people," she says solemnly with a kind of uppity tone, a tone that I know well because, like it or not, my mother is a future possibility for me and sometimes I can hear that uppity tone coming out of my own mouth. Maybe I used it right then when I told Jean I was sure it was a mistake. What can I do, though? I am Emily Milty.

But the truth is that I don't really know anything about my sister. (Hell, maybe even my dad and Junie run a damn bulldog farm in Pasadena!) I hadn't seen my sister, in fact, for a year and a half, since our grandmother's funeral. Miranda had come alone, leaving Marco, a six-month-old at the time, with a friend. (I'd only seen pictures of Marco. Every few months one would appear in an envelope with no return address.) Miranda's appearance at the funeral was like a miracle, a vision almost. It was so quick and grief-clouded. (My grandmother was a wonderful woman, and it seemed like another horrible loss in my mother's life. How many could she take?) I had wondered how Miranda had heard about our grandmother's death at all, since my mother wasn't in touch with her, but I'd been too disoriented to ask then and, until this moment with Jean, I'd put it out of my mind. I changed the subject. With girls like Jean, you can change subjects and, pretty easily, throw them off the trail.

"That homework took so long. Did you finish it?"

Jean shrugged and looked up at the clock with her pinched eyebrows and trudged off.

I wished Jean hadn't told me. I was frazzled now. I don't like being frazzled. How would I make it through biology? I had to be strong for Miss Finch, who depended on me for the limited joy in her life. Maybe it's a lie, I said to myself. But really, now that Jean had said it, I knew that it was true, that my sister was in town again. I could feel Miranda's presence, a certain closeness, as if at any moment someone would cough in the hall and I would look up and she would be standing there, shimmering in her body glitter.

I sat by the bank of crank-out windows that overlooked the parking lot. I had no idea what kind of car my sister would be driving and I had no indication that she would show up here at all, but still the least I could do was keep a lookout, and so I did it.

During biology, Miss Finch wrote on the board *He-man* and *Domestic Bliss.* You see, sometimes Miss Finch knows exactly what to say, what to do. Sometimes she tunes into my needs and she provides answers. (Like God, but the Miltys, who aren't dog people, are also not God people. Religion is a crutch, my mother says. It'll make you walk with a limp. To which I sometimes think, What if we're already limping? Because of life? And we need a crutch?) She told us that certain female animals ("The peacock," she said. "The walrus . . .") choose their mates by the first approach, meaning they look for flashy, big, virile males who would be most likely to produce strong offspring. This was the he-man approach.

I thought of Tommy Eldridge, who was loud and drove a red car. And poor Miranda, I thought, poor Miranda fell for it. (Sometimes I can feel really sorry for Miranda!) See, Miss Finch knows better than to fall for such trickery. (I kind of love Miss Finch.)

"But other animals," Miss Finch continued, "blue bills, for example, woo their mates by providing them with gifts of food to prove that they will be good fathers, protecting and nurturing their young."

I thought of my mother's stories of courtship, how my father bought her a leather-bound collection of the works by one of the Brontës, whom she loved, and pear-shaped ear-rings because they'd picked pears together once on a field trip as children. And then how he'd bought Junie a tennis bracelet (which, by the way, is made of diamonds, I came to find out, not a sweatband of some sort) with money from my parents' joint checking account.

I looked out across the class. There was Justin Gunter. My boyfriend. Or, well, at least my mother thinks he is my boyfriend . . . because I've told her that he is my boyfriend. But Justin isn't the flashy type or the wooing type. We kissed once under the mistletoe at a Christmas party at his house. I'd gotten invited because his mother and my mother work in the shoe department of Boscov's. The Gunters are dog people. They have a Lab named Arlen, a great big-headed, pink-tongued, loud-breathing dog that sniffed my crotch when I walked into the party, as dogs do.

The kiss had been almost an accident. We bumped into each other under the mistletoe. I accidentally got punch on his white shirt, and some neighbor girl yelled out, "Kiss! Kiss!" She was drunk.

I told my mother about the kiss, loosely, not the specifics. My mother had smiled shyly, had put up her hand to say, "No more. That's enough. It's private," and then kissed me on the forehead. I thought of Justin Gunter's kiss right there in Miss Finch's biology class—the tight press of his lips, the wispy brush of his light mustache. (And I thought of other things, too; that party hadn't gone perfectly well in the end. Justin made fun of me. And I snuck into his bedroom and shoved one of his sneakers into my faux-designer backpack.)

"Choose wisely," Mrs. Finch said. "Choose very wisely or, if in doubt, choose not to. Do you understand what I'm saying?"

And was it my imagination or was Miss Finch staring at me, Emily Milty, third row back on the left? Be like Miss Finch, I thought, be more like Miss Finch. She's an unlikely role model, I know that, in her cardigans—orange for Halloween, red for Christmas. But Miss Finch has a part to play in life, and you can't rely on the Justin Gunters or the George Miltys or the Tommy Eldridges of the world. Miss Finch has stuck with her role, and there was much to be said for that.

My mother never said anything against Tommy Eldridge. She was afraid of him. He never knocked at the door. He'd gun the engine, and Miranda would clomp down the stairs. She'd flip her hand up, the other hand fitting into her tight jean pocket, and say, "I'll be home late. Don't wait up."

"How late?" my mother would chirp, trying to sound casual.

Miranda would say, "How would I know? I haven't even gone out the door yet."

My mother would glance at me, her eyes shifty with fear, and I'd give her the big eyes and my shrug.

I could have learned how to come and go as I please, like Miranda. She'd already oiled the door hinges. But I didn't. Miranda would strut out the front door, the car's engine would tear open and they'd roar off, and my mother would start crying.

And then she would turn her eyes on me, Emily Milty. She would say, "Tell me what you're learning in school."

But what she meant was: *Don't ever leave me. Don't ever leave me like that.*

In fact, just last week, she'd been sad, when we were eating, just the two of us, at the table in the kitchen with seating for four. Sadness would sometimes just descend, because Miranda was gone and Marco was out there somewhere with her. My mother's grandson. She's already lost her husband and her mother. And she said, "How about something from *Oklahoma!* to brighten things up around here?"

So I stood up, opened my mouth, and sang my heart out. "Oh, What a Beautiful Morning" and "Surrey with the Fringe on Top." I smiled and sang and rocked on my heels and then slapped my knee. "Oklahoma O.K."

How can I explain it? I would stay here forever. I would make up for my father and Miranda. And, in return, she would offer me all of their uneaten portions of love . . . so much love that I could almost choke on it.

We had a deal.

I was nervous when I got home from school. I always tell my mother everything, a moment-to-moment recap of my day over doughnuts and milk. I thought it would only raise false expectations if I told her about Ed Pencher seeing Miranda at BJ's buying dog food. I knew that my mother lived on the hope that Miranda would come back (and maybe my father, too). Somewhere deep in her maternal heart, she still expected Miranda to bound through the door. No matter how wonderful I am, no matter how uplifting and simply good, each moment that slipped by without Miranda was a call for disappointment.

I decided not to say anything about Ed Pencher seeing Miranda. But I certainly couldn't say that nothing interesting happened, because every detail of my life interests my mother, everything, especially anything I have to say about Justin Gunter. "It's so nice that you have a little friend of your own," my mother says.

The truth is that I'm not so sure that Justin Gunter likes me at all. Miss Finch once told us about Inuit mothers, that they know their children so well that the babies don't have to wear diapers. The mothers can sense when the baby in the papoose is about to pee, and they then just slip them out to do so.

After the kiss under the mistletoe and before I stole his sneaker, Justin walked up to me, his teeth stained pink from the spiked punch, his upper lip wet with it, his apple cheeks shiny with sweat, and said, "I always see you with your mother. Don't you have any friends your own age?"

"Sure I do!" I get along really well with both of the girls who have lockers on either side of me. Both of them, not to mention Miss Finch.

"It's like the Inuit mothers," he'd said.

"What?"

"Does your mother know everything about you? Does she still carry you in a papoose? I saw you two at the movies together. Shouldn't you get out and live a little? And I don't just mean here at my stupid Christmas party."

"And you're living large?" I said. "You're really going buck-wild? Please!"

I kept this part of the story from my mother. It would have made her knit her brow. She would have said that men were imperfect. She might have even started to cry.

Sometimes I don't even like Justin Gunter. He's a little over-weight and sometimes he wears his shirts too tight at the neck and they seem to cut off oxygen to his big red face. He's sar-castic with everybody, and although they seem to like it, I don't. It's confusing. It sends mixed messages. What would my mother think if she knew that Justin Gunter wasn't my boyfriend? (Was my mother jealous of Miranda? As jealous as I was when she came home those nights after being out late with Tommy Eldridge and told me how in love she was, and where they did it? Hadn't my mother married George Milty when she was still young and pretty like Miranda? Couldn't she have lived a little? What does she think about when she's listening to the car radio and hums along like she does to "Muskrat Love" and "Afternoon Delight"?) What if my mother knew that I was only a coat-soup-carpeting sort of a girl who doesn't have anything better to do than comfort her grieving mother?

I walked into the kitchen through the back door, the cur-tains puffing out and then going slack. My mother was lining up the doughnuts on a tray. I decided to talk about Jean Pencher's eyebrows again. It couldn't be overstated.

"There should be a policy against penciling in your eye-brows," I declared. "A firm policy."

My mother turned then to put the tray on the table, and I

could tell that she'd been crying. Her eyes were puffed and red.

"Emily," she said, and then she smiled broadly and then the tears welled up and she covered her crinkled mouth. She walked over to me and hugged me around the shoulders. She whispered into my ear, "Miranda is back! She's back! Our Miranda!"

Over the next two days, my mother told me all the new things she'd learned about Miranda. Miranda had gotten a job at the veterinary practice on Cleveland Avenue. It was just secretarial, but she was thinking of becoming a vet herself and so she was checking it out from the inside. My mother said "from the inside" as if Miranda were FBI working undercover in the mob. Marco was in day care. He was a great talker. My mother had conversed with him about a tricycle on the phone. Miranda had three dogs, a great Dane and two mutts she'd taken in as strays.

But I couldn't process any of it. I would tell myself the old Miranda stories—how much Miranda had loved Tommy Eldridge, and when he decided to take off with the money he'd saved from working at the par-three, he wanted Miranda to come, too, because she was pregnant and he was going to prove everyone wrong and make something of himself and his new family. I remembered Miranda's long, impassioned speeches about Tommy Eldridge. There was no need for the speeches. My mother wouldn't stop her, couldn't. She wanted her to stay with us, to raise the baby at home while attending the community college, and my mother said so, calmly, unconvincingly. It was as if my mother had been pulled from the audience to help out with a scene. (It was called "performance theater" or something like that. My theater teacher had talked about seeing it in New York. It was bad.) Miranda had her suitcase packed, and Tommy was waiting at the intersection. I replayed in my mind how my mother and I followed her to the front yard, the sprinkler ticking around our shoes.

Miranda said, "Well, this is good-bye, like it or not. I know that I'm the black sheep. I know I never fit in."

"That's not true," my mother said. "It's not true." But her tone rang otherwise. She was desperate. "We love you, Miranda," she said. And although this was true, it only made the first denials more obvious lies. It seemed to be that my mother loved her despite the fact that she never fit in, or because of it.

I was desperate, too, though, and this desperation was what I remembered most of all, probably because I'd begun to feel it again every once in a while since Jean Pencher had told me the news. It was a tightening in my throat, as if my muscles were made out of elastic bands, the kind found on nightgown sleeves, and someone had just cinched them. Even out on the front lawn the night Miranda ran off, the sprinkler spraying my bare legs, my shoes soaked down to the socks, I seemed to understand that if Miranda left like this, so angrily, I would spend the rest of my life making up for it, and I would never leave.

I said, "Go, then, if you're going to go. Don't make any more out of it. Don't be so dramatic! Just go."

And I stormed inside, slamming the screen door behind me and running up to my room, where I dipped below the window and watched her run up the street under the streetlight-moons to the car at the intersection, a car that then roared away.

This is what I thought about, not any of the newfangled facts like Miranda's coming for dinner! With Marco! No. I refused to try to believe that. I stuck with the past, with the set of roles the past had well established, with what I knew had happened and was dependably true.

* * *

I was upstairs in my room, waiting, all of my stolen objects laid out on the floor, my padlocks and banners and bonnets, the office telephone, and Justin Gunter's sneaker. If my mother had knocked on the door, I would have told her to wait; I'd have shoved everything under the bed. But she wasn't going to knock. She was waiting for Miranda and Marco, who were late—not a surprise. My mother was fluttering around downstairs. She'd vacuumed the whole house, rubbed down all the wood with Pledge, and wiped the windows until they squeaked. And now, from my room, I could smell the bubbling meat loaf, the buttered carrots and green beans, the caramel dessert—Miranda's favorite.

I was looking at my loot, thinking, No one knows this about me. No one knows that Emily Milty is a thief.

When the doorbell rang, I arranged everything in the back of my closet, stood up, and looked in the mirror. I'm ordinary. I have nice eyes. My teeth aren't too big or too small. Neither is my nose. But Miranda gobbled up all of the prettiness. She was first and took more than her share. (Miranda was a thief first. I'm just reclaiming things here and there. I've been stolen from myself, you know.) I brushed my hair and walked downstairs.

Miranda was standing in the hall and Marco was sitting on the floor at her feet, taking off his shoes. He had dark hair like Tommy and lots of it, though it had been smoothed down with a comb. My mother hugged Miranda carefully and kissed her cheek the way she would our ninety-year-old aunt Sassy.

Miranda was a little skinnier than she'd been at our grandmother's funeral, softer. Her hair was a brash blond, still long, but straggly even though it had been brushed. She wore a big necklace with wood cutouts of giraffes and rhinos. And parrot earrings. She was stomping her feet as if they were cold. My mother took her coat to hang up for her. Miranda still spoke loudly. Her mouth was, in fact, bigger than the rest of the family's, and she spoke using all of it.

She was saying, "I forgot it gets chilly here. I mean, I expect

Delaware to be so much warmer than Michigan and it isn't much different." Tommy had had friends in Michigan. It's where he left her.

My mother doesn't ever really leave Delaware. It has a city, farmland, and a small slice of the ocean for vacationing. I was saying inside my head, *We've never even been to Michigan. We've never been invited or even been given a phone number or an address.* And again I thought of my grandmother's funeral: How exactly had Miranda gotten the news?

My mother said, "Oh, is that right? Is that so?"

And then Miranda looked up and she gasped a little, startled to see me standing on the stairs. "Emily, you scared me. You're always sneaking up on people!" This is the type of thing that's often said of people like me, the Emily Miltys of the world—the wool coats and gray soups and Sears carpetings.

Miranda had lipstick stuck on one tooth, but she had a perfect nose and her face was still glossy and all-American. I walked down the stairs.

"I didn't mean to be sneaking up," I said. "I was just waiting my turn." I felt like a grade-schooler. Since when did I say, "Waiting my turn"? I never had to wait my turn anymore. It was always my turn.

At dinner, Marco sang his ABC's, and everyone clapped. He slipped under the table and poked at our legs. Each time we were supposed to say, "Ouch!" But I didn't.

Miranda said things like, "I'm thinking of staying here in town for a while." And, "It's a nice town actually. I mean, I'd have never said that before I left, but it is." She said, "It's such a nice place to raise kids." She seemed oblivious to what her comments might mean to my mother.

I wanted my mother to explode at her, to say, "Of course it's nice! It's where I raised you! It's where I told you to raise Marco!" But my mother only encouraged her, talking about the parks and the recreation leagues as if she were informing a new neighbor of all that was now available to them in the land of plenty.

Miranda turned to me halfway through dessert. She said, "So, are you seeing anybody?"

I looked at my mother and then back at my plate. I could feel the cinched elastic of my throat, a small tug, a pull.

"What?" Miranda said, glancing from my mother to me and back again. "Who is it? Anyone I know?"

"No," I said, meaning *No, I'm not seeing anyone*, but also meaning *No, you don't know him*, because I knew that my mother wanted to think I'd found a boyfriend in Justin Gunter.

My mother said her lines, as I had expected. "I think that Emily has a special fella at school. Justin Gunter. He lives just three streets over from us!"

"Oh, Justin," Miranda said, pointing her fork at my mother. "The one you told me about a while ago, the one she kissed at the Christmas party."

This, I wasn't expecting—a departure from the script. I stood without thinking about it, a natural reaction to my body's stiffening up. I stared at my mother, who was tsk-tsking with a little shake of her head, meaning *Oh, no, no, Miranda, you shouldn't have mentioned it. You've spilled the beans, dear.*

I glared at one face and then the next, the next and back to the first. I wanted answers. When had my mother told Miranda about Justin Gunter's kiss? A while ago? Not at the funeral; I'd barely known Justin then. I imagined Miranda and my mother's conversations. How many had they had? Had there been months' worth of them, more than a year? I could just imagine their dialogue.

"Poor Emily!" my mother would say.

"Why doesn't she get a life?" Miranda would answer.

Had they been having these sneaky conversations since the funeral or before? Is that how Miranda knew?

I turned to my sister. "And who are you seeing these days? Tommy Eldridge types? Dirty high-school dropouts?"

"I see people all the time!" She gave a laugh that was more a bark. "I'm not like you, Emily. I've had my share. I've been there and done that!" Again, she barked loudly, but she looked tired, too, older suddenly.

I felt sick. I could feel the caramel and butter and gravy rising in the back of my narrow throat. I swallowed hard.

"Are you a dog?" I said. "Are you some sort of dog now? Barking at the table?"

I glanced at my mother, but she couldn't look me in the eye. It wasn't the best exit line, but I picked up my plate anyway, piling it neatly with my silverware and my glass. I walked into the kitchen, letting the dishes clatter in the sink.

"Emily!" my mother called out.

But I was already at the closet fishing through hangers for my coat. I heard my mother say, "Excuse me." And then her feet shuffled through the kitchen. But by the time she appeared, I had already put on my coat and was buttoning it up.

I said, "You've been talking about me? How long have you two been talking about me?"

My mother said, "Emily, no, we don't talk about you. She calls me sometimes during the day when you're at school. I just never mentioned her calls. It hasn't been easy for her. It hasn't."

She wiped her hands on her skirt and held them out to me. She wanted me to rest my head on her chest and cry and cry until the shiny duck pin on her sweater made an imprint on my cheek—just like I had after not getting a real part in *Oklahoma!*, after being pushed into the stupid chorus, where I only wandered around in a herd like a singing cow.

I shook my head. "You shouldn't have! You broke our promise!"

My mother paused. She looked confused. "What promise?"

I couldn't answer. It hadn't been the kind of promise that had been put into words. But it was a promise, an agreement.

Oklahoma O.K.! I turned and walked out the front door into the night, which was much, much warmer than anywhere in Michigan.

At first I didn't know that I was heading toward Justin Gunter's house. I could only think of how my mother had never slipped, not once. I thought back to her tearful performance in the kitchen. Hadn't she known for some time? Hadn't she decided that it was time to tell me? How long had I been lifting my mother up, sticking with her all of the time, denying my life for hers, and all the while she was keeping secrets from me? She'd lied to me. Why? Because I'm so fragile? What does she know about my life? She was a remarkable actor, I decided. Remarkable. So good, in fact, I'd never known she was acting at all!

Soon I found myself rounding the corner of Briar, starting my march uphill toward Justin Gunter's house. I wanted to see him with my own eyes. I wanted to have my own life, and in this life, I was the kind of person to march over to Justin Gunter's house if I wanted to.

It was a ranch. The first floor was nearly dark. I could hear a pumping base line coming from the basement, where Justin's older brother lived. I could hear the dog, Arlen, bark once, twice, but then he gave up, probably flopping to the floor in a tongue-lolling, heavy-breathing heap of fur.

I walked up the cement path. The screen door squeaked as I opened it. Here, tucked inside the screen door, I could imagine Justin's face appearing in the cracked door, his chin above a chain that he would quickly unlatch. I knocked. But there was no answer. I knocked again and took a few steps back, looking over my shoulder across the street to the other houses, their blank windows staring at me like a row of my classmates all screwed into their desk chairs, their implacable faces, the vacant stares. *Are you watching me?* I wanted to ask. *Can you see me?*

No, I decided, no one ever watches me, except my mother. No one could ever really see me. I was nearly invisible. How else could I steal so very many things? I stepped off the porch and onto the Gunters' lawn. I walked through the side yard to the only lit room. Ducking behind a bush next to the house, I leaned up to the window, my knuckles poised over the glass.

And there was Justin Gunter. He was sitting at his desk, his head resting on the fold of his textbook, his arms sprawled out. Was he asleep? And here I was: Emily Milty in the dark, looking in his window. Had my mother ever done such a thing? My dithering mother? Had Miss Finch ever found herself in a situation like this, breath-minty, mothbally Miss Finch? It dawned on me at that moment that maybe there was some other future version of Emily Milty, besides my mother and Miss Finch, out there in the distance . . . a crazy woman who knocked on windows in the middle of the night. *I am not the person I've always known.* That's what I said to myself. And then I knocked.

Justin's head popped up. His face was flushed and there was a line running down his cheek from the center of the book. He looked around. I waved. And he drew back, surprised, but then loped to the window and opened it up.

"Were you asleep?" I asked. This was an odd thing to say, in the dark, outside of Justin Gunter's window.

"No," he said, which was a lie.

"Well, I just wanted to tell you . . ." And here I realized that I didn't really have anything to tell Justin Gunter. "I just wanted to say . . ."

"I can't believe you're here," he said, with a hint of happiness, with a kind of I-can't-believe-my-luck ring to this voice.

"Oh," I said. "Well, I should probably explain . . ."

"Does your mother know you're here?"

"No," I said. "I don't need to have permission for everything. We aren't Inuits, contrary to what you have to say about it."

"You know, Emily Milty, I was asking you out. I was saying you should go to the movies without your mother. And, instead, with someone like me. That's what I was saying."

"Oh," I said, feeling hot and nauseous and tight in the throat and happy, too.

"But you got mad and you stormed off."

"Oh," I said again. Was I an Oh-machine? Only capable of Oh-ing?

"What did you want to tell me?"

"See, I don't know. I guess I just wanted to tell you that I'm a thief, and no one knows that."

"Are you going to rob us?" He smiled. "You don't seem like a cat burglar."

"I don't seem like who I really am," I said.

"Neither do I," Justin said.

"Oh," I said, again with the Ohs, and we looked at each other for a moment. We just kind of stared at each other the way people do, I guess, when they recognize something of themselves in the other person. "Well, I should go."

"I'll see you tomorrow, though, right? In bio?"

"Yep," I said.

"Good," he said.

And then I didn't walk away. I asked him a question: "Are you going to ask me out again?"

"I didn't ask you out in the first place."

"Well, are you going to?"

"I think so."

"Okay, then."

Then I walked away and he shut the window.

But the window quickly flew back open. "Did you steal my sneaker at the Christmas party?" he asked.

"Yes," I said. "And four bonnets from backstage at *Oklahoma!* and one of the phones from the main office, but I never told anybody any of it."

"Wow! You know, I've been looking for that sneaker. Can I have it back?"

"Sure."

And that was it. I thought of my sister's long hair swinging across her back and Tommy Eldridge's motor and how everything had changed. I thought of my mother's meat loaf and little Marco under the table. I started to cry, sharp little bites in my chest, but not because I was sad. I wasn't. Miranda was home. My sister had come back to us. And Marco was here now, and I am still a wool coat and gray soup and Sears carpeting, but not as much as I was just that morning when I woke up. I was becoming someone else. I could feel it.

By the time I walked down Justin Gunter's street, I was heading home. Soon I was at my front door, fishing a key from under a clay flowerpot. And that's where they found me, my mother, my sister, and my little nephew with his lumpy dark hair. And I realized that, no, they didn't really know me, that I hadn't ever really been all that honest with them, and maybe more important, I didn't really know them. Who was this woman with her red nose and her hands clasped nervously at her chest? What did my mother really want? And my sister. She was older now. She was tired, a little heartbroken maybe, but stronger. She was a mother, and her son— who'd stayed up too late—was wrapping himself around her leg, saying, "That's her. That's Aunt Emmy from the picture."

What picture? I wanted to know. Had my sister packed a picture of us away in her bag when she left with Tommy Eldridge? Had she missed us?

I didn't know very much of anything at all. But I was forgiven, awash in the porch light, redeemed by nothing more than my arrival. My eyes shined into their eyes, back and forth, from one to the other, like a roving spotlight.

Rutford Becomes a Man

Ned Vizzini

"Rutford! Time to get up! It's your birth*day*!"

I have no intention of getting up. I do not care what day it is.

"Rutford?"

I am not moving.

I have been awake already for a number of minutes—perhaps one hundred—but this does not mean that I am fully conscious. I like to spend my time in a blessed half-sleep where I am in touch with and in control of my thoughts but also free to let them roam. In this state I am very aware of sounds inside and outside the home. Inside sounds of food cooking and family members murmuring to one another. Outside sounds of birds and crickets that did not manage to finish chirping during the night, and small bells tinkling as patrons move in and out of local shops for early purchases. These are pleasant sounds. When loud, unpleasant voices interrupt my mental explorations I am very perturbed.

"Rut*ford*!"

Now there is the sound of steps, hard wooden steps that bang as if the person climbing them were wearing shod boots—except Ma has such tough feet and unbelievable heft that she can bang like this with her bare soles. She goes up the nine . . . ten . . . eleven stairs before reaching my door and giving it a sharp and similarly powerful bang, as if using her thick feet.

"Up!"

"I will not be getting up this morning," I announce. Except I announce it lying down, and something about that position causes the words to squeak out of my thorax. That mimics the mousy sound I make when creeping up and down the stairs with my small, weak feet.

"Oh, your voice is crackin'," she says. "Still a small one after all. C'mon, Rutford, get up, don't tryin' spoil this day for all of us."

I sit all the way up in bed to announce with full force, deeply: "I will not be getting up at all."

"Rut*ford*!" More banging.

"I told you no—" I begin, but suddenly there is a new sound, that of rapid-fire feet carelessly flapping up the eleven steps. A voice erupts that is two octaves higher than Ma's, but with the same intonation.

"*Rut*ford! Ma won't give me my special present for your birthday lessn' you get up and come down and make it like a normal birthday and I already know what I'm gettin' and I want it bad and I don't care if you're so crazy that all you want to do is spend time in your room, you still count for having a birthday so I still get a present so you might as well not even try because I've been thinking about this all—"

I wage that my mother is coaxing her, holding her hand or patting her small back. Ma knows that when there is no work with my father, one of the only ways to get me out of bed is to bring my sister into the fray and encourage her to screech; her pitch triggers low and primal responses in my brain, and it is nearly impossible for me to remain in the vicinity of its source. So I put my feet on the warm floor (an advantage to never getting out of bed in the early morning—the floor is comfortable when I finally do) and walk to the door, careful as always not to get splinters. I pull it open.

"I do not care if it is my birthday."

Ma is smiling in a dopey way that I suppose all mothers

smile. Even surrogate ones. "Well, hurry down, like it or not," she says. "We're having breakfast."

"You're odd," my sister says, holding Ma's hand, in a similar bathrobe to hers. They turn and walk down the stairs. I turn back and close the door and wash my hands in the bucket that I keep under the bed for the purposes of washing only. I do not keep any of the other kinds of buckets, the ones that some use for waste or the effluvium of self-ruination. These are reprehensible buckets.

I walk down the stairs sullenly, which is how I do everything and which I feel is a much underused word.

One can eat sullenly.

One can walk sullenly.

One can do a drill sullenly.

One can even sleep sullenly, with practice, hating the institution but desiring its release.

Sullenness is an attitude, a worldview that I espouse proudly. And I like the way it sounds. It sounds like how it is. This is a phenomenon called onomatopoeia, which is another underused word. I used to have a good dictionary in my room. It was a comfort.

Down the stairs is a wooden door frame with a hook in it but no door. I touch this hook for good luck even though it has never given me any.

In front of me, the wooden table has eggs on each plate and an orange and a cup of tea by the seat that was obviously meant for me, the one at the head of the table, because I am the birthday boy.

"Took the liberty of accommodating myself to your seat," my father says. "Since you declined to wake up at a decent hour and then gave your mother trouble." He sips my tea and gulps down the word *Happy*.

". . . Birthday," he says.

My mouth is open at his insolence.

"Shut that, you'll get flies," he says, and drinks more of his tea. *My* tea.

"Ma, why is he sitting in my seat?" I ask, putting my hands over the top of the other seat, where I usually sit on all days that are not my birthday.

"I thought that you weren't gettin' up, anyway. It shouldn't matter what seat your father's in," she says, bringing food to the center of the table. The food is always the same—eggs and eggs and biscuits and biscuits and, when we are lucky, bacon and gravy. Today we have a plate of bacon and a decanter of gravy.

"Well, I do not care," I intonate, "but why must we tamper with tradition? It is tradition for everyone in the family to sit in *that* chair on their birthday." I point at it.

"Why don't you sit down where you are?" my father says lowly and quietly, and I do because I know to listen to him when he sounds that way, even if it is in the form of a question. I know there are certain questions that one should respond to as if they were orders. They are rhetorical with an added touch of dread. There is no word for them. Gravo-rhetorical questions, I suppose. Brutal-rhetorical.

I sit. Ma sits across from me and my sister piles in at the end opposite my father. It is amazing how she can fold herself into a seat as if she were three small people, bunching up her arms and legs to make it a complex process. Once I am seated, my father's hand and my sister's reach out in unison for us to all say Grace. My father's hands have gotten rougher in the thirteen years I have known him (the first three years do not register), but they are still not proper Texas hands; they are the hands of a clerk, which makes sense, since that is what he is.

"Bow yer heads," Ma says.

Grace is ridiculous because obviously there is no God, but I have learned to make certain compromises with my family. I bow my head and Ma begins:

"Bless us, O Lord, through these thy gifts and thus to thy service. Amen."

"A-meh," I respond. I never say "Amen" fully because I feel that this is caving into the entire concept of God, and so I make myself a quiet revolutionary and drop the *n*. I do a similar feat with the Lord's Prayer—I do not say the last word or significant two words of each line:

"Our Father who art in, Hallowed be thy, thy kingdom, thy will, on earth as it is, give us this day our daily, and forgive us our, as we forgive those who trespass, and lead us not into, but deliver us." This renders the meaning of the prayer ridiculous yet very progressive; it is difficult for me not to laugh at my own cleverness when I get away with it in church every week. I have been doing it for five—no, six—years now.

I lean back in my seat and twist to crack the bones in my back. The crack is deep and extended—a good morning one—involving many bones and seven distinct pops. As I relax into my chair, it feels like something has been released in my back; soothing fluids now soak it, giving me the courage to sit through the meal.

"Don't do that," my father says. He is eating eggs.

"Do what?"

"Stress your joints. That's for old men."

"Yes, sir." There are times when this is prudent.

"So how does it feel?" Ma asks. She is eating eggs as well. Everyone is eating besides me. I spend too much time thinking to eat as quickly as these people.

"How does what feel?"

"Your birthday! Being sixteen! In'nit exciting?"

"It is important," I say. "Going from thirteen to fourteen was a big change. I felt I had entered a productive midlife period of youth. Now I am at an even higher plane. Fifteen to sixteen is perhaps larger than thirteen to fourteen. This excites me."

"You're odd," my sister says. She is eating a biscuit and forking her eggs over to Ma.

"It excites you?" my father asks.

"Yes."

"Well, you don't seem excited."

"Well, you must be misinterpreting my exuberance," I say. Sarcasm is a cousin to sullenness.

"No lip," he says.

It is so ridiculous to hear him using these rural expressions as if he can fool me. Every time I hear him, I want to get up and scream across whatever table or desk or pew or bed or piece of furniture happens to be nearby: "You are a clerk! From *England*! You have no right to talk this way! Your weakness and propensity to please others have led you to adopt the absurd figures of speech that permeate this hole in which we have settled! You are not my father! You brute!"

But I always think better of this because such outbursts lead to violence. It does not matter what continent we are on. He hit me over there, where all fathers hit their sons, and he does it over here, too, where fathers hit their sons almost as much. Part of me has been waiting for the day when I am big enough to hit back. But due to my diminutive stature, I should just forget about that. So I shut up and stay as good as I can while still maintaining sullenness. And it is through this arrangement that I have avoided being hit for two years.

"What do you remember most about this year of working?" Ma asks.

"I wish I were still in school."

"There isn't any more school," she says. "You need to remember that."

"You could send me back to England, where there is an institution called university."

Ma sighs. "You're here now. You need to stop talking like a fool."

"You're a cow," I say quietly, into my eggs. But not quietly enough.

"Don't you *dare* speak to your mother like that!" My father rises from his seat, and although he is not big, he is big enough. "I am not going to *stand* for this—"

He is standing.

"—and neither is anyone else in this family. I want you to stop eating right now—"

I'm not eating.

"—and apologize to your mother. And then I want you to tell us all something that you were thankful for this year. And then that will be the end of it, and you will shut your mouth and be happy and eat until you get your present."

One present? I look at my eggs. What is the rule for eggs? Their edibility diminishes at the square of the time they are in front of one's face. Their coldness progresses at twice the rate of tea—

"Rutford?" This is my sister, echoing my father, waiting for my statement.

I suppose I should say that my real name is William, and although there are a lot of Williams in Texas, there are very few William Rutherfords, so when you go to a new school at age eight, it is very easy as a smart, hopeless, realist English boy to get called Rutherford, which then shortens to Rutford as an insult because it sounds like what animals do to reproduce: rutting. Yet I would wage that very few boys who suffer in this manner have their own families to add to the list of assailants.

"I . . ." I begin. "I apologize to Ma for giving her 'lip.' " I look at her. She nods and keeps eating. "And in this year of eighteen ninety-seven, I was greatly enlightened by my work with Father, who showed me how to calculate accounts for the new station in Lubbock that was recently put into operation by Standard Oil."

"And isn't this the most important and lucrative business to come to this part of Texas ever?" my father asks. "Besides the mine?"

"Yes."

"And aren't you proud that your father is helping to calculate the accounts for Mr. Gummerin?"

"Yes."

"So you are proud of your father." He points his fork at me.

"Yes."

"Good. And you are sorry to your mother?"

"Yes." I already said this, but as I indicated: compromise.

"Well, Happy Birthday." My father gets up and allows me to sit at his seat. My seat. There are few eggs left but the ones here are warmer than what was in front of me because Father was served last. I eat them all.

My sister receives a stuffed dog for my birthday. This dog used to belong to the Clemenses, who live two houses down from us. When the Clemenses decided to put the dog down, my father asked if he could use it for his first taxidermy project. The result is on the table. The dog has his right eye about an inch too right, but other than that he was sewn up acceptably: no limbs missing or organs left in. My sister loves it instantly and does an admirable job pretending to be surprised by it since Ma told her months ago that it would be her present. (She told me, too. Ma is not discreet.) My sister says that the misplaced eye is lucky and that the dog is Lucky and I am kind enough not to point out that the eye is glass and the dog is dead. It doesn't seem to bother anyone else that a deceased creature is being passed around the kitchen table while plates caked with drying egg yolk collect its accompanying filth. The dog is medium-size and brown, the way I conjecture all canines would end up by means of evolution if they were allowed to interbreed (rut, Rutford) freely as they are in my town. I am a diligent believer in evolution. This is why my family disconcerts me so; it is clearly heading backward, away from the natural progress.

"Oh, he's so lucky—Lucky!—lucky Lucky!" my sister says, hugging the treated fur.

"Stuffed animals are becoming very popular in the East," my father says with his fork. "We are ahead of everyone else with them. These are going to be indispensable for children in a few years." When I hear him say *indispensable*, it reminds me that he is intelligent, and part of me burns for the set of circumstances that led him to this stifling place and shameful situation.

My father is a criminal, a common criminal, I have to remind myself when I become enamored of him while he is calculating accounts for Mr. Gummerin with an ease that none can match. What brought him to Texas were dogs, common mutts like the one he just brought to the table, except live ones, which he made extra money handling bets on in England. One day one of his clients, in whose affairs Father was helplessly tied up, ended up owing a man named Ricardo Hump so much money that he thought it would be better—an "opportunity," even; he called it an opportunity—to leave for America, where there were fortunes to be made in the West. Just as soon as my real mother gave birth to my sister, who we at that point did not know would be a sister, and whose birth we did not know would kill my real mother.

"Now, son, it's time for your present," Father says. "Emiline, you have to leave."

My sister would under no circumstances leave me to receive a birthday present by myself—it has always been imperative for her to peek into all of my affairs, and presents are of particular interest—except these *particular* circumstances have afforded her a new toy with which to play. And when Father mentions that there is a rope out in the yard that she can use to tie up Lucky and lead him on a *treasure hunt*, she is so smitten that she forgets about me and leaves the table, sliding out of her seat as if it were a carriage and dragging Lucky by a front leg, banging into furniture, toward the back door. Ma takes up the dishes.

"Son." My father stands up. I point at myself questioningly.

"No, you stay seated. Son, for your birthday you are going on a special trip."

My goodness! A trip! It must be back to England! Ma is cleaning the dishes. Silent, but meant to be there—if Father had wanted her to leave, she would have left. Maybe she has to come, too? And then my sister, too? Drawbacks, but I could not be more thrilled—

"We are going back to England?" This is a rhetorical question. O happy day!

"No, you are going to the brothel," Father says, and lowers his eyelids and twists his chin.

"The what?" I stand up now, and I see why I was told not to before—this sort of news would make me stand on the table if I were standing already, to make my point, which is forming quickly: "What? Why? You! *You!* You are sending me to a house of prostitution as a *birthday present*?! What has overtaken you? Are you . . . are you testing me to see if I am some sort of miscreant? Where are your senses? Why—"

"Son," he says, pushing his palm downward. "There is nothing wrong with it. I believe that you deserve to go. You did good work with me this year. You're a man now and it might help you become normal."

Ma speaks up with an "Mmm-hmm" from her washbasin.

"You agree with this plan?" I turn around "You reprehensible harlot! You surrogate Jezebel! You call me your small boy, and then you want to make sure that I am a big 'man'—Ack!"

My father hits me across the face, spoiling two consecutive years of safety. "Apologize to your mother!"

She's not my mother, I say, but this is in my own brain. "I am sorry," I say out loud, but the slap was so stinging, so alive, that it has energized me, and so I reengage my father: "But I am a responsible young man, an intellectual, a hard worker, and I would *still* be an industrious student if I were afforded the opportunity in this unspeakable . . . pigsty! I do not see any conceivable reason why I should be forced down to this place of ill repute—"

"Son, do you even know what goes on at a brothel?"

"I know that it is terrible and morally repugnant."

"Yes, but do you know *what*?"

"Absolutely. Sex."

Ma makes a disapproving sucking noise at the sink.

"But you don't know how any of it works," Father continues.

"Well, I am not going to explain it here." I do very much know how it works.

"You need to know." Father puts a hand on my shoulder. "You really are a young man now, and you have to learn about these things firsthand, and your mother and I . . . we refer you to the professionals. And you are going to love the entire experience, and when you are done with it, it's quite possible that you won't be the exacting little twat"—Ma laughs—"that we've all come to expect and tolerate in this household. Maybe you will stop worrying about death, evolution, your education, my profession, your mother's and my speech patterns—"

"The economy—"

"The economy—"

"Infectious disease—"

"Right, that, too—"

"My own entrapment in this prison of idiocy—"

"Yes, all those things. Maybe you'll stop, and make an actual friend or two, and end up as something of a functional human being. Yes?"

"I am already functioning."

"Of course you are, son. Of course. So relax. Sit down."

I obey. "I hope you both know that I am entirely opposed to this absurd notion that I need female companionship, or indeed, companionship of any kind, to solidify my place in the world and placate the needs of the entirely ordinary and imprudent individuals with which I live and interact. Whom. With whom. Wait . . ."

Ma continues washing dishes.

"Put your nice clothes on in the afternoon," my father says. "We're going this evening."

This is ridiculous and unspeakable. I go to the dictionary in my room (under my bed, next to my honorable bucket) to look up the word *brothel*. This is one of many words that when I heard it uttered by boys at school—although usually they used much worse words, words I cannot even begin to conjure up—I would turn away so as not to hear what it meant. Now, however, I want to know with scientific precision. I know that a brothel houses prostitutes, but perhaps there is another sort of brothel, a less shameful one, that I can lie about and tell others I have been to. (Or I could not go at all; I could run away, but I do not want to be found and hit again.) Maddeningly, however, *brothel* is not in this dictionary, which has been sanitized by the Christians. I agree with the Christians' position that brothels are wicked, but I wish they had allowed me to know what they were.

As for sex, I know what that is. A woman unfurls her ovarian tubes and inserts them into my belly button until a special fluid leaks from *me* into her belly button. If I want to simulate the experience, I can use a hole in a fence and a stick of butter, apparently, according to the boys in my class. But in order to clarify, I look for *intercourse* in the dictionary. *Intercourse: the sexual act as performed between a man and a woman.* I look up *sexual* and find *pertaining to arousal or intercourse.* This is an infuriating loop, and as I ponder it, a certain dread—or rather, a dread certainty—comes to me and I know that other boys, the literate ones at least, must have already encountered this circuitous dictionary sham and I feel left behind.

I long for my old *Oxford English Dictionary*, the one that I snuck into my room back in England and Father did not miss. It is becoming the standard and I feel someday it will be legendary. I could not bring it on the trip over because it was so large, so instead I have this smaller, sanitized *Harmonious Children's Dictionary* that I purchased in New Orleans from a street vendor over the hearty protests of my father. I lugged it all the way into Texas because I needed *some* dictionary to make sure I ended up an educated man and not some nameless lout.

The *Oxford English Dictionary* was so large.

It was so exact.

I loved it and it loved me back; I never stained or mauled it.

I lie on my bed in the hateful Texas heat and try ever so hard to put myself back in that state of half-sleep where I am my own master and the world cares somewhat what I say and think. But it is eleven o'clock, and it is difficult for nondrunks to sleep at this time, I believe, so I get up and tell my parents that I am going for a perambulation.

"You're lucky not to have to work on Saturdays," Ma says.

The street is dusty and horrible. All dust. This was a quick town—it is not nearly as old as me—so the dust hasn't settled yet. And there are ruts in the road, which make me think of my name, which makes me think again of dogs rutting and Lucky the dead dog and the brothel where I will be expected to rut tonight. The houses—even the brick ones—sag under the sun.

Toward the end of town I turn off into an alleyway to avoid the porch of Murphy &c., where the boys congregate. The boys' chief preoccupation is hitting me in the side with small rocks; once, last year, the richest one threw an egg at me. The idea of throwing one . . . it was disgusting and wasteful, and yet the boy's egg flew down from the Murphy &c. porch and right into my back with what must have been the most satisfying crunch, for him. My clothing became soaked in gelatinous filth and I was forced to run home to change, weeping. This boy had discovered a missile superior to small rocks.

Above the road, above the boys, above the defeated and slanted roofs, is the sky. It deserves the songs. It spreads approximately ten degrees farther into the horizon than any other sky I have seen. (Admittedly, I have seen quite a bit of the English sky, which is not really a sky so much as a background for clouds.) It impinges upon the land, but then the land remains huge and open, so it is as if the sky combines with the land, lends it some acreage, a landlord/tenant relationship. I look up at the blue—no clouds today—and waste time on the stupid wish that I could fall into it when I die and have my own constellation up there, one so bright that it shone even during the day.

"Are you ready?" my father asks.

I sit on my bed in my church outfit: black shirt, then more black for a vest, then brown for the shoes, impeccably put together with a hat, of course. I always look wonderful at church as I say my truncated Lord's Prayer. I have been rocking on the bed and comforting myself with the knowledge that I am going to see something new. Ultimately, I may find explanations that I cannot in the *Harmonious Children's Dictionary*. The prospect of this knowledge is the only thing that intrigues me. It is night.

"Come down," Father says, and I work my way down the stairs and touch the hook for good luck. We leave into the hot, dry, black air; we walk swiftly and there is no speaking for minutes.

"You are not going to know precisely what to do," he says finally, triggered by some fatherly duty. "But the madam has assured me you will have fine instruction."

I am looking at the sky again. "Yes, Father."

He grabs my shoulders and turns me to my right. "This is it."

It is a simple, low building, not noticed by me on my walk midday or indeed at any other time during my tenure in this disgusting town. It is not marked.

"This is it?"

"Yes. See?" My father nods his head. In one window—the upper right—a woman sits on a sill fanning herself. The terrace under her appears rotted away, so she must stay in the window, fanning with a rhythm that I would wager is very close to the human heartbeat but I have no time to check. She wears black, like me, and is lit by the room glow, with a stylish triangular hat. I would never have noticed her.

"Come." Father walks to the door below her and I follow. He knocks in a way some might think was coded but I know is simply his manner: *rap rap-rap-rap rap*. He has a nervous condition.

"Yes?" A woman comes to the door, pulls it open slightly, and speaks quietly with my father. I am amazed that they can hear each other because behind the woman—heralded as she opens the door—is a room full of drunks. There is yelling and clinking and music but no windows to confirm the scene; the windows must be on the back and sides of the building, where the new part of the town has just been erected for miners in the last eight months. I wonder what it looks like inside, but the woman has enough respect for the respectable side of town not to completely open the door.

"William Gainor; I had a special arrangement," my father says.

"Oh, yes," the woman answers. "Around the side and up the ladder." She closes the door.

"We aren't here to get you drunk, Lord knows," my father says, which is another expression he has picked up. "You stay out of the saloon."

"Yes, sir."

We move around the right of the building and there, preposterously, is a rope ladder. It seems to lead up . . . right up to two iron pegs next to a window. And this window shares its terrace with the window in which I saw the woman in black! Will this be my prostitute? How disgusting! Have I already *seen her*? Do I know what she looks like?

"I cannot," I say, looking at the ladder, then at my father.

"Why? It's good." He tugs it.

"No! I cannot bring myself to *do this*!"

"Son, get on the ladder."

"But I have seen her! I have seen the woman I am going to defile!"

"I don't know if you can defile anything. Get up and shut your lip."

I look at him and make a promise. "I will never forget this."

"I know you won't, Rutford." And my father stands under me with his hands cupped at my buttocks to ensure that I do not fall on the first few "rungs," and then he stays there making sure that I reach the metal pegs and the terrace. I test with my foot to see if it is rotted and find it acceptable but worthy of censure; I step off the ladder and peer over the terrace at Father, hissing about it. He stops me:

"When you're done, send for me. The madam knows this is expected. Do not come home alone."

"Do you mean bring . . . *her*?"

"*No!* Do not come home until I *take* you home."

"Ah." I nod, trying to think of something to say, but it is difficult for me to see my father as he turns into the night and there is a voice to my right as he leaves, perfectly timed.

"Hallo, Mr. Gainor."

The woman in the window is looking at me.

She's yellow! Oh, the Yellow Trade—I have read about this in the newspapers that make it here. So sad. They bring these women in from the Chinese lands and they do not know what to do with themselves and end up in these terrible prostitution situations and it's all too horrible and I am scared and ready to fling myself off the terrace, from guilt, when the woman stands up and takes my hand and pulls me in the window so fast I do not really know what is happening. We are inside a small, nearly unfurnished bedroom, and the woman in black—who has a bustle in the rear of her dress, fluffy to make her buttocks appear to jut out—is motioning to a woman in red to replace her in her spot on the windowsill. There are two doors in this room, the one that the woman in red just came out of (noise comes from it) and another that appears appropriately sized for a dwarf or perhaps a cat. This is the door that the yellow woman takes me to, turning sideways as she opens it to fit through (although we are both so small, this seems like a theatrical flourish). She closes it behind us and the room we are now in is *very* quiet and *very* small, almost like a prison cell, as I would imagine.

The woman lets go of my hand and sits on the bed. The only object in this room is a bed. "Conjugal bed" is the term that comes to mind. I do not truly know what it means, but I know that this is one.

"Greetings," she says again. "Your name is William, yes?"

"Rutford," I admit. "People call me Rutford."

"William Rutford?"

"No, just . . . Rutford."

"Instead of William."

"Yes."

"Are you certain you would you like me to call you Rutford?"

"If you call me William, I might not know who you were speaking to. It has been a long time since anyone referred to me by that name," I say.

"I see. Well, hallo, Rutford."

"Hallo," I say. "It is a pleasure to meet you, Miss . . ."

"Annabelle."

"Annabelle. How pleasant."

"Never . . . anything?" she asks.

I nod in a way that I hope makes clear that I do not quite understand what she is asking but I am eager to please. Her hair is dark and straight and tied back behind her head, but then somehow it spills over her shoulders in a sort of sheet, shining like a shaped mineral in the candlelight. There must be quite a lot of hair, if it were to be untied.

"You want me to take my hair down?" she asks. Perhaps she sees that I am looking at it.

"I don't know," I say.

"You like it this way?" She grabs it and pulls all of it up, so that her neck is open.

"I don't know," I say.

"You like it this way?" She lets it all out and it flows over her.

"I don't know."

"You like like this?" She pulls it out to the side, being silly, looking like a lioness. She smiles but I cannot grasp the humor right now.

"I don't know."

"Do you like anything?" she asks. "Anything at all?"

"No." I know the answer to that. I have been saying it my whole life. "I hate everything."

"Oh," Annabelle says. "Well, this is going to be easy. Come here on the bed and we will talk and find out if you are truly hopeless, and then, if not, we'll find what you like!" She pats the bed next to her. I sit.

"You seem smart," I say.

"I am."

"How did you get here, then?"

"By boat." She smiles.

"I mean, *why* did you get here? If you're so smart? Why not get married? More foolish girls than you get married."

Annabelle shrugs. "I did not want to get beaten."

"Ah. I understand. Ahm. Where are you from?"

"China."

"Why did you leave China?"

"I had to. My father got in trouble. I had to go. Why do you hate everything?"

"It's all hopeless and disgusting."

"Life is?"

"Yes."

"You feel people are stupid?" she asks.

"Yes."

"No one understands you?"

"Yes."

"I do."

"You do not," I say.

"How come not?"

I sigh and lean back on the bed. She is being paid for this time. She cannot leave. So I say the Basic Premise: "We are all going to die. We are going to die, and once we do, we will not get to go anywhere and we will not get anything permanent, not our gravestones or the love of our friends or families or our art . . . it will all crumble and fade. The only permanent things are the constellations and we will not get one of those—they are all used up. Do you understand?"

"Yes. Except the word *constellations*."

"It's the stars. In the sky. The shapes that they make."

"Oh. I had different ones. I do not know the ones here."

"Well, no matter, the point is no one will remember us when we die, and even if they do, it will be for only a short while. And while we are here we suffer idiots who know *nothing* and cannot comprehend the greatness that lives inside us, and often these idiots are not only our friends and teachers but also our family, our parents, with no expectations for us other than to grow up and breed like animals, and we really are just animals—"

"I never knew my parents," Annabelle says.

"That is unfortunate. My mother died," I say.

"Your father remarried? You have a false mother now?"

"Yes!" I smile. "She's terrible."

"False mothers are the worst. I am happier to have none." She is lying back on the bed, looking up at the ceiling, same as me.

"Look at that stain." I point. "Looks like China, yes?"

"Where?"

"That one."

"That?"

"Yes."

"I can't . . ." She pauses. "I don't know what China looks like."

"You don't know what it looks like?!" I jump out of bed. "You really *are*—" I am about to say *a simpleton, a fool, a silly prostitute, deserving brothel dweller,* but looking at her in the face in the bed, I find this difficult to undertake. "You are denied some basic knowledge," I say. "Let me show you."

"All right." She sits up.

"Are there writing materials in the room?"

"Only this." She leans over the bed and reaches under, pulling out a small, capped container of ink.

"Nothing to write on?" I ask.

"You want to write?"

I nod.

"Write on me!" Annabelle says, and she puts herself back on the bed with her arms spread to the wall and her torso stretched out. "You can see, don't worry." She unbuttons her dress from the back very quickly and has it off in a pile like a small dog by her feet, and under it there is some sort of undergarment that I don't notice so much because I am looking at her bare breasts, which have nipples on them, and it feels as if large blocks are falling into place in my mind and I shake quickly as if I have an illness.

"Uhgag . . ." I believe I say.

"Don't be scared," Annabelle says. "I enjoy your company, Rutford. Come and write on me. What were you going to write?"

"I was . . ." I look at her. "I was going to depict China . . ."

"Do it! Please!" She cranes her neck to look me in the eyes. "Please." And she puts her head back down and splays her body out like a young tiger, I would imagine. In a book I saw a drawing of one stretching; I never expected it to have a human application.

I sit next to her on the bed and open the bottle of ink. "It's . . . it looks like this . . ." I say, dabbing the ink onto my fingers. This will be difficult to wash off, but some part of me remembers something, playing with clay in a stream somewhere in my old home, pressing it and feeling it flatten in my hands. It was difficult to wash off, too. I dash my fingertip against Annabelle's skin—

"Ack!" She giggles. "Cold!"

I keep going and, staying very concentrated, not looking at the breasts, I make a more-than-serviceable map of China. I have seen it in atlases enough that even the curvature of the skin is no impediment; I end up with a fine representation.

"Now look up at the stain again," I tell her.

"Yes," she says.

"And now look at your stomach!"

She lifts up on her elbows. "That's China?" she asks.

"Absolutely."

"It looks just like the ceiling!"

"As I said."

"That must be why this is my room, then!" she says. "With my country all over it." The ink is drying on her. She turns to me. "You are a very kind young man; I like you very much," she says. She rolls back and forth on the bed and the ink on her body presses another print onto the bedsheet. "A third China."

"I— Thank you," I say.

"It is your birthday, the madam says, but you are very kind to *me*."

"I . . . Gugkle."

"I can be kind to you as well. You wish to do things now?" She touches her breast to show me that I can do that, if I would like.

"I do not . . ." I think about who this really is. She may be alluring in a different way from anything I have seen before— certainly more than any dusty schoolgirl with teeth missing or my false mother—and she may smile and look at me, but she is *paid* to do these things, all of them, paid by my father, a worker like everyone else in this world, working toward money, never wanting to know anyone or anything. How can anyone touch these women? They are a constant reminder of what they are. I look at the rash of color in her face.

"Come . . ." she says. "If you do not touch me, the madam will be angry."

Well, I cannot say anything to that. I do not want to anger anyone. I reach down.

"No bussing, no kissing usually," she says. "But since you are so young and kind, I can do this." She leans up to do this thing that I have heard and read about so much but never seen performed. I was not aware of the mechanics of a kiss. What she does scientifically is maw at my lips for a few seconds before prying them open with her tongue, which is unexpectedly warm and eager and soft and pointed at the end. Then she uses her tongue inside me to loop around while saliva—that is what it is, I wish there were a more beautiful word for it—drips out of me into her. Such a strange ritual. I pull back.

"You don't want?" she says.

"I liked showing you China better," I say.

"Forget it." Annabelle sits up quickly on the bed and reaches under it again, maybe for more ink for me to write on her. I look at her hair and question what went wrong in the room while she fiddles about and comes up with a new object, a pipe made of ivory.

I have never seen such a thing before. The pipe is long and dirty. It has a smell that is unlike any smell I have smelled on earth, but once I smell it I definitely have a recollection of it somewhere—I always *knew* that this smell existed; I just had not come across it before. Annabelle puts the pipe in her mouth theatrically and sucks in at it, showing me what I have to do. I am not certain whether this is a part of the sex act, but having been unable to find a suitable definition in the dictionary, I am willing to accept that copulation could involve a pipe.

Annabelle stands up and walks across the room, which intrigues me greatly—it is as if her legs and torso are moving sideways and back again, opposed to one another, on a hidden set of pendulums. Her body swings. I stand up to see if I can imitate it—

"What are you doing?" she asks. She is now at the corner of the room by the candle on the floor. "Sit on the damn bed!"

I do so. It is difficult for me to synthesize and accept that I have disappointed a prostitute. But part of me is very proud.

"Now listen." She comes forward with the pipe, puffing at it just slightly, enveloping me in this smell that is, I realize, a bit like a new spice in the kitchen, a secret spice that there was no occasion to take out and partake in previously. "You aren't ready for any women, Rutford. You need to relax first many, many times."

"Yes, Annabelle."

"That isn't my real name. Take—"

"What is?"

"What is what?"

"Your real name!" This is important.

"Rutford, never mind. Take this pipe and put it in your mouth."

I do so.

"Now pull the smoke up into your mouth."

I do so.

"Now hold it there, just hold it."

I do this as well. I want to ask why—

"I see your mouth moving and you better not be talking or thinking. Just hold that smoke in there. Let it go when you need to."

I do. I hold it for three and one half seconds. Then I pull the pipe out and let it go. I look back at Annabelle, whose name is really not Annabelle, and put the pipe on the floor.

"You are supposed to pass it to me." She smiles.

"I will remember," I say.

"Better?" she asks.

"No."

"Oh, you'll be fine." She smokes from the pipe herself, then puts it back under her bed. Then she moves next to me and holds my shoulders with her small soft arm.

"My shoulders are very bony," I apologize.

"Shhhhh, just relax," she says, and while I have never written it down or told it to anyone, I have a theory about how my brain works. I have always thought that each one of my thoughts must, deep down, be represented by a particle, just as the scientists know that all matter is particles deep down and that these tiny particles are indivisible, which is why they are called atoms. I know that I must have brain particles as well, one for each of my thoughts, because when thoughts run in my brain, I can feel them butting up against one another, clashing and merging and flipping in circles, or breaking through, as is the case when I am thinking clearly, busting out of my mouth in a coherent mastery of concept and going out into the world.

But now I am lying on the bed with the woman I know as Annabelle and all of the thought particles in my brain are moving much more slowly. She has increased gravity in my spine and they are pulled down and only the thoughts that register pleasure are allowed to circulate. I turn to her and stare at her pretty face and realize that she is a very special girl; she knew my secret. She knew that I liked to be half-asleep and she has put me there again. I look up at China on the ceiling and China on her stomach and the China on the bedsheet and think that maybe with her I can be like this more often.

The Grief Diet

Emma Forrest

He was at the kitchen counter eating peanut butter with a tablespoon when I asked him the question that had been nagging me since I learned how to talk.

"Are you going to die one day, Papa?"

I had on OshKosh B'Gosh dungarees, red with hundreds of tiny falling ice cream cones that he'd jokingly try to lick. Although I was only seven, they were for age ten. I wore all my clothes too big, willing myself to grow. He was wearing a battered caftan and a three-day stubble.

Dad flicked the spoon clean with his tongue, stalling for time. Then he put it in the sink and said, "Never. No. I will never die."

"And Mummy will never die?"

"No, your mother won't die."

"And I will never die?"

"No. None of us will ever die."

I remember my mother, in the doorway hissing, "*Adam!* You can't say that to a child! You're giving her a totally false—" and I don't remember the rest because he shushed her and took me to the park to ride the swings.

And then, the fucker, he has a heart attack and drops dead. Nine years after the promise, it's true, but a promise is a promise. Of course, a lot of stuff happened first. The investigation. Dad's court case. Him winning but Mum leaving. The divorce. Mum's remarriage. Dad's demotion. And then . . . and then . . .

One day I woke up and all I could think of was the way my dad used to wipe bread in butter. He misappropriated many foods (salt and vinegar potato chips crushed and used as sandwich filling, golden syrup spread on toast) and I've given them up one by one.

I can't eat the food he ate but I can listen to the records he loved. I rolled my first joint to "Rain Dogs" by Tom Waits. My dad taught me how. He had awesome taste in music, cataloged in an immaculate vinyl collection. I was a whiskey-grizzled middle-aged man trapped in the body of a little girl. Dad led me to my peers: Leonard Cohen, Bob Dylan, Kris Kristofferson, Townes Van Zandt.

Dad liked my records, too. He liked Jeff Buckley and Primal Scream and he loved Chan Marshall, especially her song "Good Woman," which he played over and over. We played it at his funeral, but the tape sounded tinny and no one could really make out the words that explained why he thought Mum had left him:

'Cause I want to be a good woman.
And I want you to be a good man.

The idea seems so novel and so obvious: that you leave when you love someone, because you love someone. That kind people try hard and it's still not enough. That song came out the year Mum moved out. But he was wrong to apply it to her. He looked at her photo and played the song over and over until he could believe it. But he was wrong. She didn't leave because she loved him. She left because she didn't love him anymore. It goes off, I guess, like milk. My new stepfather and my stepbrothers, well, they were good people, nice people, but to me they were mere holograms, facsimiles of family, cutout paper dolls I couldn't be bothered to cut out.

"Good Woman" is how I met Lara. I had left Mum one Saturday to go shopping in town and found myself in the basement of a chichi West End boutique looking at dresses I couldn't afford, stroking them longingly like a pervert on the subway. Lara leaned behind the counter, laughing on the phone, her feather-cropped black hair nibbling at her long dark neck. The cordless phone pressed against her ear and I noticed that her red shift dress had sleeves that extended all the way down her wrists and hooked over her thumbs. Combined with her voluminous bosom, it leant her the air of a medieval wench who spent her days toiling on the land, not a modern-day shop girl folding overpriced underwear.

A mix tape blared from the speaker and I could tell she had made it herself. I could also tell that she was a motivated person, as the tape was full of instructions: "Call Me!" snarled Blondie, "Express Yourself!" shrieked Madonna, "Don't Stop the Rock!" intoned an early eighties breakdance outfit that I remembered but could not place. I caught myself dancing in the mirror, then I saw her dance behind me and we exchanged glances and smiled. Her teeth were white and Chiclet small.

I went into the dressing room and pulled over my head a succession of cotton minidresses. Then the eighties instructional tape shifted gears in the most alarming way, and out of fucking nowhere, "Good Woman" started playing and I lost my fucking shit. I was halfway into a blouse when I wandered out of the dressing room, unbuttoned, my bra showing, people on the floor staring. And, again, I caught a glimpse of myself in the mirror, but this time I was not dancing, I was sobbing, sobbing hard enough, it was almost like a dance.

Lara was so kind to me. I didn't know she, too, was only sixteen, on a summer job, visiting London from New York, or that the manager had gone for a long lunch and left her in charge, and she was probably freaking out. She made me herbal tea ("You want chamomile, ginger, lemon zinger?"), and just the flatness of her American accent soothed me.

What draws us to people is what we eventually hold against them. The American accent came to drive me mad. When I met her I loved her softness, those acres of chocolate truffle skin. By the end the very chocolate truffleness seemed a cruel joke—for an extremely rich person she ate the nastiest, cheapest chocolate bars.

She told me she was rich the third time I saw her. In fact she told an invisible girl who had bothered her in line at the cinema, conjured after-the-fact in the comfort of her Sloane Square pad because she had not been able to think of the fitting response at the theater. It came to her in a flash:

"I'm rich and you're not. Ha-ha!"

The conjured girl, suitably chastened, vaporized.

The wealth on her Colombian father's side was vague and mysterious; on her WASP mother's, public and dull old money. Her father was sexy as hell but seemed sad. He wanted to be whiter than her mother, as though to spite her for taking so much in the divorce, and so he wore monogrammed Savile Row suits and never spoke in Spanish.

Dad would have been impressed with the apartment in which Lara and her mother lived that summer, although he'd have tried to hide it. Dad grew up in East End poverty and taught himself to read when he was nine because no one else was going to. He used to read two books a week. Lara was very well read because the wealthy get to be well read. They get to study art and learn languages. As a child she took sailing, rock climbing, and ice skating lessons: the world's free geographic beauty condensed into monthly payments and required uniforms.

Our trip to Paris was one of several holidays she would take in a year, this one to reward her new best friend for getting through the grief of her father's death. That's what she implied when she handed me the first-class train ticket. That it would be a healing distraction. But that was forgotten somewhere in the planning and it morphed into a full-on sixteenth birthday celebration for Lara, even though she had only four months to go before she turned seventeen. Lying together in her four-poster bed, we planned what we would wear for her birthday dinner. She pinched my hip.

"You're getting thinner."

"I'm thin."

"You're thinner than you were."

"Well, I don't know what to tell you. Christ, do you think they picked on Audrey Hepburn like this?"

"I bet," said Lara, hugging me, "she had at least one friend who did."

She fell asleep next to me and I watched her snore, the way her mouth fell open in an obscene O, a reminder of the blow jobs she gave freely—she had hooked up with three boys in the month she had been in London. Curious, the American belief that oral sex is somehow not intimate. She once told me she would rather blow a man she didn't know than kiss him. Lara loved sex. She felt slightly offended that I didn't, and she was also slightly offended that I wouldn't drink with her. I just was never a drinker. And I always liked getting people home, putting them in cabs, tucking the sheets under their chin. I had a history of doing that for best friends.

I had traveled the Channel Tunnel with dad once. As I marveled that we were really and truly under the ocean, he took a box of Crayola and drew fishes on the window of the train.

"I want your first trip to Paris to be with the one man who will love you for the rest of your life," he said.

He fucked up and the hotel didn't have a record of our reservation, so we had nowhere to stay and ended up at dinner somewhere dreadful, where I threw up in the dingy bathroom. Then we went to a shitty hotel across the street from the train station. They had one room left and, to my thirteen-year-old dismay, it had no TV.

It was different with Lara's dad. He had reserved two suites at the Hôtel Georges V, one for me and Lara, one for him and his girlfriend, Jessica. Jessica, like his ex-wife, was blond and elegant, slim, coiffed, immaculate. She tried frequently to engage Lara in conversation but Lara would have none of it. She had been pretending not to hear her for three years.

Even Lara was impressed with our room, which boasted a cornucopia of fine antiques, among them a real Georges de la Tour on the wall, and a claw-foot tub with gold faucets in the marble bathroom. Our first night in Paris we stayed in and Lara took photos of me in the tub. She said she was trying to prove to me that I was anorexic. I had taken to going to bed hungry, it was true, but I wasn't anorexic. I knew I was skinny and furthermore that the bones jutting from my hips actually suited me.

My whole life, the life in which I knew him, my dad was overweight. But in all the photos from before I was born, he was built like a Greek god. Did it change the second my mother got pregnant with me, as though he, ever the gentleman, had opted to lose his figure instead of her? Inspired by the Greek god photos, I used to tell people my dad was Freddie Mercury. I had a history of outlandish lies rooted in truth. The truth was, like Freddie, he had a mustache and a lot of teeth. I also used to tell people I had won the London Marathon, when, in truth, Dad had carried me on his shoulders for a children's fun run when I was five.

The next night had been officially designated Lara's celebration. Her father took us to a five-course dinner of crab, steak, snails, and foie gras—a checklist of things you would never want to put in your mouth—followed by three birthday cakes. Lara tried to bully me into having a forkful of angel food cake, but I kept my mouth shut, even when, in front of the adults, she forced a fork jokingly toward my pursed lips as if playing a game of choo-choo train. Soon the waiter poured her enough champagne that she was distracted half out of her dress, her father tugging up the straps as she danced on her chair.

By two A.M. she was splayed drunk on the bed in her Galliano gown. Her dark hair was sticking to her forehead in clumps. Her lids were growing heavy and her mouth was falling into its familiar O. I watched her breathe, her milkmaid bosom straining at the green satin that encased it. It took fifteen minutes to muster the courage.

Finally, "Lara," I breathed. "Lara? Can I kiss you?"

"Mmmpf," she answered, and since it wasn't a no, I very gently touched my lips to hers. Her mouth moved imperceptibly against mine and I grew bolder. Moving a hand to the buttons at her chest, I slowly, painstakingly, as though afraid of waking a giant, freed one of her breasts. Placing my mouth on the dark brown nipple, I sucked, ever so gently, waiting to feel her wealth, her confidence, her happiness slide down my throat and into my heart. But it didn't. And when I heard her begin to snore, I stopped, and crawled into the bed, my arm around her waist.

In the morning Lara was briefly hungover, but after scrambled eggs and coffee, she was ditzy with exuberance. Either she was pretending not to remember what had happened, or she really didn't remember. Either way she said nothing. We swam in the hotel pool, she in a fifties vintage costume, me in a tank and shorts. Her father dove from the deep end, a blur of broad shoulders, tan, thick black hair. Jessica climbed neatly down the steps, displaying the kind of body that would have been beautiful if it didn't betray such vanity: You could see each and every hour with her personal trainer, each dollar shading each muscle. Such an abundance of rude health, it made me think of Dad. . . .

All those nights I sat up crying because my parents would die one day and still I had not inoculated myself one bit. He's fat, I thought; he lifts heavy things for a living. And then it happened. I was in the house. I was the one who called the ambulance. And he was talking . . . he was walking even when he got in. He said he was going to be okay and that I should go to school. So I let him go to the hospital alone. I didn't go with him. And he never came back.

Looking at my tearstained face in the gilded mirror of the marble hotel bathroom, I noticed frown lines on my forehead. Lara was on a private shopping excursion with her father, so I called down to housekeeping and charged a hundred-dollar jar of face cream to the room. Then I felt for my soul like a packet of cigarettes—where did I leave it?

For dinner, Lara wore the midnight blue Prada dress her dad had bought her. I had on a gray silk dress that had belonged to my mother a decade earlier. She had it taken in for me. I fumbled my way through dinner, pretending to dip forkfuls of filet mignon in béarnaise, bringing them to my mouth and then putting them back on the plate as though it were all an elaborate acting exercise under the watchful gaze of Lee Strasberg.

When dessert arrived—tiramisu and chocolate gâteau because Lara couldn't choose—I went to the ladies' room and on the way back slipped my debit card to the waiter. I signed the bill with a flourish and no idea how it translated. It could have been forty dollars, four hundred dollars, or four thousand dollars. I didn't care anymore. I knew I had Grandpa's money in my checking account and that I was supposed to use it one day to travel. "Here I am," I reasoned to myself, "traveling."

When Lara's father realized what I had done, he pleaded with the maître d' to reverse the charge and put it on his black Amex, but they couldn't. Jessica looked at me quizzically. Lara was inexplicably enraged. She could hardly make eye contact, she just kept shaking her head. Her dad took Jessica to the hotel bar and in the elevator back to the room Lara hissed, "You don't get it, do you? It's rude. It's an insult to my father."

Sometime during her shopping expedition with her dad, Lara had managed to slip away to score a bag of coke. She looked so sad, in her beautiful thousand-dollar dress, with her luxurious dark skin and cheap white flakes around her perfect nose. Soon enough, she wanted to go clubbing and decided it would be amusing to check out the hotel disco. I knew what to expect: banality and bad dancing. Strange aristocrats grinding against one another like outtakes from an unfinished Stanley Kubrick movie. Italian girls with bleached hair and Arabs with bleached teeth.

Hoisting her new dress around her thighs, Lara danced furiously to "Who Let the Dogs Out," which seemed to be the urgent query of the night, so often did the DJ play it. It was too awful. I left her with a floppy-haired Hugh Grant type and went back to the room. As I put the key in the door her dad came out of the elevator. I could see he was drunk, his bow tie askew, top buttons open, dark hair sprouting like rumors on his chest.

"Hello there, moneybags," he said when he saw me. "Where's Lara?"

"Dancing with a man who looks like Hugh Grant's afterbirth. Where's Jessica?"

"Mad at me. Stormed off into the Paris night in a huff . . . which is, at least, cheaper than a limo."

I laughed.

"So thanks again for dinner. I don't know when a girl has ever bought me dinner before."

"You're welcome. Thank you for bringing me to Paris."

"It's my absolute pleasure. We love having you here."

Then somehow I—because it was I who started it, that's the honest truth—was kissing him, as he steadied himself against the corridor wall.

In his suite, he locked the door and unzipped his pants and took it out. It was huge, just offensive really. What is seen is different from what is felt and I knew I couldn't do it. He held it in front of my mouth and I looked at it and said, "I'm sorry,

I can't . . . I just . . . I can't." Not in Paris. Not in a hotel room.

I remembered the dingy room without a TV, the way my father had pleaded and then cried. He hated himself. He couldn't help it. "If you loved me," he said.

And I did love him.

"Hey, that's okay." Lara's dad stroked my hair. Then he asked, "Can I eat you?" and I said, "Yes." That was what I wanted since I could not eat: to be eaten. I wanted to disappear and maybe he could help me. He kept asking me if I wanted him to stop and I said no, it was okay, as though I were being very brave. I made too much noise. I heard it, like hearing yourself say something dumb but not being able to control yourself. When he was finished I scooped my dress back over my head as fast as I could. Once all your clothes are off, there is nothing left to do but put them back on again. I crept back to my room.

That night I dreamed about falling. I know falling dreams are supposed to be terrifying, but I didn't mind. I let myself fall. When I woke up I felt cheated. I didn't get to hit the floor. I didn't get to watch myself burst.

I slid in bed beside Lara and stroked her hair, which seemed to have grown three inches in the three months I had known her. Her eyes popped open like a Victorian doll's and she slapped my hand away.

"You went off with that guy!"

"Which guy?" I asked, nursing my whipped fingers.

"The Hugh Grant guy!"

"I did not!"

"Well, you left and then he left and then I was alone. I went back to the room but you weren't there."

"I didn't go off with that guy."

She climbed out of bed.

"Girls don't do that to each other," she huffed.

Lara went into the bathroom and brushed her teeth so angrily, I thought they would drop out of her head. Lara and her father were going on to Switzerland. My train home left the station in an hour.

"I'm sorry, Lara," I said. "I'm sorry. I only went off because I wanted to be with you and it didn't seem as though you wanted to be with me."

"I don't want to be with you!"

Before I left, Lara's dad gave us both little Eiffel Tower pendants encrusted with diamonds. By that point she was no longer speaking to me. As I stepped into my taxi I thanked her for taking me on holiday and tried to hug her, but she wouldn't let me. I knew what she was thinking: I took in a damaged person. I sat next to a fat man on the Channel Tunnel home. He had a musky odor that, over the course of the journey, I pinpointed as the smell of sour defeat. When I got back to my mum's house, I stuffed my jeans and T-shirt in the washing machine.

For the longest time I wanted to see the pictures Lara took of me in the bathtub at the Hôtel Georges V, naked and skinny. It nagged at me for ages. I could think of nothing else. Then, one day, when I was cleaning out my closet, I found something more important to think about.

My dungarees. The red ones with the ice creams. Age ten. I found them in a box of old clothes beneath the shoe rack. I freed them gently from the tumble of sweaters and summer dresses, as though working on an archaeological dig. And, incredibly, they fit. Once I discovered I could get them on, I wouldn't take them off. Mum pleaded with me to get out of bed and she pleaded with me to eat, but mainly she pleaded with me to change my clothes. I heard her talk with my stepfather about hospitals and what they might be able to afford.

The doctor says that I will starve. Maybe I will and maybe I won't. My mum called Lara's mum and she told me Lara promised she would visit. She never did. Lara is somewhere in New York now, doing rich-people things: skating, vacationing, giving insincere blow jobs. I don't like that a girl I loved and will never see again has a photo of me naked in the bathtub of the Hôtel Georges V. But I don't need to see it anymore. What's the point? I know what I look like.

Mona Lisa, Jesus, Chad, and Me

Carolyn Mackler

I first noticed that something was weird when Mona Lisa showed up at my sixteenth birthday party wearing a *Little House on the Prairie* dress. Seriously. It was straight from the banks of Plum Creek. Calico print, modestly high neck, hemline way below the knees.

It was barely even a clothed gathering. My boyfriend, Chad, and his best friend, Jonathan, were wearing their swimsuits. I had on my padded bikini top, jeans shorts, and a straw hat because the sun was descending toward the western shore of Cayuga Lake and the glare always kills my eyes. We were hanging out on the deck of my family's rented summer cabin, drinking Pepsi, snacking on chips, and spitting cherry pits over the cliff. My mom was starting up the coals on the grill. My dad was inside, frosting the chocolate cake. When I went into the kitchen to get a round of sodas, he'd already written *Happy Birthday, Emmy*. Now he was squirting the decorating tubes to create a painter's palette across the top of the cake because art has become my big obsession this year.

"So when does your friend arrive?" Jonathan asked, shading his hands over his eyes and squinting at me.

Chad puckered his lips, went, *"Tfoooooo!"* and blasted a cherry pit off the deck. He kept trying to spit them all the way to the water, but so far he'd only reached the stony beach.

I shrugged. "I e-mailed her yesterday and said to come

around sunset. Her plane lands in Rochester in the late afternoon and then she's got an hour-and-a-half drive."

Jonathan grabbed a fistful of chips. "Mona Lisa *is* cute, right?"

"Da Vinci!" Chad exclaimed.

Leonardo da Vinci painted the famous portrait that is her namesake, so Chad had been saying that ever since I mentioned the idea of fixing up Jonathan with Mona Lisa. But as much as Chad was joking about her name and as frequently as Jonathan was questioning me about her level of attractiveness, they had to admit it was a great idea.

Mona Lisa was my best summer friend. Ever since we were little, we'd spent the first two weeks of July on the same unpaved road, in cabins that overlook Cayuga Lake. Mona Lisa's grandparents rent her cabin. When we were younger, she used to come up from Georgia with her mom, dad, and older brothers. Then her parents got divorced and she came with her mom and brothers. Then her brothers joined the military and her mom got some all-consuming job, so for the past few summers she'd come by herself.

Mona Lisa and I were always inseparable during those two weeks. We'd swim in the lake and lay out on the deck and read magazines and scout for cute boys whizzing by in speedboats. In mid-July, when she'd return to Atlanta and I'd head back to Rochester, we'd promise to stay in better touch. At first, we'd e-mail every few days and then every few weeks and then it'd get patchy until I received a note from her with the date she was flying to Central New York for another summer, usually right around my birthday.

The only thing different about this July was Chad. We'd been going out since January and it was really serious by this point. We'd even had sex. Chad was seventeen and had his license, a used Toyota, and a lifeguarding job that gave him relatively flexible hours.

My parents had agreed that Chad could drive up to the lake and spend his days off with me. *Day* being the operative word because as soon as the sun disappeared, so must Chad. At first I begged my parents to let him sleep over on the lumpy couch in the living room, but they said absolutely not. Then I thought, Hmmm, what if I turned it into a group thing—like Mona Lisa, Jonathan, Chad, and me—and we went on a camping excursion in the woods behind the cabin? My parents are always urging me to be more outdoorsy, so I knew they'd nibble. Sure enough, when I floated the idea, they said maybe, which of course beats absolutely not.

I showed Jonathan a picture of Mona Lisa from last summer. Her blond hair was flowing past her shoulders and she was wearing low-rise shorts and a bikini top, except she doesn't need the padded variety because she's got boobs the natural way. Jonathan said, "Sure, hook me up." So I e-mailed Mona Lisa to ask when she was coming and, hey, did she have a boyfriend? A few days later, she wrote me only with the date and time of her flight, so I took that as No Boyfriend. I e-mailed her and told her to stop by for my birthday barbecue as soon as she got to the lake.

"You sure she's coming?" Jonathan asked a half hour or so later.

I lifted up the brim of my hat. The pink-orange sun was sinking into the horizon. We'd finished the chips and my mom had just put the shish kebab on the barbecue. Chad took another cherry. I sipped my warmish Pepsi. Jonathan was making some comment about Georgia peaches when I heard Mona Lisa say, "Hey, Emmy."

The three of us craned our heads around. There was Mona Lisa, standing on the edge of the deck in her *Little House* dress. Actually, only one of her feet was on the deck. The other was on the grass. The second thing I noticed, after the dress, was that Mona Lisa was wearing sandals. We always go barefoot at the lake, even if the stones murder our feet at the beginning, because after a week our soles become impenetrably tough.

I jumped out of my lawn chair and ran across the deck. But when I bear-hugged her, she gave me the overcooked-noodle-semi-squeeze treatment.

"How's it going?" I asked.

"Great," she said.

"Come join us." I gestured to the guys. Chad waved. Jonathan half-smiled as he fiddled with the drawstring on his swimsuit. "Want a Pepsi or something?"

Mona Lisa nodded. "Sure."

After I went inside to the fridge, I introduced Mona Lisa to the guys. Chad said, " 'Sup?" Jonathan double-knotted his drawstring. My parents came out to greet her and then retreated back to the grill/kitchen. Mona Lisa sat in a chair a few feet off to the side, quietly sipping her soda. Chad and Jonathan started joking about this last-day-of-school bash we'd all gone to the previous week and, basically, how I got so wasted on Jell-O shots I was clutching the walls and tripping over my feet. I hissed that they should shut up because my parents were in earshot. Chad let it go, but Jonathan kept singing things like "It wiggles, it wobbles . . . J-E-L-L-O!"

Mona Lisa didn't say much while we were goofing around. She watched us, smiling now and then, almost with that strained patience my parents exhibit when they're driving me and a friend somewhere and we're being loud and you can tell it's pissing them off but they don't want to be the buzz killers.

Mona Lisa didn't say much during dinner, either. She complimented my mom's shish kebab and politely answered questions whenever my dad or I asked her about her year. And then, when my parents went inside to light the birthday cake, she touched my shoulder and said, "I'm going to head back to my cabin."

"Are you okay? Don't you want to stay for cake?"

Mona Lisa shook her head. "I'm really tired. Let's catch up tomorrow, okay?"

"Okay," I said, shrugging.

Mona Lisa called out good-byes to my parents. Chad reached across the table and scooped the last cherry out of the bowl. I watched Mona Lisa walk across the deck, her dress swishing from side to side. I could hear Jonathan mumbling something about how you could barely see *anything* with that frock she had on. I glanced back at them just in time to see Chad go, "*Tfoooooo!*" A cherry pit cannonballed through the air and landed with a distant *plink* in the lake.

"Da Vinci!" Chad sang as the two of them high-fived.

Since it was my birthday, my parents let Chad and Jonathan stay late. I ended up sleeping until eleven the next morning. When I woke up, my dad was out in the kayak and my mom was in the garden, searching for bugs. That's her latest thing. She spends hours gaping at daddy longlegs and caterpillars and iridescent beetles.

I ate a cinnamon Pop-Tart and sat on the deck, my sketch pad in my lap. I attempted to draw a willow tree with streaks of black charcoal, but I kept smudging my hand across the page and messing up the perspective and making it look more like a mushroom cloud or an obese porcupine. Finally, I set my supplies on the chair next to me and stared out at the lake.

I couldn't stop thinking about how strange it had been to see Mona Lisa. Any other year, she would have hugged me hard, stolen the straw hat off my head, flirted with Jonathan. She would have leaned down to scratch her ankle, deliberately giving him the opportunity to check out her cleavage, which would *not* have been covered in calico fabric. She would have matched my Jell-O story with some tale about getting high or going to a keg party. She would have whispered in my ear that the shish kebab was too weird and did we have a hot dog to throw on the grill?

I grabbed my pad and charcoal pencil and headed down the dirt road toward her cabin. We'd only been here a few days, so I walked on the grassy center, wincing as stray rocks poked into my feet. Her grandparents' car wasn't in the driveway and no one answered when I knocked, so I walked around to the front yard.

Mona Lisa was sitting in an Adirondack chair, reading a book. She was wearing shorts and a T-shirt. In summers past, she would have been in a skimpy bikini, but it was a definite improvement over the frock.

"Hey!" I said, skipping across the grass.

Mona Lisa smiled. "Hey, there."

I flopped down next to her. "How's it going?"

"Fine. How about you?"

"Fine," I said.

I glanced at the book on her lap. It was called *Simple Faith*. Last summer Mona Lisa was devouring the *Gossip Girl* series.

"Is everything okay?" I asked.

"What do you mean?"

"You just seem . . ." I paused. "You left so early last night."

"I was tired."

"You didn't look like you were having any fun."

Mona Lisa shook her head. "That's not really my thing anymore."

Huh?

"I was hoping you and Jonathan would hit it off," I finally said. "He's Chad's best friend, you know."

Mona Lisa ran a finger up and down the spine of her book.

"What did you think of Chad?" I asked.

"He seems nice."

I grinned. "Isn't he cute? We've been together since January."

"I know . . . you told me in *that* e-mail."

She said the word *that* as if it were an odor. I had a feeling she was referring to the e-mail I sent her in April, when I told her Chad and I had done it. She'd already lost her virginity, so I hardly thought she was going to get judgmental on me.

"I've gotten into a new relationship this year, too," Mona Lisa said.

"Really? Why didn't you tell me? When I asked if you had a boyfriend and you didn't reply, I thought it meant—"

"Oh, no," she said, shaking her head. "Not like that."

"Okay, I'm confused. Who's it with?"

"Jesus."

I was dumbfounded. I mean, what *do* you say? *Jesus is such a hottie! But isn't he a little old for you?*

As I stared at her, my jaw hanging, Mona Lisa told me how she'd been having a really hard time this past winter and then a friend took her to a Bible-study group and it was so great and then she started going to that friend's Christian church and it was so great and how she's been talking to God every day and it's so, so, so great.

I still didn't know what to say. *Great?*

But I didn't have to say anything because Mona Lisa went on to describe how Jesus had saved her. She told me that he'd changed her life and how, if I were searching for answers, she was sure I'd find them in God as well.

As she talked, I began sketching her profile on my drawing pad. I used a moderate dark line for her forehead and the skinny side of the pencil for her eyelashes. I scribbled a shadow along the side of her nose. But when I got to her mouth, I was perplexed. I couldn't figure out what expression her lips were making, almost as if they were changing every second. For some reason, this unknowing bugged the hell out of me.

Over the next few days, I avoided Mona Lisa. I guess you could say she freaked me out. I'm usually good at fielding random tidbits, but that whole Jesus thing came hurtling from out of nowhere. Well, not *completely* out of nowhere. Sometimes in e-mails, Mona Lisa used to put song lyrics at the bottom. Other times, she'd include quotes from the Bible. I'd always dismissed it as her coming from the South, where that kind of thing is probably more normal.

Truthfully, I'd never thought much about religion. My family puts up a tree at Christmas and sings about silent nights and mangers, but that's as far as it goes. We don't go to church. My dad has told me outright that he doesn't believe in God. My mom says she thinks God is a feeling inside all of us, in nature, in the universe. I side more with my dad. God seems about as realistic to me as the Easter Bunny.

When Mona Lisa called to see if I wanted to take a walk, I said I was beat. When she stopped by the cabin and invited me down to the lake, I said I'd just been swimming. When I was tanning at our beach, I spotted her and her granddad at their dock, pushing a rowboat into the water.

"Want to come along?" she yelled over to me.

"Maybe some other time," I shouted back.

My parents kept asking me why I wasn't spending time with Mona Lisa, but I didn't know what to say, so I shrugged it off and said she was busy and I was busy. As if there was anything to do at the lake but shuck corn and listen to Jet Skis droning in endless circles and swat at horseflies.

One morning, my mom and I were in the garden. She was watching a spider spin a shimmering web. I was painting a watercolor of my foot. When my mom asked again about Mona Lisa, I told her the truth this time. I told her how she's gotten all into Jesus and how she practically tried to convert me.

My mom surprised me by not being surprised. She said how Mona Lisa had a difficult childhood, with her parents divorcing and her dad moving to Arkansas and her mom never being around and her older brothers being bullies. She talked about how sometimes, when people are feeling vulnerable, they turn to religion for comfort and support.

I dipped my paintbrush into a Dixie cup of water. "But I just feel like I can't even relate to her anymore. It's like she's all brainwashed."

My mom poked at the spiderweb with a blade of grass. "That's one of the sad things that happens as you get older. Friends sometimes slip away from each other and there's nothing you can do to stop it."

As I painted my foot this deep red, I thought about how at least I should *try* to yank back the old Mona Lisa before she disappeared entirely.

That afternoon, the sky was cloudy and the air was heavy, like a thunderstorm was on its way. But when I saw Mona Lisa swimming in the lake, I headed down our stairs and walked over to her dock. I sat on the pebbly shore until she spotted me and stepped out of the water. She was wearing a one-piece suit and mesh shoes. As she grabbed her towel, I cut right to the chase.

"What did you mean when you said that it wasn't your thing anymore, hanging out with Jonathan, Chad, and me?"

"Hi to you, too," she said, cracking up.

"I'm not joking. I want to know what you meant."

Mona Lisa flipped her head upside down and began toweling off her hair. After a minute, she said, "I guess that you guys are all into sinning, you know, drinking and fooling around and stuff."

"Are you *serious*?"

Mona Lisa stood up straight again and twisted her hair into a knot. "Unless you can let Jesus into your heart, you're going to go to hell."

My pulse sped up. I couldn't believe she'd actually said that.

"But it's not like you've been any better than me," I said.

"What about the guys you've been with? What about the partying you've done?"

"But I've asked Jesus to save me, so it's all okay now. You can do that, too, if you want."

I was getting frustrated by this point. "Mona Lisa," I snapped, "can you quit it with Jesus for a second?"

There was an awkward silence. I could tell by her expression that I'd hurt her feelings. I picked up a flat stone and flung it into the water. It skipped three times. Mona Lisa and I used to have skipping contests down here. Whenever either of us skipped a rock, the other one would shriek, "I can do better!" And then we'd throw and throw until our shoulders were sore and our voices were parched.

"It looks like a storm's coming," Mona Lisa said. "I'm going to head upstairs. Want to come?"

I shook my head.

Mona Lisa secured her towel around her waist. "I'd be happy to talk more about this, if you want. I can even loan you some books."

I bit my bottom lip. It was probably best for me to shut up right now.

Mona Lisa stood there for a moment before heading toward the staircase that leads up to her cabin.

I watched as the clouds got darker and the wind picked up. A major storm was about to hit, but I remained on the beach, staring at the thrashing water, my eyes stinging and my throat tight.

It rained the entire next day, a constant downpour. I loafed around the cabin, cranky and depressed. By mid-afternoon, my mom offered to take me into Ithaca. In an effort to cheer me up, we swung by the Department of Motor Vehicles and got a driver's manual so I could start studying for my learner's permit. Then we went to an art-supply store and she bought me a new sketch pad and some pastel crayons. As we were walking out, she gestured to a bookstore and said she wanted to look for a guidebook to insects, so we held up our umbrellas and raced across the street.

While my mom was in the animal section, I browsed the art books. I was thumbing through a book about Renaissance painters when I came to the chapter on Leonardo da Vinci. I flipped a few pages until I came to the portrait of Mona Lisa. I leaned against the bookshelf, studying her black hair and dark eyes and flushed cheeks. I skimmed the text underneath—about how it's oil paint on pinewood and was most likely done around 1506—until I came to a paragraph that jumped out at me:

> *One of the most highly discussed aspects of the Mona Lisa is her delicate smile, which blends into the gentle atmosphere. To achieve this, da Vinci invented a technique called "sfumato," which he applied to the corners of her mouth. "Sfumato" is the gradual blurring of forms. It lessens the perception that a still image is entirely still and therefore suggests that we are observing her face as the expression is changing.*

I closed the book and returned it to the display table. I couldn't stop thinking about the profile I tried to draw of Mona Lisa—*my* Mona Lisa—the day after my birthday, when I couldn't figure out how to do her lips, or even what expression she was making. Maybe I needed to use *sfumato*. Maybe I shouldn't have tried to capture her on paper, unchanging, forever and ever. Maybe I had to accept that she's changing, that I'm changing, that we're all changing, and that's just the way it is.

By Sunday, Mona Lisa and I still hadn't talked, not since she'd told me I was going to hell. Chad drove down from Rochester that morning and we headed right to the water. We crawled under a willow tree and I let him undo my bikini top. Around noon, he was lolling in an inner tube, his eyes closed and his head tilted back. I was sitting on the shore, sketching his shoulders and arms, blurring the charcoal where his elbow kept dipping in and out of the lake.

I glanced at Mona Lisa's empty dock. Chad had said that when he was driving in on the dirt road, he'd passed Mona Lisa and her grandparents heading out in their car. He said she was wearing her prairie dress again, so I had a feeling they were going to church.

"Watch out, Emmy!" Chad shouted.

He slapped his hands into the lake, pelting my legs with water. A few droplets hit my sketch pad. I was about to yell at him, but then I noticed that he was grinning irresistibly, so I flung off my straw hat, set my pad aside, and bolted into the lake. I drenched Chad with water. He kicked water back at me until I squealed for mercy. Then he grabbed my hands and pulled me toward him. As I leaned down to kiss him, I realized that it didn't even hurt my feet anymore, standing on the sharp rocks. At least some things about summer hadn't changed.

The Alumni Interview

David Levithan

It is never easy to have a college interview with your closeted boyfriend's father. Would I have applied to this university if I had known that of all the alumni in the greater metropolitan area, it would choose Mr. Wright to find me worthy or unworthy? Maybe. But maybe not.

Thom took it worse than I did. We had been making out in the boys' room, with him standing on the toilet so no one would know we were in the stall together. Even though I was younger, he was a little shorter and had much better balance than I did. Dating him, I'd learned to kiss quietly, and from different inclinations.

He found the letter as he searched through my bag for a Certs.

"You heard from them?" he asked.

I nodded.

"An interview?"

"Yeah," I answered casually. "With your dad."

"Yeah, right."

The bell had rung. The bathroom sounded empty. I looked under the stall door to see if anyone's feet were around, then opened it.

"No, really," I said.

His face turned urinal-white.

"You can't."

"I have to. I can't exactly refuse an alumni interview."

He thought about it for a second and then concluded, succinctly, "Shit."

I had almost met Mr. Wright before. He had come home early one day when his office's air-conditioning had broken down. Luckily, Thom's room is right over the garage, so the garage door heralded his arrival with an appropriately earthquakian noise. Thom was tugging on my shirt at the time, and as a result, I lost at least two buttons. At first, I figured it was just his mom. But the footsteps beat out a different tune. I did the mature, responsible thing, which was to hide under the bed for the next three hours. Happily, Thom hid with me. We found ways to occupy ourselves. Then, once the family was safely wrapped up in dinner, I climbed out the window. I could've gone out the window earlier, but I'd been having a pretty good time.

The trick was getting Thom to enjoy it, too. I wasn't his first boyfriend, but I was the first he could admit to himself. We'd reached the stage where he felt comfortable liberating his affections when we were alone together, or even within our closest circle of friends. But outside that circle, he got nervous. He became paralyzed at the very thought of his parents discovering his—*our*—secret.

We'd been going out without going out for three months.

I'd picked my first choice for college before Thom and I had gotten together, long before I'd known his father had gone to the same school. Thom couldn't believe I wanted to go to a place that had helped spawn the person his father had become.

"Your dad wasn't in the drama program," I pointed out. "And I think he was there before Vietnam."

It helped that my first-choice college was in the same city as Thom's. We'd vowed that we wouldn't think or talk about such things. But of course we did. All the time.

We were trapped in the limbo between where we were and where we wanted to be. The limbo of our age.

The day of the alumni interview, we were both as nervous as a tightrope walker with vertigo. We spun through the day at school, the clock hands spiraling us to certain doom. We found every possible excuse to touch each other—hand on shoulder, fingers on back, stolen kisses, loving looks. Everything that would stop the moment his father walked into the room.

Thom gave me a ride home, then drove back to his house. I counted to a hundred, then walked over.

He answered the door. We'd agreed on this beforehand. I didn't want to be in his house without seeing him. I wanted to know he was there.

"I've got it!" he yelled to the study as he opened the door.

"Here we go," I said.

He leaned into me and whispered, "I love you."

And I whispered, "I love you, too."

We didn't have time for any more than that. So we said all that needed to be said.

I'd never been in Mr. Wright's study before. The man fit in well with the furniture. Sturdy. Wooden. Upright.

It is a strange thing to meet your boyfriend's father when the father doesn't know you're his son's boyfriend—or even that his son *has* a boyfriend. It puts you at an advantage—you know more than he does—and also puts you at a disadvantage. The things you know aren't things you can let him know.

I was not ordinarily known for my discretion. But I was trying to make an exception in this case. It seemed like an exceptional situation.

Thom stood in the doorway, hovering.

"Dad, this is Ian."

"Have a seat, Ian," the man said, no handshake. "Thank you, Thom."

Thom stayed one beat too long, the last beat of linger that we'd grown accustomed to, the sign of an unwanted good-bye. But then the situation hit him again, and he left the room without a farewell glance.

I turned to Mr. Wright as the door closed behind him.

I can do this, I thought. Then: *And even if I can't, I have to.*

Mr. Wright had clearly done the alumni interview thing a hundred times before. As if reciting a message beamed in from central campus, he talked about how this interview was not supposed to be a formal one; it was all about getting to know me, and me getting to know the college where he had spent some of the best years of his life. He had a few questions to ask, and he was sure that I had many questions to ask as well.

In truth, I had already visited the campus twice and knew people who went there. I didn't have a single question to ask. Or, more accurately, the questions I wanted to ask didn't have anything to do with the university in question.

Thom says you've never in all his life hugged him. Why is that?

What can I do to make you see how wonderful he is? If I told you the way I still smile after he kisses me—the way my head feels like helium and my heart feels like a song, not because it's a sexy kiss, but because it's a kind kiss—is there any possible way you'd understand what he means to me?

Don't you know how wrong it is when you wave a twenty-dollar bill in front of your son and tell him that when he gets a girlfriend, you'll be happy to pay for the first date?

And then I'd add:

My father isn't like you at all. So don't tell me it's normal parent behavior.

I am not by nature an angry person. But as this man kept saying he wanted to get to know me, I wanted to throw that phrase right back at him. How could he possibly get to know me when he didn't want to know his son?

Taking out a legal pad and consulting a folder with my transcript in it, he asked me about school and classes. As I prattled on about AP Biology and my English awards, I kept thinking about the word *transcript*. What exactly did it transcribe? My life. No, not that. It was a bloodless, calendar version of my life. It transcribed nothing but the things I was doing in order to get into a good college. It was the biography of my paper self. Getting to know it wasn't getting to know me at all.

Sitting in that room, talking to Mr. Wright, I knew I had to get all of my identities in order. I realized how many identities I had, at a time when I really should have been focusing on having one.

"Have you taken economics?" Mr. Wright asked.

"No," I answered. It had never occurred to me to take economics.

"Why not?" he harrumphed.

I explained that our school offered only one economics class, and I had a conflict. A complete lie, but how would he know?

"I see."

He wrote something down, then told me how important economics was to an education, and how he would have never gotten through college—not to mention life—without a firm foundation in economics.

I nodded. I agreed. I succumbed to the lecture, because I really didn't have any choice. Judgmental. I considered the word *judgmental*. The mental state of always judging. His tone. I knew he wasn't singling me out. I knew this was probably the way he always was.

There were times I had gotten mad at Thom. Argument mad. Cutting-comment mad. Because his inability to be open made me a little closed. I didn't want to be a conditional boyfriend. I didn't want to be anybody's secret. As much as I said I understood, I never entirely understood.

Can't you just tell them? I'd ask. After they became the excuse for why we couldn't go out on Saturday. After they became the reason he pulled his hand away from mine as we were walking through town—*what if they drove by?* But then I'd feel bad, feel wrong. Because I knew this was not the way he wanted it to be. That even though we were sixteen, we were still that one leap away from independence. We were still caught on the dependence side, staring over the divide.

Now, bearing the brunt of his father's disapproval, I understood. Not all of it. But a little more.

". . . too many of you students ignore economics. You dillydally. You spend your time on such expendable things. Like Thom. You know Thom, right? No focus. He has no focus. He wouldn't be right for this university. You show more promise. But I have to say, you need to make sure you don't spend time on expendable things. . . ."

And suddenly I was sick of it.

I looked to the door and saw something. A shadow in the keyhole. And I knew. Thom had never left. He was on the outside of the door, holding his breath for me. Trying to keep quiet. Stay quiet, because his father was around.

I was sick of it.

The economics lecture was over. Mr. Wright didn't alter his tone when he asked, "What are your interests?"

"Your son in my room," I said.

"Excuse me?"

"The sun and the moon," I said. "Astronomy."

Mr. Wright looked pleased. "I didn't know kids liked astronomy anymore. When I was a child, we all had telescopes. Now you just have telephones and televisions instead."

"You couldn't be more right, sir." I nodded emphatically, as if I believed for a second that he hadn't watched television or spoken on the telephone as a child. "A telescope is a fine instrument. And there's something about the stars. . . ." I paused dramatically.

"Yes?"

"Well, there's something about the stars that makes you realize both the smallness and the enormity of everything, isn't there?"

Thom had first told me this as we lay on our backs on a golf course outside of town, too late for the twilight, but early enough to catch the rise of the moon, the pinprick arrival of the stars. His words were like a grasping.

Now here was his father, agreeing with him, through me.

"Yes, yes, absolutely," Mr. Wright said.

I looked to the keyhole, to Thom's shadow there. Knowing he was near. Speaking to him in this code.

Saying to his father what I've said to him.

"Sometimes I wish we could open ourselves up to each other as much as we do to the sky. To the smallness and the enormity."

"I see," Mr. Wright said, looking back at his notes. "And do you have any other interests?"

Must interests be interesting? That is, must they be interesting to someone other than yourself? This is why I hate these interviews, these applications. *List your interests.* I wanted to say, *Look, interests aren't things that can be listed. My interests are impulses, are moods, are never-ending. Sometimes it's as simple as Thom holding my hand. Sometimes it's as complicated as wanting to be able to hold his hand in front of his father. That want is an interest of mine.*

"I swim," I answered instead.

"Are you on the swim team?" Mr. Wright looked vaguely interested.

"No."

"Why is that?"

"I like to do it alone."

"I see."

He wrote something else down. *Not a team player,* no doubt.

"Thom is on the swim team," he added.

"I know," I said.

"Very competitive." As if that was the marker of a fine activity.

"So I've heard." I had grown so tired of competitions. Of sacrificing the nights of stargazing in order to make the paper self as impressive as possible.

"Do you know Thom well?"

"We're friends," I said. Not a lie, but not the whole truth.

"Well, do me a favor and make sure he stays on track."

"Oh, I will."

He picked up my transcript again, frowned, and asked, "What is the GSA?"

It had now gone from uncomfortable to downright fierce. I tried to imagine him coming to one of our Gay-Straight Alliance meetings. I tried to imagine that if I told him what it was, he would understand. I tried to think of a way to avoid his shiver of revulsion, his dismissive disdain.

Thom had tried to signal him once. I'd placed a pink triangle pin on his bag after a meeting, and he didn't take it off when he got home. Instead he put the bag in a spot where it could be seen. But it didn't work. Mr. Wright brushed past it. He didn't notice or didn't say. When all Thom wanted was for him to notice without being told.

"GSA stands for God Smiles Always, sir," I said with my most sincere expression.

"I didn't know the high school had one of those."

"It's pretty new, sir."

"How did it start?"

"Because of the school musical," I earnestly explained. "A lot of the kids in the musical wanted to start it."

"Really?"

"It was *Jesus Christ Superstar,* sir. I think we were all moved by how much of a superstar Jesus was. It made us want to work to make God smile."

"And the school is okay with this?" Mr. Wright asked, his eyebrow raising slightly, a vague irritation in his voice.

"Yes, sir. It's all about bringing people together."

"It says here you were on the dance committe for the GSA?"

I nodded, imagining Thom's reaction behind the door. "I was one of the coordinators," I elaborated. "We wanted to create a wholesome atmosphere for our fellow students. We only played Christian dance music. It's like Christian rock music, only the beat is a little faster. The lyrics are mostly the same."

"Did Thom go to that dance?"

"Yes, sir. I believe I saw him there." *In fact, he was my date. Afterwards, we had sex.*

"It also says you were involved in something called the Pride March?"

"Yes. We dress up as a pride of lions and we march. It's a school-spirit thing. Our mascot is a lion."

He did not look amused. "Do you march in costume?"

"Yes. But we don't wear the heads of costumes."

"Why not?"

"Because we're proud to be wearing them. We want people to know who we are."

He looked back down at my application.

"It says the Pride March is tied to Coming Out Day."

Damn. The transcript might as well have been written in lavender ink.

I faked a laugh. "Oh, that. It's another school-spirit thing. First day of the football season, someone dresses up as a lion and comes out from under the bleachers onto the field. If we see its shadow, we know the season will be a long one. If not, we know it's pretty much over before it's begun. The whole school gets really into it."

"I can't recall Thom mentioning that."

"He hasn't? Maybe he thought it was a secret."

"I know what's going on here."

Mr. Wright put down the transcript.

Now it was my turn to say, "Excuse me?"

"I know what's going on here," Mr. Wright said again, more pronounced. "And I don't like it one bit."

"I'm sorry, sir, but . . ."

He stood up from his chair. "I will *not* be ridiculed in my own house. That you should have the *presumption* to apply to my alma mater and then to sit there and *mock* me. I know what you are, and I will not stand for it here."

I wish I could say that I hurled a response right back at him. But mostly, I was stunned. To have such a blast directed at me. To be yelled at.

I couldn't move. I couldn't figure out what to say.

Then the door opened and Thom said, "Stop it. Stop it right now."

Suddenly Mr. Wright and I had something in common—disbelief. But I also had faith. In Thom.

"If you say one more word, I'm going to scream," he said to his father. "I don't give a shit what you say to me, but you leave Ian out of it, okay? You're being a total asshole, and that's not okay."

Mr. Wright started to yell. But it was empty yelling. Desperate yelling. And while he yelled, Thom came over to me and took my hand. I stood up and together we faced his father. And his father fell silent. And his father began to cry.

As if the world had ended.

I could feel Thom shaking, the tremors of that world exploding. As we stood there. As we watched. As we broke free from limbo.

And I wanted to say, *All you need to know about me is that I love your son. And if you get to know your son, you will know what that means.*

But the words were no longer mine to say.

Except here. I am writing this to let you know why it is likely that you received a very harsh alumni interview report about me. I'm hoping my campus interview will provide a contrast. (Thom and I will be heading your way next week.) I do not hold it against your university that a person like Mr. Wright should have received such a poor education. I understand those were different times then, and I am glad these are different times now.

It is never easy to have a college interview with your closeted boyfriend's father. It is never easy, I'm sure, to conduct a college interview with your closeted son's boyfriend. And, I am positive, it is least easy of all to be the boy in the hallway, listening.

But if I've learned one thing, it's this:

It's not the easy things that get you to know a person.

Know, and love.

Cat Got Your Tongue?

Sonya Sones

It Feels Just Like I Dreamed It Would

My skin misting all over,
my T-shirt clinging to me,
my breath coming in short, soft gasps,

my heart hip-hopping in my chest,
my hands trembling
and reaching out,

my fingertips buzzing as I take hold of it,
gripping it for the first time,
slipping around it as if it were a trophy—

my very own driver's license!

_Every_body Sing!

Happy Birthday to me,
Happy Birthday to me,
Happy Birthday, dear Bria,

Happy Birthday
to deliriously happy, totally independent,
sixteen-year-old, licensed-driver

me!

Actually, My Real Name Isn't Bria

It's Umbria.
And just in case you're wondering *why*
I have such a bizarre yet fabulously exotic name
it's because my parents named me
after a region in Italy.

Which, supposedly,
is the very region in which I was conceived.
So, as you might well imagine,
every day I thank my lucky stars
that I *wasn't* conceived

in Oxnard.

My Parents Told Me That It Happened in a Car

Not that I had even the eensy beensiest desire
to *know* that.

Mom says maybe that's why learning how to drive
came so easily to me.

But it *wasn't* easy trying to figure out
California's teen driving rules.

I'm still not real sure about it.
I think it goes something like this:

For the first six months after you get your license you
can't drive around with anyone under the age of twenty in
the car unless there's also someone over twenty-five with
you, except for your siblings or unless you have special
permission to take your friends to school, but only if you
get it in writing and even *then* you have to have it signed
by *their* parents and by *your* parents and the principal,
and probably the pope, too, but after you've had your
license for six months, it's okay to drive other teens
around without an adult in the car, as long as their
midriffs aren't showing and there are absolutely no
poodles present, though for the whole first year I'm pretty
sure that it's a no-no to go cruising between midnight and

five A.M., especially during earthquakes, unless a licensed driver over the age of twenty-five or under the age of ninety-seven and three quarters is in the car, too.

And under no circumstances can you *ever* drive to an IHOP on a Tuesday.

So That Means

That even if my big brother, Paris
(can you guess where *he* was conceived?),
wasn't twenty-one years old

it'd still be okay for *me* to be the one driving us up
to Aunt Ginger's place for my birthday luau
(*her* idea, not *mine*),
as long as we could prove that he's my brother.

And even if a practically blind cop were to pull us over
he'd be able to see that Paris and I are related.
Because we look more like twins
than twins:

same green eyes flecked with gold,
same shoulder-length wavy brown hair,
same annoyingly adorable dimple in left cheek.

Levitating to My Luau in Paris's Mustang

Shooting through the night
like an arrow on the wind,
we're zooming past the orchards
with the top down.

Breezing down the road,
listening to rap,
my fingers have to tap,
have to dance to the music of the ride.

The car and I are one,
swaying through the dark,
awaying to the rhythm
of the drums.

I could drive like this for hours,
I could drive us *any*where,
drive us right up past the moon
to the stars.

Both of Us See It

This bullet of fur,

this tiger-striped shadow,
this smudge, this blur

that darts from the dark like the tongue of a snake.

We see it streak out.
But it's just

too sudden,
too fast,

too—!

I Slam on the Brakes

Slam them so hard
that wheels scream,
rubber burns.

"Oh, no!" I gasp.
"Did I hit it? I didn't hit it.
Did I?"

Paris doesn't answer.
He doesn't need to.
I already know.

I know.
But I don't *want*
to know.

And I sure don't want to turn around
and see it lying in the middle of the road.
But I swivel in my seat and there it is—

a mangled mound of tiger-striped fur,
one delicate paw extended out of the heap,
as though caught in mid-swipe,

a small white moth
fluttering above it
in the bloodred glow of the tail lights

as if trying to coax the little cat to life,
trying to lure it back
to the chase—

I rest my forehead
on the steering wheel
and cry.

I Guess Paris Must Feel Pretty Sorry for Me

Because he doesn't even call me Dumbria.

He just reaches over and switches off the ignition,
silencing the CD and filling the night
with the sudden echoing choir of crickets.

He lets me cry it out for a few minutes.
Then he hands me a Kleenex,
tousles my hair, and says, "Geez, Bria.

I know you aren't particularly fond of kitties,
but don't you think you've gone
just a tad too far this time?"

Now I'm laughing instead of crying.
And thinking to myself
how much I love my brother.

But then *that* gets me thinking
about the people
who probably loved that cat.

And I break down all over again.

Paris Sighs

Then he puts his arm around me and says,
"What a rotten thing to have happen
your first time out of the box."

He says that I should try not to take it so hard.
That there wasn't anything I could do.
That it really wasn't my fault.

"Believe me," he says, totally deadpan.
"Even if a *good* driver had been driving the car,
the same thing would have happened."

It takes me a second to realize
that I've just been insulted.
Then I start laughing again.

He says, "Well, we better get going
or we'll be late to your birthday luau."
"Okay," I say. "But *you're* driving us the rest of the way."

"No. *You* drive," he says. "It's only five more blocks.
You've got to get right back on
that Mustang that threw you."

He's giving me that look of his,
the one that means,
"Don't even think about defying me, lowly baby sister."

So I blow my nose one last time,
switch on the ignition,
shift into drive,

and flee from the scene of the crime.

Two Minutes Later

We pull up in front of Aunt Ginger's house.
Paris commends me on my courage,
my fortitude,
and my parallel parking.

We head toward the front door,
but before we can even knock,
it sweeps open and Aunt Ginger yanks us inside,
hurling herself into our arms.

It's like being hugged by an unusually friendly octopus
who just happens to be wearing a hula skirt and
one of those bras made out of coconuts.
(Ouch! Ouch!)

"Aloha, my darlings!" she cries,
flinging a lei over each of our heads.
"I want you to meet Leon,
my fifth and final husband."

Leon stops strumming his ukulele
and steps forward to pump both our hands.
He's a Buddha-esque little man dressed only in a pareo,
with a belly as round as his gleaming bald head.

"Which one is the birthday girl?" he says with a grin.
This is apparently Leon's subtle way
of letting us know that he's noticed
the length of my brother's hair.

"I am," Paris says,
with a seductive bat of his eyelashes.
This totally cracks Leon up.
"You're going to get along great with my son!" he says.

His son? No one said anything about a son.
I hope he's not as obnoxious
as her fourth husband's little brat was. . . .
"Flynn?" Leon calls. "Where are you hiding?

Get on out here, boy."

Flynn Walks Through the Door

Wait a minute.
This is no little brat.
This is—

Suddenly
I'm staring deep into a pair
of swimming-pool-blue eyes,

these huge, dreamy,
heavy-lidded miracles
fringed with a forest of feathery black lashes.

I'm just standing here dumbstruck,
staring straight into Flynn's soul,
while the room spins out of focus around us,

and my heart starts dancing the hula.

I've Read About This Sort of Thing Happening

This hokey love-at-first-sight thing,
this sparks-flying-fireworks-exploding-
ohmigod-I-think-I'm-about-to-melt-into-a-puddle-
right-here-and-now-
all-over-the-floor thing.

I've read about these mushy moments dozens of times.
And I've heard about them, too,
from some of my friends.
But mostly from Paris.
And in *way* more detail than I actually wanted to hear.

Like when he was crushing on Ava.
And then when he swooned for Emily.
And when he swore his undying love for Nicole.
And then there was Monica and Maggie and Brooke.
Although not necessarily in that order.

I've read about all this sappy stuff happening.
And I've heard about it happening.
But I never thought
it would *ever* happen
to *me*.

Or That When It *Did*

It would be with a boy
named Flynn.

A boy whose hungry eyes
are holding so tight to mine

that they're making me feel
as if we're exchanging our genetic codes. . . .

We aren't speaking.
But we're *saying everything*.

It's as if in this one kaboom of a glance
my fate's been Krazy-Glued to Flynn's

forever.

I Let My Eyes Drift Down to Flynn's Lips

"Hau'oli la hanau momona 'umi kumaono," he says.
"Huh?" I say.
"It's Hawaiian for 'Happy Birthday, sweet sixteen.'
I've been practicing."

"Wow . . ." I say, temporarily stunned into monosyllables
by the husky sound of his sexy voice.
But a second later I manage to pull myself together
and purr, "I love it when you talk Hawaiian to me."

This makes Flynn laugh.
And the sound of it bubbles up
and washes over me like cool spring water,
quenching a thirst I didn't even know I had.

I notice Flynn's eyes doing some drifting of their own,
and suddenly I'm *very* glad that I decided to wear
my slinky little Hawaiian print dress,
the one that clings to all my curves like shrink-wrap.

Then Paris says, "Hey, Flynn.
Can you teach me the Hawaiian words for
'How about them Lakers?' "
And Flynn cracks up, as Leon herds us into the kitchen.

Aunt Ginger Tells Us She's Been Secretly Yearning

To throw me a luau for my sixteenth birthday,
but that she hadn't suggested it
because she didn't want to be intrusive.

So she was happy to help when my mom called to say
that she and my dad had been
"unavoidably detained" in Turkey.

(Thank goodness
their *conceiving* days
are over.)

Then she slips on an apron and asks my brother
to help her chop the onions and tomatoes
for the lomi lomi salmon.

Leon opens the oven to check on the kalua pig.
He asks Flynn to peel the sweet potatoes.
I offer to set the table, and head out onto the patio.

Lilting Hawaiian music drifts from the speakers.
Strings of lanterns, shaped like tiny pineapples,
twinkle on and off, like tiny pineapple-shaped lanterns.

Alone at last,
under a full moon,
with my fantasies of Flynn . . .

I'll be setting out the plates
when he'll come up behind me and whisper in my ear,
so near that I'll feel the tingle of his breath on my skin,

"Do you need any help, Bria?"
But I won't answer.
I'll just lean back, pressing my body tightly to his.

He'll wrap his arms around me,
holding me so close
that I'll feel his heartbeat's wild drumming.

Then he'll start kissing my neck,
my shoulders,
my—

"Do you need any help, Bria?"
I whirl around—
Ohmigod!

It's *Flynn*.

I Can Feel My Cheeks Flushing Hibiscus Pink

"Sure," I say,
trying not to stare at his lips.
But they're like eye magnets,
so tempting they should be illegal.

"How about if *you* put out the napkins," I say,
trying my best to sound nonchalant,
"and *I* put out the plates?"
"Okay," he says.

I begin circling the table,
placing a dish in front of each chair.
Flynn trails after me, setting down the napkins.
I can feel his eyes burning right through my dress.

I continue circling,
placing a fork on each napkin.
Flynn follows behind me, a seductive shadow,
putting down the knives.

Wherever I go,
Flynn goes, too,
gliding along next to me
as though we're doing the tango.

I put down the spoons
and Flynn sets out the glasses,
his thigh hovering
dangerously close to mine now.

He begins passing me
the little paper umbrellas for the glasses.
That's when it happens—
his fingertips brush my wrist!

Suddenly, this quivery sort of shiver
is fluttering all through me
and Flynn's taking a step closer to me,
his fingers finding mine, lacing us together.

The heat that this is generating
could melt Alaska!
Now *I* take a step closer to Flynn,
lifting my chin toward his and—

"Hey, kids," Paris calls.
He's standing in the kitchen doorway smirking,
with his arms crossed over his chest,
one eyebrow raised.

"Can you give us a hand grating these coconuts?"

I Muddle Through the Next Half Hour

Avoiding eye contact,
avoiding *any* contact
with Flynn the Magnificent.

Because it's entirely too weird to be falling for him
while his father is watching,
not to mention my aunt *and* my nosy big brother,

who for some strange reason
has decided that his baby sister is off-limits
to every boy on the entire planet.

At least Aunt Ginger and Leon
are still way too into each *other*
to notice what's going on with Flynn and me.

They don't even seem to see
all the lightning flashing in the charged air
that's crackling between us.

But no matter what I'm doing,
whether I'm helping Aunt Ginger and Leon
dice the chicken for the adobo,

or stirring the coconut pudding over low heat,
or wrapping up the butterfish in the ti leaves
for the lau lau,

all I can think of is Flynn—
because he's so completely and utterly
wow wow!

When We Finally Head Out onto the Patio to Eat

Flynn practically breaks into a trot
to grab the seat next to mine.
This totally goose-bumps me.

Paris flops into the seat on my other side,
while Aunt Ginger and Leon
settle in across from us.

They're too entranced by each other
to be able to hear the cymbals crashing together
when Flynn presses his thigh against mine.

I wish the same thing could be said of Paris.
"I think maybe we're crowding Flynn," he says.
"Let's give him a little more space."

And he scoots his chair over
six inches to the right,
embarrassing me into doing the same thing.

Oooooo . . .
When I get that brother of mine alone
he's gonna be dead meat.

But Flynn Won't Give Up Without a Fight

He rises casually from his seat,
and lifting the pitcher of Mai Tais from the table,
he offers to pour the rum-laced drinks
for the twenty-one-and-older crowd.

I can't take my eyes off Flynn's long fingers
as he circles the table filling each of their glasses,
doing this really funny impression
of a drunken bartender.

A second later, when he sits down again,
he somehow manages to surreptitiously
slide his chair back in *my* direction,
successfully closing the awful gap between us.

And when his thigh touches mine for the second time,
and I feel the delicious heat of it,
an entire marching band
suddenly starts playing in my chest.

We Share a Secret Smile That Lasts a Nanosecond

Then,
while Paris is passing the adobo chicken to Leon,
Flynn slithers his hand into mine under the table,
and a dizzying current of energy surges between us.

"So, Flynn," Paris asks,
"were you in Maui with your father when he met Ginger?"
But Flynn doesn't answer.
He doesn't even appear to have heard the question.

"That son of yours," Aunt Ginger says fondly,
resting her head on Leon's shoulder,
and smiling across the table at Flynn.
"He's such a daydreamer."

"What's the matter, boy?" Leon asks gently.
"Cat got your tongue?"
"Hey, speaking of cats," Aunt Ginger says,
"has anyone seen Bitsy?"

Did she just say "speaking of *cats*"?!
"Who . . . ," I ask warily, ". . . is Bitsy?"
Aunt Ginger heaves a dreamy sigh and says,
"Only the most wonderful kitty on the face of this earth."

"She really *is* terrific," Leon says.
"I wonder where that little rapscallion could be.
It's not like her to be late for supper.
She's *always* home by eight. . . ."

I check my watch—

It's *8:25!*

My Heart Freezes in Mid-beat

Under the table, Paris grabs my other hand.
We sneak a quick peek at each other.
He's obviously thinking what *I'm* thinking.
I squeeze his hand in panic.
Paris knocks back the rest of his Mai Tai in a single gulp.

"I hope that dear little cat hasn't gotten herself
into any trouble . . . ," Aunt Ginger says.
And a line creases her forehead.
"Don't you worry, doll," Leon says.
"I'm sure our Bitsy's just fine."

"She better be," Flynn says,
finally emerging from his love trance.
"I've gotten *way* attached to the Bitster.
I can't wait for her to get home
so you can see her, Bria."

"Me neither," I barely manage to croak.

Paris Pours Himself Another Mai Tai

As Aunt Ginger's eyes start misting over.
"You know," she says, "if it weren't for Bitsy,
I never would have even met Leon."

Then she tells us this long story about
how she was taking a walk on Hamoa Beach in Maui,
and she was feeling *so* sorry for herself,

because there she was,
all alone in this tropical paradise,
letting this fabulously deserted beach go to waste,

when she heard this tiny mew coming from behind her.
So she turned around and there was this scruffy kitten,
following right along after her.

"She could easily fit into a single one of my footprints,"
Aunt Ginger says.
"She was such an itsy-bitsy little thing."

"Hence . . . the name?" Paris asks,
with a visible lurch of his Adam's apple.
"Exactly," Aunt Ginger says,

not seeming to notice his oddly strangled tone of voice.

There's a Question Burning in My Throat

A question that has to do
with whether or not
a certain little wonder cat is tiger-striped
But I'm way too scared to ask it.

"I figured she was lost," Aunt Ginger continues.
"So I picked her up and started knocking
on all the doors of the houses nearby
to try and find her owner."

"When Flynn and I answered our door," Leon says,
"there was this absolutely gorgeous woman
standing there, smiling at us,
holding this scrawny little feline in her arms."

Well, apparently,
one thing led to another,
and the three of them spent the rest of the day together,
searching to no avail for the kitten's owner.

But before the moon rose that night,
Leon was in love with Aunt Ginger.
And they *all* were in love
with Bitsy.

"Which Was Totally Strange for Dad and Me,"
Flynn Says

"Because both of us had always been allergic to cats.
And neither one of us had ever really even *liked* them."
"To be honest," Leon adds with a little chuckle,
"we'd never even liked the *people* who liked cats."

Aunt Ginger snuggles up to Leon and says,
"But that was before they met Bitsy and me."
He gives her a hug and says, "A couple of weeks later,
your aunt and I were married by a justice of the peace."

"At sunset, right there on Hamoa Beach,"
Aunt Ginger says, getting all dewy-eyed.
"With Flynn as the best man
and Bitsy as the flower cat."

And Flynn says that even though he and his dad
had been sneezing their heads off for two solid weeks,
the three of them decided right then and there
to bring Bitsy home to live with them.

"We knew it would be hard," Flynn says.
"But Dad and I decided that we'd rather spend
the rest of our lives on antihistamines
than have to give up the Bitsinator."

And Flynn
squeezes my left hand,
while Paris
squeezes my right one.

My Stomach's Doing the Jitterbug

I can't take this anymore.
I've *got* to find out if Bitsy's the one I hit.

I'm trying to muster the courage
to ask them what color she is, when Leon says,
"Then the most amazing thing happened."
"Two weeks ago," Flynn says,
"we stopped being allergic to Bitsy!"

"The allergy doctor says
my boys must have somehow managed
to build up a resistance to her," Aunt Ginger says.
"But *I* say it was a real bona fide miracle!" Leon cries.

"It's a lucky thing, too," says Flynn,
"because I was wheezing so bad
I couldn't sleep at night.
I was willing to put up with it, though,
because Bitsy's . . . Bitsy's . . ."

"One cat in a million?" I squeak.
"She sure is!" Flynn says,
stroking my knee under the table
as if he's patting a cat.

It's a shame I can't enjoy it.

But How Can I Enjoy *Anything*

When I still don't know for sure?
I *have* to ask them. . . .
I *have* to ask them. . . .

Just then, Paris takes a swig of his Mai Tai,
and, in an offhand sort of way, he says,
"What does the Bitserino look like, anyway?"

"Yeah," I say hopefully.
"What color is she?
Gray? Calico?"

"Nope," Flynn says,
pulling out his wallet, like a proud father,
to show me her picture.

"She's a cute little tiger-striped thing."

No!

Suddenly I'm choking on my lau lau.
Or is that my heart that's stuck in my throat?
Paris and Flynn start slapping me on my back.

"Dang hairballs," Paris says.
And everyone laughs.
Even Paris and me.

But anyone who took a close look at either one of us
would be able to see the *ohmigod!!!*
in our eyes.

Flynn Reaches for My Hand Again

"Why don't you come into the living room, Bria,
and I'll show you some more pictures of the Bitster?"
And he leads me inside, away from the others,
sitting down real close to me on the couch.

He reaches for the thick photo album
on the coffee table and places it on my lap.
I can't *do* this.
I can't look at any more pictures of my *victim*. . . .

But Flynn doesn't open the album.
Instead, he slips his arm around my shoulder
and traces a circle on my lips with his fingertip. . . .
At least if I faint, I won't have far to fall.

Maybe Flynn *would* like to show me
some pictures of Bitsy,
but I think there's something *else*
that he'd like to do *first*!

And *I* Want to Do It, Too

I want to kiss Flynn
just as much as Flynn wants to kiss me.
Maybe even *more* than Flynn wants to.

Maybe even more
than anyone in the whole entire world
has *ever* wanted to kiss anybody before.

I turn my face to meet Flynn's gaze.
Those eyes of his—
melting into mine.

Telling me exactly what he wants to do.
Asking me if I want to do it, too.
And I do.

Do I *ever*.
I do.
I *do*!

But I can't.
I *can't* kiss him.
Not until I tell him the hideous truth

about what I've done.

But If I Tell Him

He'll hate me.

And then I'll never find out
how his hands would feel
slipping into my hair,
how his fingers would feel
at the nape of my neck,
guiding my mouth toward his,
how his lips would feel,
pressing onto mine. . . .

Maybe I could kiss him *first*.
Just kiss him *one* time.

And *then* tell him.

But That Wouldn't Be Right, Would It?

No.
It would be evil.

Ohmigod, though.
I'm *sooooo* curious.

But you know what they say about curiosity. . . .
Oh, the irony of it all!

I've got to find out what it would feel like to kiss him.
I've just *got* to know.

I close my eyes,
letting my face drift toward his and—

Suddenly,
we hear footsteps approaching!

"Hey, Flynn," Paris calls from down the hall.
"What have you done with the birthday girl?"

"Bria," Flynn whispers urgently,
letting his lips thrill against my ear.

"We can look at these pictures later.
Let's take a walk to see if we can find Bitsy, okay?"

Find Bitsy?!
Oh, man . . .

"Sure," I gulp, as Flynn takes my hand
and yanks me out the front door,

before Paris even sees where we went.

I Try

To steer Flynn
in the opposite direction
from the scene of the crime.

But he says that Bitsy sometimes visits
the cat that lives at the apple farm
a few blocks down the road,
so we ought to check there first.

Now it's just the full moon dappling the lawns,
the echoing of the cricket choir,
and Flynn's long, warm fingers entwined with mine,
as we stroll together through the summer night
lit with stars and fireflies
and possibilities. . . .

The only problem is
that every step we're taking
is leading us closer and closer still

to a certain heap of roadkill.

"Here, Bitsy, Bitsy, Bitsy . . ."

Flynn's calling softly to her,
in that devastating voice of his.

One block . . .
Two blocks . . .

Now Flynn's telling me stories about his life.
Funny ones.

Stories that make me like him
even more than I already did.

The sound of his laugh, the feel of his hand,
those lips, those lashes . . .

"Here, Bitsy . . .
Here, Bitster, Bitster, Bitster . . ."

Three blocks . . .
Four blocks . . .

Now Flynn's letting go of my hand,
slipping his arm around my waist,

and I'm slipping my arm around Flynn's,
lightly pressing my hip against his

as we walk down the road,
linked together in perfect sync.

I'm trying not to think.
Trying not to think.

Trying not to think
about *anything*.

But I Can See It in the Distance Now

I can just make it out at the far end of the block—
the lump that's lying in the middle of the road!
The poor little kitty that *I* snuffed out . . .

Then, without warning,
Flynn slows to a stop
and pulls me around to face him.

But I keep my eyes trained on the ground.
Because if I look up into *his*,
I know what will happen.

And I can't *let* that happen.
Can I?
Can I?

He Takes a Step Closer to Me

And brushes his lips against my forehead.
"Flynn," I whisper.
"Yeah?" he whispers back.

I swallow hard,
trying to force my heart back down to where it belongs.
"There's something I have to tell you."

"What is it?" he asks softly,
giving my hands an encouraging squeeze.
"I . . . I don't know *how* to tell you," I say.

"It's okay, Bria," he murmurs,
folding me into a knee-wobbling hug.
"You can tell me *any*thing."

"But this is so awful," I whisper.
"Because I . . . I . . ."
I can't tell him—I *can't*!

I sneak a peek at Flynn's face
and see the light that's in his eyes
flicker and start to fade away.

"What is it, Bria?" he asks.
"Is there someone else?"
"No," I say, closing my eyes tight.

"It's nothing like that. . . .
It's . . . it's about your . . .
your . . ."

Suddenly,
something brushes against my ankle.
I leap back and then I see it—

it's something furry,
something soft,
something *tiger-striped*!

"Bitsy!"

Flynn cries, "Where have you been?"
scooping her up and burying his face in her fur.
"We've been looking all over for you."

"Bitsy . . . ?!" I gasp.
"But . . . but *I* thought . . .
Ohmigod! *Bitsy*! It's *you*!"

"Mew,"
Bitsy says matter-of-factly,
gazing at me with her big yellow eyes.

I lean in to rub my cheek
against the softest fur in the universe
and then I find Flynn's lips

and *kiss* him!

The Day I Turned Chickenhearted

Steve Almond

I was sixteen when I started dating Jodi Dunne. It astounds me now to think of myself at sixteen. It astounds me to think of sixteen. I see these kids in my neighborhood, scuffing along in their giant boots, their hair all sculpted with gunk, like they'll never take one on the chin. It makes me sad.

Jodi was a year behind me. We sat across from each other in second-period art. The class was taught by this old guy, Mr. Park, who was famous at our school for being a flamer. He walked around in a beret and called us children.

"Children," he would say, "who on earth is going to pull down those shades?"

We were all totally terrified of him. The whole class was just us looking at slides of paintings while Mr. Park walked around and talked about how delicious they were. So, what I'm saying, there was a kind of intimacy to that class. You can't put a bunch of teenagers in a dark room and show them Gauguin's nudes and not expect the sap to rise.

Jodi sat pretty near the screen, and I can still remember the way the colored lights from the paintings revealed the subtler aspects of her beauty, the articulation of her nostrils, the pink curve of her underlip. She had a small, exceptionally expressive mouth. If I close my eyes I can still see those things. And her hair. She had the greatest hair I'd ever seen, a pale orange that turned blond in summer, and if you examined each individual hair (as I later did), what you saw was that the color went from rust, at the roots, to a burnished gold.

The one thing about Jodi, she was a pretty big girl. Not fat. Not even close to fat. But wide-bottomed and fleshy. The problem was that in high school, as you know, you're either thin or fat. There's no real in-between category. Also, she played volleyball and hung out with the girls who played volleyball, many of whom were dorks. She sometimes wore sweatpants to school. She wasn't interested in trying to doll herself up, which suggested some kind of inner strength, which, of course, most boys wanted nothing to do with. We wanted the pliant ones, who wore makeup and flipped their hair and chewed gum at all times so their breath wouldn't stink. The main thing, the thing I'm most ashamed to mention, is that Jodi's family didn't have a whole lot of money. I knew this because I'd asked Sean Linden about her one time and he told me she lived over by Los Robles, which was this crappy part of town with one-story ranch houses.

None of this should have mattered, especially her finances. But it did. You should know this: From the beginning, I was making certain kinds of judgments about Jodi, holding myself above her a little. It was a kind of disease in our family, a way of casting out weakness by assuming superiority.

I knew I was attracted to Jodi the first week of class. But I put off asking her out. I started to second-guess myself. I'd see her and her friends camped in front of the gym in kneepads and think, She *is* kind of heavy, her friends *are* sort of lame. Four months of this nonsense. I did manage to stare at her every day. And she stared back. So that was kind of our courtship. We sat in that darkened room staring at each other. There was even kind of a language that developed between us, an initial stare that was like, *Hello, good morning!* then another one, with a little more smolder, which meant *Lookin' good!* and some eyebrow work if Park said something especially swishy, or, if one of us made a comment in class, a respectful little nod, like *Nice goin'!* The whole thing was so Hello Kitty.

I remember one day I got caught cheating in my math class, first period, and I was so ashamed that all I could do was glare at Jodi, which of course confused the hell out of her, and she looked back at me with such tenderness—*Are you okay? What's wrong?*—which made me even madder, so I did this silent scoff, and she got fed up and turned her eyes away, then I panicked and tried to stare an apology at her—*Oh hey, I'm sorry, just having a rough day*—but she wouldn't look at me, the bitch. So then I didn't look at her. Fine. We had this whole week-long spat, a really dramatic little emotional event I mean, without having actually spoken.

Lord knows this episode should have goaded me to ask her out. It did not. What happened was this: Brent Nickerson pulled me aside one day after class.

"Your girl's got herself a sweet new ride," he said. "A Ford Mustang."

"She's not my girl," I said.

"Check it out," Nickerson said. "Some very cherry shit." Then he punched me in the shoulder.

Nickerson was a popular kid, one of those guys who finds himself in the pursuit of girls. He had gone all the way with Melissa Camby and Holly Kringle, allegedly at the same party. That he had taken notice of Jodi placed her on a different level in my mind. And the Mustang. These things suggested that she wasn't just what she seemed, that she existed outside the little box I'd placed her in and puzzled over day after day.

I can't remember how it all started, how I finally broke through my own doubt, only that at some point we were in the parking lot behind Swensen's with our shirts off. We spent a lot of time in parking lots, kissing, touching each other. We weren't experienced, but we were eager to learn. We understood that sex was our surest path to intimacy, to being able to feel more sure of ourselves in the world. And we were kind to each other. That's what I remember most vividly. We had things to talk about—friends, classes, plans for college—but we were too young to talk about what really mattered, the secret miseries our families inflicted on us, our half-realized plans for escape.

We loved our families, after all. Jodi loved that my dad had once sung opera, that my mom wrote books for a living, that my older sister was in the Peace Corps. I couldn't explain to her that there was something merciless in their achievements.

The Dunnes were a joyride by comparison. Jodi was their youngest child by ten years, a happy mistake. You got the feeling that raising the other three had worn them out. They seemed delighted to have this sweet young woman around to keep them company. Bill spent most of his time in his workshop, designing the boat he hoped to build when he retired from Ford, where he was an engineer. (This explained the Mustang—he leased a new one every year.) He'd served in the navy long ago and he moved like a sailor, with a wide, rolling gait. He was missing certain teeth. He had big, rough hands, stained yellow from his Newports, and a sardonic way of dealing with the world that obscured the fact that he was actually shy and socially awkward. I guess the word *crusty* applies. Jodi's mom, May, watched her TV shows and laughed a lot and hugged me whenever I came over.

They were both alcoholics. I didn't see this, of course. They just seemed more relaxed and affectionate than my parents, a little more sentimental when they got going, Bill with his tumbler of whiskey next to the cigarettes on his workbench, May with her glass of red wine. Happy drunks. So what? Most of the world is happy drunks.

Jodi's older brothers and sister were a little less happy. They were all divorced, and they had money problems. Sometimes, later on at night, when I was sneaking out of her room, through the little courtyard next to the Dunnes' bedroom, I would hear May on the phone, singing out in her wine-blurred alto: "I know, honey. It's hard. I know."

Jodi's older sister, Sue, spent a few months at home, with her two boys. Jodi and her mom loved this at first. They got to fuss over the kids. But these guys were out of control. They drew stuff on the walls, pooped in the bath. Sue took one of those multilevel marketing jobs, selling health products made from apricots and seaweed. This made her desperately happy for about a week. She'd bought six hundred dollars' worth of the stuff and was going to make ten times that. I can still remember her sitting at the dining-room table with a bottle of wine, stabbing at her list of debts. She had the same beautiful hair as Jodi, though her face had gone puffy.

Jodi had a brother, Dave, but I didn't hear too much about him. He'd gone to Europe with a Belgian woman and her son. They were street entertainers, jugglers or something.

Billy, the eldest kid, lived on a houseboat up around Half Moon Bay. He invited the family for lunch one time and we trolled to this little lagoon near the harbor so Sue's kids could angle for sunfish. Billy was a handsome guy, a charmer, but he had that same agitated quality as his dad. After lunch, those two went down into the galley. He wanted Mr. Dunne to go in on a charter boat with him. That had been the whole point of the invite, it turned out. We could hear Billy setting out the plan, his voice rising through the registers of imploration. But his dad wasn't sure. Billy'd had some scrapes with the law, some problems with drugs, whatever it was.

Billy reappeared, surly and squinting, and everyone gave him a wide berth. One of the kids, Devin, complained about the fruit plate Billy had set out. He didn't like pineapple. Billy walked over and picked up the platter—it was one of those plastic deals you get from the grocery store—and hurled it over the side of the boat.

"No more pineapple," he said.

So then Devin pitched a fit and Mr. Dunne started to holler

at Billy to settle down and Billy snapped back at him, then Sue got in on it and Jodi's mom, who was in her cups by this time anyway, went downstairs to cry. Jodi and I took this opportunity to paddle the dinghy out into the cattails, where we groped at each other. It was what we did when the family traffic got too thick.

This was the life of the Dunnes, besotted and needy and a little tumultuous. At their parties, people got drunk and sang songs and flung the dip around. They flirted with one another. I secretly loved the mess of their lives, the brazen displays, the emotion flowing sloppily from one human to the next. When my parents had friends over it was for intellectual discourse, little concerts, linzer torte. They were people of the mind, not the flesh, and incredibly boring to a teenager.

The Dunnes liked me. They understood that I was leading their daughter into the deep sexually, but they also understood that somebody was going to get to her eventually, and they could have done a lot worse than me. I was from a good family. They could smell the ambition on me, though, and it always made them stiffen a little when I showed up.

My family really wasn't so much richer than hers, by the way. But I guess it's important to know a little bit about the town I grew up in, how much attention was paid to the subtle gradations. There was a rich part of town, and a super-rich part of town, and a big, prosperous university where my mother worked. There was a set of kids who had their own cars and others who were destined for the Ivy League. There were mansions with lawns so green I wanted to eat them. Some afternoons, I pedaled through these neighborhoods on my way to work and felt that old American itch to pull a Gatsby.

I didn't want to be rich. (It's not what Gatsby wanted, either.) What I wanted was the sense of ease that I imagined the rich kids possessed, of being able to relax, not having to try so hard all the time. I wanted to be loved, of course, but more than that I wanted to be able to *receive* love.

Jodi did what she could to help. She rescued me from what might have been a terrible misery. All around us, we could see the cruel theatrics of our classmates, the breakups and minor betrayals, the public humiliations of unsteady love. One night Jodi and I hung out with Sean Linden and his girlfriend, Tess, and it was terrible to see what he did to her, how he tore her down a little bit at each turn. She'd gotten a new perm that hadn't set quite right and he kept calling her Shirley (as in Temple), pretending it was affection. He stroked the soft flesh of her stomach and made a blubbery noise. She drank a bit too much and wound up spilling some Chex Mix on the fancy new rug and Sean made her pick up every piece. Or, actually, it was worse than that, because Tess did this herself, without his prodding. I can still see her down there, on her hands and knees, a pretty girl in loose curls, digging around my feet for Rice Chex.

One of the reasons I hate Hollywood so much is that they portray the travails of teen life as so innocuous and fun-loving, some kind of idyll before the mean business of adulthood. People forget how much it all hurts back then. Someone pinches you and you feel it in your bones. They don't want to face what a bunch of sadists teenagers are, wounded narcissists, killers. All these folks who acted all shocked and outraged about Columbine—where the hell did they go to high school?

My point is only that Jodi and I protected each other from a lot of that. We were in that dinghy, floating away from the tribulations of our friends and families. We were the bodies in that dinghy, streaked in sweat, tender from the sun, braced against the gunwales, taken up by the awkward contortions of love.

I can remember Jodi walking into the music room one

night as my father was rehearsing his lieder. It was something I would never have done. To intrude on such a moment of vulnerability—that was not how we did business. My father had failed as an opera singer, after all. That was why he sold sheet music. But Jodi didn't see him as a failure. She sat primly on the piano bench as my father released the somber notes that lived within him. He was a baritone, though he often sang in the low tenor ranges, and when he did his face tilted up and his eyes took on an almost unbearable yearning (my sister called this his Figaro face). His nostrils flared, as if he could smell his lover racing toward him through the *Schwartzwald*.

When he finished the song, my father looked up. He hadn't realized Jodi was there.

"It's so beautiful," she said. "Your voice."

My father smiled shyly. He smoothed the wisps of hair onto his brow. "I was just warming up."

"What's he saying?"

"That he loves too well and not enough, something like that."

"He's singing to his lover?"

"Yes."

"Beautiful," she said. "Thank you."

"Well," my father said, "I didn't write it."

Jodi leaned forward on the bench. She looked as if she might want to touch his arm. "John told me you used to sing, in New York."

There was a moment when I thought my father might relent, might open his chest of shy memories and lay them before Jodi. But he seemed to catch himself. He took a step backward and leaned against the piano and inhaled through his nose. "You're sweet," he murmured. "A sweet young lady."

She had this effect on people, an optimism that struck me as close to magic. And there were moments when I felt ready to receive the full weight of her love, when I believed that we could live quite happily together, one of those lucky couples who find the cure early. We breezed through junior year and into senior year, and when it came time to apply to college, I chose five schools, four schools back East, plus UC Santa Cruz, Jodi's intended first choice.

In our town, among the bright young sires and dames of the landed gentry, where you *got in* carried the weight of a life sentence. Several years earlier, a kid had tried to kill himself when he got wait-listed at Harvard. I myself tried to affect an air of nonchalance about the whole thing. Or maybe it would be more accurate to say that I was simply avoidant. Whatever the case, I took it harder than expected when, on a single afternoon in early May, I got rejected by three of the East Coast schools.

My mother, who had gone to great pains not to appear overly concerned about where I applied, called me into her study that evening.

"I hope you're not going to take this personally," she said.

"Oh, no," I said. "It's not like they rejected me *personally*."

"I've sat on these admissions committees, Johnny. It's all a formula. I don't mean to denigrate the process, but it's riddled with quotas. Diversity is the new mantra."

"I guess Lisa was more diverse than me."

This was a somewhat self-pitying reference to my sister, who had been accepted by every school on the eastern seaboard, including the ones she didn't apply to.

"Your sister—" my mother said. Then she stopped herself. "It's gotten more competitive, significantly so. I see the application figures, kiddo. I know about this stuff."

"I'd like for it to have been my choice, that's all."

"You've still got a chance."

"Plus Santa Cruz," I said. "Jodi would be pretty happy if I wound up there."

"Yes, I imagine she would." My mother sighed. She took off

her glasses and fixed me with a sober look. "Now listen, Johnny. You know how fond we are of Jodi. She's a wonderful girl. This isn't about her—"

"What isn't?"

"We would love it if you went to Santa Cruz, to have you nearby, your father and I. We want you to be happy. But you need to make sure you're thinking about what *you* want to do. Do you understand me? You and Jodi, you're both very young."

I could feel something squeezing in my chest. "So you're saying to disregard Jodi?"

"That's not what I'm saying at all," my mother said. "I'm saying to *regard* yourself. You make the decision that's best for you. It's as simple as that."

I looked at my mother, at the massive bookshelf above her, the volumes of Marx and Freud and Spinoza, all those big-ticket Jews in worn bindings.

"She's a wonderful girl," she said again. "You know how fond we are of her."

I don't remember the exact chronology on the rest of the college shit. I got into that last school back East—a smaller, second-tier place—and Santa Cruz, of course. That's all you need to know. No need to go over all the moaning that came later. You have your own version, I'd expect.

What I need to tell you about is this one night, a week after the talk with my mother. It was a Friday and my parents were away at a conference. Jodi and I were going to spend the weekend playing house, cooking ourselves meals and screwing wherever we pleased. Jodi was supposed to swing by after volleyball practice, but by eight she still hadn't appeared.

When she did finally call, I could hear loud voices in the background. "Hey, baby," she said. "Can you come over and pick me up?"

I figured she and her pals had started the weekend early, that she was maybe drunk, and this both excited and annoyed me. Then I heard someone scream, an angry male sound, and the sound of something slamming.

"Where are you?"

"Home," she said. "My house."

"What's happening over there?"

"Nothing. No big deal. But it's better if I don't use the car."

"Are you okay?"

"I'm fine." She laughed her patient laugh. "Just a little family drama."

"Is this a bad time?"

"No, I want you to come by. Or—just honk."

So I got in my dad's car and drove over to her house. I figured that either her mom or dad, maybe both of them, had hit the sauce a little too hard. When I pulled up to her house, I could see the new Mustang in the driveway and a car I didn't recognize, right up on its bumper. The Mustang looked a little off-kilter, and when I passed by I could see why: The left rear tire had been slashed.

The front door of the house was flung open. This was often the case. But the frosted-glass window next to the door was busted and the shards were scattered on the pebbled cement of the courtyard. I walked over to the sliding glass door. I could see right through the kitchen and living room to the backyard, where there was a little pool. Billy Dunne swung into view. A little string of blood was dripping off his hand onto the flagstone. He had a glass in his other hand and he was glaring down at his father, who was perched on the edge of a chaise lounge. These faint blue ripples kept washing across them, from the light in the pool.

Billy was screaming all kinds of crap. "Get up! Get up! Fucking sailor! Fucking phony-ass sailor!"

Mr. Dunne had his jaw set, but I could see, from the smoke coiling off his Newport, that his hands were trembling.

Then I heard another voice, a distressed, female voice, and I thought: Jodi, it's my Jodi! She's back there! I had this sense that I should do something, rush into the backyard and make sure Jodi was okay. I could step between the men and get them to cool off, make the peace. I felt the adrenaline kick in and reached for the door. But Billy Dunne raised his highball glass and smashed it on the flagstone and the sound was like the report of a rifle.

I stepped back. There was another shriek. A woman lurched into view, her blond hair up in a ponytail. "You're ruining it!" she screamed. "You're ruining everything!" Then May appeared and pulled her away from the two men. Bill Dunne dropped his cigarette and started to get to his feet, but his son struck him, a soft, quick blow above the eye, and Bill Dunne slumped back down onto the chaise lounge. He looked stunned and helpless, like a child.

Something turned in me, just then. I lost my nerve. Rather than leaping forward, into the fray, I turned and hurried back to my car and leaned on the horn. I told myself that if Jodi didn't appear in a minute or so, I'd head back inside. When I've thought about this moment in the past, taken it apart, I've made the kind assumption that I knew the woman with the ponytail was Sue, not Jodi. The truth is I wasn't sure. It might have been Jodi I was running out on.

And then Jodi did appear, a big, sweet dumpling of a girl hurrying toward me. Her hair was wet and loose across her shoulders.

"Hey," she said.

"Is everything cool?" I said. "I heard some screaming."

"Oh, it's so stupid. Let's just go, baby. Okay?"

"I don't know," I said. "Should I—"

"Please," she said, as I knew she would. Then she looked at me and took me in her arms and hugged me, hard. "I love you," she whispered. "I love you so much."

You reach a point in every relationship where you have to decide to be brave, to move forward into the dangerous territory. Or you retreat.

It didn't happen immediately. We had ourselves a fabulous weekend of kissing and fondling and slurping. Jodi was grateful for these pleasures. We both were. I managed to convince myself that I'd shown admirable restraint in the matter. It wasn't my place to interfere in family politics.

I knew what a load of crap that was, but I wasn't ready to face my cowardice. So I started making judgments. The Dunnes were drunks, failures, makers of tawdry scenes. Their poor breeding had finally revealed itself. And how long would it be before Jodi met the same fate? Here was my bigotry rising again to rescue me, the idea that I was above Jodi, that my family had more money and more sophistication, that our blood was a little purer, our minds more refined.

What was I really afraid of? I was afraid of love. I was afraid of Jodi because she offered me love, a pure, unconditional love, and this made me feel like a traitor to my family, which doled out love only as a reward for heroism. I viewed accepting her love as beneath me when, deep down, it was more than I felt I deserved.

So this isn't some kind of after-school special where the booze is the culprit. My family was just as sick as hers, beset by envy and guilt and a need to withhold, all the polite violence of the modern suburb.

There were some other things I could mention—minor acts of infidelity—but I'm not sure they matter so much. They were more effect than cause. By summer I'd decided to head back East for school and started to pursue other girls who were going East, thinner models who doled out the abuse I was seeking.

The worst part, of course, is that Jodi didn't hold any of this against me. She was totally, maddeningly forgiving. She understood that I wasn't ready for the happiness she was offering, that I needed to get away from my family.

The last time I saw her, the last memorable occasion, was the next summer. Bill Dunne had commissioned his boat.

He'd even agreed to let Billy—back from rehab and looking contrite—take it out for charters. They threw a party at the dinky little public marina near the marshlands, and Jodi sent me an invite, with a note informing me that her father insisted I be there. It was a rousing affair, with margaritas and platters of salty salami and dancing. Jodi came and hugged me. I felt the solid warmth of her flanks against me. The breeze moved through her hair, which was golden with sun. It was strange to see her again only because it didn't feel strange at all. It felt perfectly natural, as if we'd never missed a beat. Then May came and gave me a hug and Bill threw his giant straw hat on the dock and gestured for me to dance around it. I didn't get it. Couldn't these people see me for the heel I was?

Later, at dusk, Jodi slipped away from my side and went down to the launch. She and her mother smashed a bottle of Mott's against the hull and they climbed aboard for the maiden voyage of the *Jodi May*. Everyone let out a cheer and May hugged Bill and the rest of the Dunnes waved like mad.

I felt the oddest sensation then, as they puttered out under the high, distant streaks of cloud—as if I were the one drifting away from land, from the happy crowd on the dock, from the wine and song, from the simple human pleasures of fellowship. And it's true, I was.

Venetian Fan

Cat Bauer

I'm crying and it's Titian's fault.

I sit at the top of the Doge's private staircase inside the Palazzo Ducale, alone except for one cuff-linked man who stands near the foot of the steps, his back to me, black hair tumbling to his collar. He cannot see my tears.

Today is my birthday. I am sixteen. I am alone, on the day I was born, in front of an ancient fresco in Italy and I have never been kissed.

The steps are smooth stones, chilly beneath me on a hot July afternoon. My sketch pad is beside me, my fingers too unsure to draw. Outside the open door, tourists shuffle by, blank and unaware. I listen to the babble of voices that bounce off the bare walls:

"What's a Doge, anyway?"

"I dunno. I think he was sort of like the president of Venice."

"Devo fare pee pee, Mama! Adesso!"

"Basta!"

On the wall above the door in front of me towers Titian's fresco of St. Christopher, child perched on his shoulder, a colossus striding across the Venetian lagoon. His biceps are toned, his thighs, strong and muscular. His head tilts up at the child, who rides him like a victor, little legs wrapped around St. Christopher's neck. The child is serene. St. Christopher is determined, lusty jaw, noble nose. I think: I want to float up over the doorway and press my mouth against St. Christopher's stony lips.

The Palazzo Ducale, the Doge's Palace, was once the center of the government, rising like a rose-colored fairy tale in the waters of the Venetian lagoon. Now it is just another Italian museum, trampled by foreign footsteps looking for a glimpse into the past of a crumpled Republic.

The guidebook says that the Doge was the head of the government. He walked down the staircase (where I sit) from the Senate (where he worked) to his private chambers below (where he lived).

Titian painted the St. Christopher fresco for the Doge's eyes to light upon as he descended the stairs—a billboard to remind him of his majesty. I think: I could use a few frescoes splattered across the walls of our house in Florida to remind me who I am.

I have been here an hour, swallowing the image, but I'm still hungry for more. I had two fathers back in America; together they do not equal one St. Christopher. Maybe that's why the fresco moves me.

"They say Tiziano painted the fresco in just three days."

The man's voice, soft, in accented English, cuts through the tangle of languages outside the door. I am startled. I had forgotten he was there. He has turned and looks up at me.

With my index fingers, I spread the tears on my cheeks from a single trickle to a glossy sheen. I nod. "I've never seen anything so beautiful."

"You're young."

It is a statement, but I answer as if it were a question. "I'm eighteen." I lie. I don't know why.

"A student? From America?"

"Yes."

He indicates my sketch pad. "An artist?"

"I try."

The man's beard is trim; his black hair is tousled. He wears a blue tie. I raise my eyes to meet his. They are chestnut eyes, polished and moist, with deep creases in the corners where remnants of his own tears still gleam. I don't look away; I can't. We are connected for a weighty moment.

"Is it the fresco?" I am hoping.

He nods. "*Sì*. Sometimes, when I am overwhelmed, I come to see it. It always gives me . . . the word is not *comfort*. It gives me . . . power. *Sì. Potenza*. Potency. In the sense that I can carry the weight."

I wonder what his burden is. He looks tired. His clothes are dark and graceful, but his tie is loose. There is a lion of San Marco on his tie clip, so I assume he is Venetian. Venetians hold themselves separate from other Italians, I've learned, still angry that Napoléon conquered their Republic more than two hundred years earlier. Even the word *Venetian* sounds like an alien from another planet.

"It would be nice to feel as confident as the child," I say. "If you had St. Christopher holding you up . . . I guess that's why some people pray to saints."

The man climbs up two steps and stops. "You don't pray?"

"I look at art. It's like praying."

"If you like art that touches the soul, there is another Titian, my favorite here in Venice, across the piazza on the ceiling in the library." The man moves up another step. "It is called *Allegory of Wisdom*. It is interesting to me because Titian has painted Wisdom as a young woman, confident and mysterious. Have you seen it?"

I shake my head. "I don't have a clue what you're talking about." I decide there is something attractive about him in a schoolteacher type of way, even though he is probably three times my age. There are green flecks at the edges of his chestnut eyes.

"I can show it to you, if you like." The man hesitates. "If you have the time."

"I would like that," I say. I am feeling bold on my sixteenth birthday.

A British family, two adults and a matching boy and girl, enter the stairwell, attached by four headsets plugged into two cassettes. They talk too loudly, their hearing muffled by the recorded voice in their ears. The little girl is the first to turn to the fresco. She points: "There's the Titian!" She runs up the stairs, forgetting the cable that connects her to her brother. Her headphones tumble to the floor.

The mother pulls off her own headphones and follows her daughter up the stairs, leaving the male members of the family with their cords dangling.

They sit two steps down from me. The girl wiggles between the mother's legs and perches on her lap. The boy bounds up the stairs and presses close to his mother, who wraps her arm around his shoulders. She is Mother Goose, about to tell a tale. It is impossible for me to imagine a family outing like this. In Florida, my mom and I are lucky if we make it to Wal-Mart.

"It's St. Christopher," the mother explains. "They say the Christ child he's carrying on his shoulders represents the weight of the world."

The boy asks, "What's a fresco?"

The father has climbed up the steps but doesn't sit; he leans against the railing. He touches his chin as if he's smoking a pipe. "You paint straight on the wall." Their English sounds exaggerated, pompous and strange.

The girl asks, "How did Titian get up there?"

The father says, "On a ladder."

The boy says, "He was a priest."

The mother says, "No, that was Vivaldi, the composer. Titian was just an artist."

I think: Yeah, and Einstein was just a scientist.

The father says, "He lived to be very, very old, to his nineties. That was very unusual for those days."

I think: Ain't too common these days either, mate.

The mother says, "They say the fresco brings luck. Whoever looks at it will have luck all day."

The father says, "Well, we could all use a bit of luck, couldn't we?"

I think: We certainly could.

I watch the family lean into one another, comfortable, a single unit, and I am sad. I feel like a jigsaw puzzle missing a few key pieces.

I see the black-haired man move to the bottom of the steps, his place conquered by the British. Some Americans wander in past him, led by a tour guide. They are dressed in sneakers and windbreakers, as if they're going hiking.

"Three days, huh? I could paint that in two." Their words are Southern, slow and drawling.

I pretend I am French and shrug my shoulders, disguising myself from my countrymen.

"Why do they call him Titian if his name was Tiziano?"

"I guess it was his nickname."

"I read van Gogh's story about four years ago. I should have read it like, four weeks ago."

I want to snicker, but I don't.

"Well." The tour guide hesitates. He decides to be kind. "That wouldn't have made much of a difference. Van Gogh was born in 1853, almost four hundred years after Titian. And he was Dutch, not Venetian."

"Whatever."

A group of German university students pour into the stairwell, nudging the Southerners out the door. They climb the stairs, backpacks knocking into one another. They sprawl out over the steps, unzip their backpacks, and take out bottles of water and candy bars. It is a palazzo picnic. The leader of the group, tall and dressed entirely in black, barks out guttural orders, but no one pays attention. He bounds up the steps two at a time and stands right in front of me, blocking my view.

"Excuse me," I say. He either ignores me or doesn't hear. I tap his ankle. "Excuse me."

He whirls around and glares down at me. "What? What do you want?"

"I'm sorry, but I can't see."

"So stand up! What do you think, you own the world?" He turns away from me and defiantly spreads his legs.

My first instinct is to challenge him, but I am an American in Europe, and my rhythm is the beat of another continent. Instead I take a deep breath and wait, peering between his legs. I try to catch a glimpse of the black-haired man, but a crowd of Birkenstock sandals blocks my view.

I listen to the potpourri of languages. Three gray-haired Frenchwomen wearing flat heels have joined the crowd. *"Voici le Titien!"* These different cultures are comfortable with one another, meeting on a stairwell in Venice. They stand close together, strangers touching. Now that the Southerners have gone, I am the only American. The space around me is greater than the rest.

Finally, the German students pack up their backpacks and titter out the door, pulling the Frenchwomen along in their wake. The British family connects itself back together and shuffles out behind them, leaving me alone with St. Christopher. It takes me a moment to realize that the black-haired man is gone.

I stand, surprised that I am disappointed. I pick up my sketch pad and walk down the stairs. Outside in the great hall stands the man, hands in his pockets, waiting, I hope, for me. He seems agitated.

"Sometimes the crowds irritate me," he says. "They show no respect."

I ask him, "Are you Venetian?"

"I am. . . . Yes. I am." The man waves his hand as if he were a king dismissing his court. "I shouldn't let it annoy me. Come. Let us see the other Titian."

He puts his hands on my shoulders and turns me toward the exit. I feel a small thrill at his touch, though he does it in a fatherly sort of way. But then, after a profusion of proxies, I have only been confused by the touch of a father's hand and what, exactly, that is supposed to feel like.

We walk through the main floor of the palace and down the Scala d'Oro, the Golden Staircase, all gilded stuccos and white marble, and head out to the courtyard.

"My name is Marco." His pace is fast, and I scurry to keep up. "My parents were not very creative, I'm afraid. I think every other man in Venice is named Marco, after our patron saint. He is symbolized by the lion, the Lion of St. Mark."

I know this, but I don't tell him so. We pass underneath the Porta della Carta, the magnificent marble entrance with its seventy-five lions. "My name is Fan," I say. "My mother named me after Ebenezer Scrooge's dead sister in 'A Christmas Carol.' My father wasn't there to stop her."

Marco pauses and holds out his hand. "Pleased to meet you, Fan." His fingers are long and spindly, like the bow of a violin. "Are you here on holiday?"

I notice he wears no rings. "Sort of. I'm visiting my aunt Ziggy, my stepdad's sister. She lives here—she's an artist. Well, she's not really my aunt, and he's not really my stepdad, he's my mom's latest boyfriend, but I call him my stepdad, so I call her my aunt. He sent me here for my birthday. Though I think they really just wanted me out of the house. They're having problems." I have no idea why I am revealing all this personal information to a stranger.

The brick bell tower, the Campanile, looms up in front of us; the Basilica, looking more like a magic castle than a cathedral, its four bronze horses galloping over the entrance, is to the right.

"Ziggy?" Marco pronounces it "Zeegy," and his accent

charms me like a snake. He takes my hand and tucks it through his arm. I know this is not unusual in Italy, friends linking together, men and men, women and women, fathers and daughters—but his touch throws me off balance and I stumble. Marco squeezes my hand with the inside of his elbow and steadies me.

"Ziggy is a nickname. I forget her real name." My voice from the Florida suburbs sounds nervous and nasal, and I think I must speak more softly and accent my consonants.

"I believe I've met your aunt Ziggy," says Marco. "At an exhibition. The Biennale, perhaps."

"You have?" I am startled. "At the Biennale? The art festival?"

"It is not so unusual. Venice is a very small town. And Ziggy is a very distinct name."

We weave our way across Piazza San Marco, the immense central square, which is crammed with visitors. We pass the outdoor cafés, with their dueling violins and pianos. An elderly couple, with pearls and white-tipped cane, dances a waltz. Dozens of languages from hundreds of people waft in between the notes; the bells on the Campanile chime six o'clock. I feel dizzy, as though I've stepped into an exotic painting, not quite real.

We stop at the opposite end of the square in front of an enormous double staircase. I know this is the Correr Museum.

"Napoléon tore down a church to connect the buildings in the square," I say, wanting to impress him with my guidebook knowledge.

"Yes." Marco smiles. "You've been studying our history." I score two points. The green flecks in his eyes catch the sun, emeralds surrounding a dark stone setting. Again, he touches my shoulder to direct me forward. A finger tangles in my hair. He gently unravels it. "Your hair is the color of Titian's paint."

Now I really start to wonder if he's coming on to me. I decide that would be okay. I touch the tips of my tresses and smile back at him, hoping I look demure. "Thanks." My hair is burnt red and thick, like a lush, foreign material falling from my head. Sometimes I feel like nature made a mistake, and this shawl of curls was supposed to be given to someone more flamboyant.

We climb the stairs and enter the lobby. "The entrance to the library is at the very end of the museum these days, so we will actually walk all the way back to where we came, across from the Palazzo Ducale." Marco ushers me toward a woman guarding the entrance to a long corridor. "It seems that entrances and exits are always changing in this city, like some madman playing a game. I have no control over it."

I think that is an odd thing to say, especially when the woman at the entrance straightens up at the sight of Marco. "*Buena sera, Sindaco.*"

"*Buena sera.* I am taking this young lady to see the Titian in the Marciana." Marco's tone is authoritative, a superior to a subordinate.

The woman, however, smiles, as if she knows his secret. "Of course, *Sindaco.* Enjoy your visit." She glances at me and winks, and I wonder what she's thinking.

We set off again, hurrying past marble sculptures and antique maps, Renaissance paintings and ancient coins. Marco flings brief descriptions of each room over his shoulder.

"What does that mean, '*Sindaco*'?" I ask as we speed past a room filled with weapons and armor.

"Mayor."

I stop. "You're the mayor? The mayor of Venice?" Now I remember that Aunt Ziggy and her expatriate pals have gossiped about the mayor over evening spritzes at the bar in the neighborhood square, calling him a dangerous man. Aunt Ziggy said he'd licked her hand.

Marco nods and seems amused. "As you say, Fan—I try."

We have arrived in a cool, dark room, curtains drawn,

glass-encased manuscripts beneath a gilded ceiling. A gallery of canvases watches us, philosophers and gods, inventors and prophets. Aside from a spectacled fellow sitting behind a desk, we are alone. I think: I am alone with the dangerous mayor of Venice on my sixteenth birthday and I have never been kissed. I hear my heart beat. I hear myself breathe. Marco leads me through the room and into a smaller chamber. He positions me in the center of a large mosaic star on the floor.

"Okay, Fan. Look up."

I realize I am trembling and try to get a grip. I take a breath. I raise my eyes. There is a single painting on the ceiling, a young woman floating on a cloud, bare feet dangling, nipples erect and poking through a billowy white blouse. Her head tilts toward a large, square mirror hoisted by a cherub. One hand holds a scroll; the other steadies the mirror. She lolls back, confident and contemplative, an elbow resting on a puffy piece of cloud.

"It is Sapientia, the patroness of wisdom." Marco speaks softly. His murmur resonates off the chamber wall. "Eros, the god of love, holds the mirror."

"She looks . . . in control." I am aware, very aware, of Marco standing next to me. The fabric of his jacket brushes against my arm.

"She acquires wisdom by looking inward, with love." Marco puts a hand on my waist as he speaks. "It is love that allows her to look in the mirror. It is power that allows her to harness her passion and examine the possibilities."

I move closer, just a breath closer to Marco. I am in Venice beneath Wisdom and Eros, the god of passion and love. I think I am a pagan at heart and should embrace my Sapientia within. I want to gaze into the mirror held by Eros and float around the ceiling, dangling my toes off a fat, fluffy cloud. Marco turns his chestnut eyes down on me as I look up at the painting. Please, I think. Please . . . And then Eros answers my prayers and I feel his lips on mine, gentle and soft, a kiss from the gods, born in Mount Olympus and transmitted by way of Marco's lips.

"Happy Birthday, Fan." Marco wraps my tumbling curls in his hands and pulls the hair back off my face, forcing me to look at him. I see myself reflected in the mirror of his eyes and wonder just how wise I am.

Kissing Lessons

Joseph Weisberg

The summer after seventh grade, I went to the Busby Berkeley Camp for the Performing Arts in Pinewood, Wisconsin. I went there because I liked to tap-dance. I liked to tap-dance because I had no friends, and when you have no friends, you gravitate naturally towards hobbies and interests which ensure that you will never have any friends.

The boys at Busby Berkeley were misshapen, bewildered, and talented. Beefo Kellner was tall and blubbery, spent most of his free time in his bunk clipping his toenails, and had a gorgeous tenor voice. Ed Waxman was squat, cross-eyed, and had numerous facial tics, but completely transformed into a sexy Brando-esque actor the moment he stepped onstage. Greg French had red hair gurgling up from his head like lava, never said a word to anyone, and tap-danced with grace and total abandon. The rest of us were hapless variations on these same themes.

The girls at camp were as perfect and put together as the boys were clunky and poorly assembled. Their hair was curled into loose ringlets that tumbled down to their shoulder blades, or blow-dried into lightly feathered Dorothy Hamill bowls. They wore diamond earrings and makeup with blue jeans. Some of them—Suzi Tefler, Shawn Coe, Nancy Rothstein—had women's bodies, and moved around camp in a charged fourth dimension, like sexy ghosts. Only junior coun-

Birth of a Tap Dancer

When I was ten, my cousin Tess took me to see a double feature of *Singing in the Rain* and *Top Hat* at the Biograph Theater. After that, I went to every Fred Astaire and Gene Kelly movie I could. I renamed my goldfish Fred Kelly. I taped the poster from *That's Entertainment!* over my bed. I got a pair of tap shoes.

Every day after school, I went down to our basement, put on the sound track from one of my favorite shows, and danced. I would clack away on the old chipped floor for hours, arms flying, body spinning, little clouds of slate dust kicking up around my feet. I'd arrive at dinner dripping with sweat.

After a year of this, my parents carpeted the basement. I tried dancing on the carpet, but they'd bought a particularly thick, spongy one. I tried dancing in my bedroom, but I wasn't allowed to wear my tap shoes there because they would scuff up the linoleum tile, and tap dancing in sneakers is unfulfilling.

Soon my focus started shifting to *Battlestar Galactica*. I named my new hermit crabs Starbuck and Apollo, after the handsome fighter jet pilots in the show who streaked through the sky fighting Cylons. Cylons were members of a master race of robots that wanted to keep Captain Adama

selors could talk to them. Most of the others were wafer thin, had tiny round butts, and tucked in their T-shirts to stretch them tight over their crab-apple breasts. In their own way, they were just as beautiful as the other girls, Kate Jacksons to their Linda Carters. All of them came from the suburbs of Chicago—Winnetka and Highland Park, Northbrook and Glencoe—and they seemed more open and sexual than the and his crew from reaching Earth. Instead of eyes, they had red beams in their silver heads that slid incessantly from side to side. I wanted to kill them.

The following spring, my parents decided that I should go to summer camp. Sales reps came to our house from places with names like Loxahatchee and Nebagamon. They showed slides of boys water-skiing and playing baseball, shooting arrows, turning Popsicle sticks into what appeared to be glued-together stacks of Popsicle sticks. The boys were always shirtless, completely flat from waist to neck, with little lines indicating where their chests were going to be.

Then Horace and Sylvia came. They were the owners of the Busby Berkeley Camp for the Performing Arts. Horace seemed to be about ninety years old, and had a pea-sized growth just above his upper lip. He'd had a stroke, and it

city girls I was used to. They made no secret of the fact that boys were the center of their universe. They talked unself-consciously about the nose jobs they were planning for the end of the summer. And they flirted constantly. At home, nobody ever flirted with me, and now girls were winking at me from across rooms, giggling while they talked to me, hugging me. I felt like someone who's been raised by a colony of apes, then returns to civilization and suddenly finds himself surrounded by the species he is truly meant to love.

Our show that summer was *How to Succeed in Business Without Really Trying*. Because the camp directors wanted as many kids as possible to get a chance to play a lead, the main roles were divided into four parts at Busby Berkeley. This meant that a tall kid with dark hair would come out for the was hard to understand him. Sylvia was somewhat younger, very robust, and made occasional jokes in Yiddish (which my parents laughed at, but I didn't think they really understood).

In their slides, groups of kids were onstage, performing old musicals. In *South Pacific* the girls were in grass skirts and the boys in sailors' uniforms. In *Oklahoma* the girls wore checkered blouses and jeans, and the boys wore cowboy hats and had guns on their belts. Every time a new slide came up, Sylvia would throw her arms out and burst into whatever song the kids were singing.

"We have a sports program, too," Horace said, showing one slide of a chipped Ping-Pong table with a sagging net.

My parents looked at me, and in the dark, we communicated a silent "Yes."

first quarter of a show, then a short kid with big red hair would come out in an identical costume for the next three or four scenes, and so on. I was cast as J. Pierpont Finch in the third quarter of *How to Succeed*. My big number was a college fight song called "Stand Old Ivy" that J. Pierpont sings with his boss. After the song, I had to go over and kiss Rosemary, the leading lady.

Rosemary was being played in the third quarter by Suzi Tefler, the most beautiful, most popular, and tallest girl at camp. She was a foot taller than me. The idea of kissing her filled me with a constant, jittery dread. I had never kissed a girl, and I didn't really know how, and I didn't know if when you were doing a show you kissed in rehearsal or waited for the actual performance to do the kiss for the first time.

For the first two weeks of rehearsal, we didn't get to that scene. Then the day came. Everyone my age at camp was in the show, so they were all there, most of them sitting in the audience watching. I sang my song, a rousing anthem about how the Old Ivy Groundhogs were going to destroy their rival Chipmunks in a football game. Then I walked over to where Suzi Tefler was standing. I turned my back to the audience, closed my eyes, and moved my face towards her, praying that kissing would result.

I felt her breath. Then the electric tingle in front of her lips. Then Suzi jumped back and at the top of her lungs yelled, "HE BIT ME!"

The audience burst into a loud, punishing laughter. It went on and on, and every time it seemed like it was dying down, it built up again. I wanted to run off the stage but knew it would be a mistake to surrender whatever tiny piece of ground I had left.

Manon Guastafeste was my best friend at camp that summer. Guastafeste means "spoiler of the party" in Italian. Manon was short and hyperactive and had a big, beautiful nose on a Jewish-Mediterranean face. I had a crush on her, but she was going out that summer with Billy Zane, who would go on to play the handsome villain in *Titanic* twenty years later, and who looked exactly the same then as he does now. I accepted that I had no chance with her, and we settled into a friendship.

Manon saw how depressed I was after the biting incident. A few days later, as I was shuffling around the no-man's-land between the boys' and girls' cabins, she came up to me and said, "I've solved your problem."

"What do you mean?" I said.

"I got Nina Steinberg to agree to give you kissing lessons."

Nina Steinberg was our friend. And she was cute. Although the idea of kissing lessons wasn't particularly less terrifying than actual kissing, I said, "Okay."

"She'll meet you at Brigadoon tonight at nine o'clock."

Every building at camp was named after an old musical. My cabin that summer was South Pacific. The dining hall was Carousel. And the prop shed was Brigadoon.

That night, I rubbed Old Spice deodorant on my underarms and put on my best T-shirt. I opened the barn doors to Brigadoon ten minutes early. It was just a little clapboard shack, behind the main camp building. A chunk of roof from *Fiddler* leaned against one wall, a buggy from *Oklahoma*

My First Fight

There were two bullies at Busby Berkeley, Hank and Russell. They couldn't sing, they couldn't dance, and neither of them liked to act—it seemed like they'd gotten on a bus to the wrong camp and just decided to stay.

Their main victim was John Poderanski. John was a small, high-strung kid who wore black plastic glasses. Hank and Russell called him Numb Nuts. All day long they'd punch and slap him, pinch him on the neck until he started to cry, drag him over to girls and tell them he was "a faggot." In the cabin before lights-out, someone would say, "Do the professor," and Russell would snatch John's glasses from his face, put them on his penis, and dance around singing, "Professor Cock 'n' Balls! Professor Cock 'n' Balls!" Once, they got all the boys to piss in a bucket they were going to dump on his head, but a counselor intervened in time.

One day, John got in my face and started yelling. "Hey, Numb Nuts!" over and over again, trying to impress Hank and Russell. I shoved him, and he shoved me back. Hank quickly stepped between us. "We'll settle this at the archery

field after lunch," he said. Then he turned to John and said,
"I'll be your second." Russell looked at me and said, "I
guess I'll be your second."

After lunch, I went out to the archery field, where my second was already waiting with John and his second. John
and I squared off. Hank immediately shouted, in disappointment, "Come on!"

We went at each other. He grabbed, I grabbed. A second
later, we were on the ground. A second after that, I was on
top of him. John twisted and writhed, but I had him
pinned. Eventually, he stopped moving and stared up at
me. His glasses were still on.

"Say you give up," I said.

"No," he said.

"Say you give up or I'll hit you," I said.

"No," he said.

stood in a corner. The only light, from a street lamp on the bas-
ketball court outside, filtered in through one small window
near the ceiling. I sat down on an old foot locker and waited.

At nine o'clock, Nina slipped in through the barn doors.
She closed them behind her, then she came and sat down
next to me on the trunk.

"Hi," she said.

"Hi."

We sat quietly for a little while.

"So you want to practice kissing?" she said.

"Ummm . . . yeah," I said.

She leaned towards me. I leaned towards her. And then I
was confronted with a problem I hadn't anticipated—Nina

My First Fight

I pulled my fist back and tried more menacingly, "Say you give up on the count of three or I'll hit you. One. Two. Seriously! It's coming!"

He lied there, impassive.

"Okay, I'll give you another chance," I said. "But this time, give up by the count of three, or I'm really going to hit you. One. Two! Two!!" I shook my fist, as if I was just about to slam it down on him. "Two!!!"

I looked imploringly at our seconds. Hank had his arms crossed in front of his chest, and was watching us with an almost intellectual interest. Russell shrugged.

"Well, I can't hit a guy in glasses," I finally said. And I got off him and walked away. As I reached the edge of the field, John called out, "Hey."

I turned around.

"Fuck you, you fucking pussy," he yelled.

had huge breasts. As we moved towards each other, I knew it was my responsibility to avoid making any contact with her breasts. I reached my arms wide around her, pulled my chest back, and craned my neck in, but as we got closer, it became clear this wouldn't help—our lips could not meet without her breasts being mashed into me.

Which is what happened. And in the same instant, our lips were together. Then her lips were pressing and pulling. They were plump. And wet.

She went back and forth between my top and bottom lips, taking each one between her lips and squeezing it. After a little while, I started squeezing back.

Then she turned her head sideways and came at me at an

angle. She affixed her face to mine and her tongue darted into my mouth. It started moving in and out, this way and that, thick and fast. I lifted my tongue and sort of . . . blocked it. Then I started moving my tongue haphazardly, startled each time it collided with hers. After the tenderness of the lip squeezing, this was chaotic. In a place that felt like outer space, I thought, *I'm French-kissing!*

Finally, Nina pulled away.

"Okay," she said. "You're a natural."

"Really?" I said.

"Yeah, you're good at it."

I didn't believe her, but I was glad she said it.

"Okay," she said again.

Then she got up and went to the door. She turned and waved before leaving.

"Thanks," I said.

Manon lived in Glencoe, a suburb an hour from Chicago, and although we never saw each other after camp, we talked three or four nights a week on the phone. The conversations were mostly her talking about her day-to-day life, and me "uh-huh"ing. I still didn't have any friends at school, and these conversations reminded me that there was an alternate universe where people liked me.

I went back to camp the next summer, but Manon didn't. I played Sky Masterson in the fourth quarter of *Guys and Dolls*. I wore a double-breasted suit, and I sang "Luck Be a Lady Tonight," crouching and pretending to throw dice on the final "Tonight" of each chorus.

When I got home at the end of the summer, Manon called and told me her family was moving to Chicago, and she was transferring to New City Day School. We were going to be freshmen together. She shrieked and laughed about how great it was going to be. I was ecstatic, too.

On the first day of school, I waited against the wall in the big front entryway. All the kids I'd known for years were bouncing through the doors, practically hopping into each other's arms. New City Day went from kindergarten through twelfth grade, but the move into high school still felt like a new beginning, and everyone was excited.

Manon came in the door, one hand gripping a Le Sportsac that hung from her shoulder. She scanned the entryway, and then her big, beautiful mouth spread wide when she saw me. She ran at me and threw her arms around me, jumping up and down while we hugged. "Oh my God! I can't believe you're here! I can't believe I'm here! I can't believe it! Oh my God! I can't believe this!"

I looked down into Manon's eyes and said, "You can't hang out with me."

"What do you mean?" she said.

"Nobody likes me here. If you hang out with me, nobody'll like you, either."

"That's ridiculous!"

"No it isn't."

"We're hanging out all the time. You're my best friend."

"We can't."

"We're going to be together all the time."

I shook my head.

"This is crazy," Manon said. "I don't know anybody else. I love you!"

"No," I said.

Then I pointed to a group of popular girls clustered together across the hall. Each had a different-colored Le Sportsac. "They're popular," I said. "Go hang out with them."

"No," she said.

"Go."

"No, this is ridiculous."

"Go."

Manon looked up at me. She was crying, and she opened her mouth to say something. Then she turned and left.

I waited in the entryway for a little while, then went in to start high school.

Junior year, I started to fall into people. First Kevin Dorst, who I was in chorus with, invited me out to dinner one night. Then Bill Fritz, who was on the soccer team with me, started sitting next to me in Latin class. We both thought the word *expugno* (*are, atus*—to take by storm) was funny, and we

Dinner at Papa Enzo's

One day after chorus, at the beginning of junior year, Kevin Dorst asked me if I wanted to come over that night and go out to dinner. I had never gone out with a friend before.

We took a bus to his building on Chestnut Street, dropped our stuff in the foyer of his apartment, and went around the corner to Papa Enzo's. It was a neighborhood Italian restaurant with red booths and candles on the tables. Kevin confidently told me that the ravioli was excellent.

After we ate, we went back to his apartment. With the constant exhale of the central air, dim track lighting, and long, white-carpeted halls, it felt vast and desolate, Kevin's corner bedroom like a far-flung outpost at the North Pole.

In his room, we sat on the floor and looked at his favorite *Playboy*—the Playmate had breasts that swelled out to cover her entire torso. Kevin offered to let me borrow the magazine (I never gave it back).

I took the 151 bus home through the deserted park. The walking paths twisted into the trees, the antique street lamps glowed, and the magazine in my bag pulsed secretly, like uranium. I could still taste the ravioli in my mouth, and the structure of my loneliness buckled.

started making as many jokes as we possibly could with it, chief among them simply repeating and declining the verb. (When a teacher has you convinced you're being disruptive by declining Latin verbs, you are in the hands of a master.)

Eventually, my relationship with Bill spilled out of the classroom and into his father's apartment on Lake Shore Drive, a bachelor's lair with a huge sculpture of a penis in the front hallway, a bearskin rug in the living room, and a Jacuzzi and sauna in the back bathroom. This was an environment totally different from my own, and going there felt as magical and exhilarating as walking into a rain forest.

Bill and I played soccer with a guy in the popular clique, Jonah, and at lunchtime we started going to his house, which was only a few blocks from school. Jonah's friend David usually came, too. I used to go to Shmendel's, where I'd eat hot dogs and play pinball by myself. Now I went to Jonah's basement, where I'd eat Chips Ahoy and play video games with a whole bunch of guys. Jonah could hiss exactly like the snake in the Dungeons and Dragons video game, and something about the frequency he hit was so creepy and primal that it gave us chills. It also made us laugh so hard we stopped caring about the game and played just to hear him hiss.

Once Bill and I were friends with Jonah, becoming friends with the girls in the clique was as effortless and quick as a sponge soaking up water—one moment you were talking to Jonah in the hall when they arrived en masse, the next you were sitting between them at Sarah's house and watching *Days of Our Lives*.

Manon had been a member of the clique since I had pointed her to it freshman year. Now we were around each other all the time again. Our friendship regrew from the old root. We went back to talking on the phone for hours. We sat next to each other in class and at lunch, we snuck away from parties for conspiratorial discussions of whatever was on her

Bill's Dad's Apartment

Bill's dad was a lawyer, but not the kind of lawyer the rest of our fathers were. He worked at home in sweatpants, he played tennis every day, he had "deals" instead of cases. One of his clients was Seka, the most famous porn star in the world at the time. I fantasized that on my eighteenth birthday Bill's dad would arrange for her to have sex with me.

One night, after taking a Jacuzzi, Bill, Jonah, and I were heading toward the kitchen in nothing but towels wrapped around our waists. We were winding through the narrow, cool hallways of the apartment when we turned a corner and ran into Bill's father and Seka. She had a sweet, plain face and, stretching a white T-shirt into horizontal ridges, breasts that we knew were heavy and oblong.

"This is Dottie," said Bill's dad.

Seka was Dottie.

"Hi," Jonah said.

"Uh, hi," I said.

"Hi, Dottie," said Bill.

"Hi, boys," she said.

There was a great awareness of towels.

Dottie then scanned each of our chests.

"How come you're so much tanner than they are?" she said to Jonah.

"Um . . . I just am," he answered.

"Okay, that's enough," said Bill's dad.

Dottie smiled slyly at us and furrowed her brow in comic suspicion.

We turned our backs to the wall and sidled past her, three half-naked boys in formation, fully understood.

mind. We were constantly huddled together, talking about love, complaining about school, reminiscing about camp. The only thing we never discussed was our separation. There was an unspoken agreement between us that it hadn't happened.

Near the end of junior year, Manon and I were going to a party together at Jonah's house. It was my sixteenth birthday, and I was vaguely entertaining the thought that it might be a surprise party for me. It was around eight o'clock, and we were parked on one of the quiet side streets of Lincoln Park, a few blocks from Jonah's. We were talking for a while before going in, in the way we always talked—her going on and on, me absorbing little bits and pieces of what she said.

At one point, when Manon was saying something I wasn't listening to at all, I saw her eyes narrow and focus in on me. "You know, you're a very confident guy," she said. "And confident men have big penises."

There was a quiet moment while her comment filtered through me. I could feel my mind reaching for it, but there was nothing there except blackness and the faint, fading echoes of *confident* and *penis*. Then, for just a second, I felt a whirring in my head. And then I shut down. I stopped hearing anything, seeing anything, feeling anything. My head slumped a little, and my eyes locked blindly on the dashboard.

Time passed.

Something clicked. The world came back on. The inside of the car, full of an electric darkness. The trees outside, crisp and still. I sat up straight, and I looked over, and Manon was still talking. I felt something in my toes, and it started climbing, working its way up my body. A feeling of action. Of one fear breaking against another. I started moving across the seat. As I got closer, Manon turned her head and looked at me, all eyes now. And then I was there, and my lips were on hers. Her lips were there. And then they were gone.

She pressed the back of her head against the car window, went a little bug-eyed, and said, "What are you doing?"

I said, "I don't know. I'm sorry."

We sat there for a few minutes, silent.

Then Manon said, "Well, it's not a big deal."

Surprisingly, I believed her.

Only her.

A few minutes later, we walked into the party. Nobody yelled "Surprise!" There were boxes of pizza, Cokes, and Diet Cokes (which the girls called "Dokes").

After we finished eating, the room went black, and everyone started singing "Happy Birthday." Sarah and Cindy came in carrying a cake. In the dark light of the candles, I saw David's mouth wide open as he hammed up the song. Sarah'eyes locked on me, as if they were searching for something inside me. And Jonah, still eating a piece of pizza, brimming with optimism and joy.

I didn't really know why these people had taken me in. But tonight they were singing to me. It didn't feel like love, but it felt like hope.

A Cab Ride

When I was in my late twenties, my father died. I had moved home to help take care of him, so I had to deal with his death and the exhaustion and agony of spending an entire year watching him die. It was too much for me, and I fell into something that might be called a depression. I continued to function, to get up in the morning and eat and work and see friends, but in an emotionless, empty-headed way, as if I'd been unplugged from the world. This lasted for a year.

Then I went into therapy, where I learned that you have to face and share the full weight of your grief. But this made me feel even worse, because my family was dealing with things differently, and didn't want to constantly discuss how horrible we all felt.

I was visiting Jonah in New York, and we were riding in a cab together down Ninth Avenue. I started to explain to him that I felt as if I'd died along with my father, and that I didn't know how to make it back to this world. I told him that the worst part was that my family wasn't interested in digging into their feelings the way I was, and so I was left to grieve alone, and I didn't see how I could do it.

"I'll do it with you," he said.

Nebraska 99

Jacqueline Woodson

Tommy's cursing about the baby screaming. I don't say nothing, just pull the sheet up over my head. Cold tonight. We put two coats on the bed on top of the sheet and thin bedspread. Got it at Super Kmart and it's got purple and gold flowers going over it but it's not warm. Tommy yelled about it. I told him it cost less than it did, but I don't even know why I lied 'cause it's not like it's his money I'm spending. Once a week I do inventory at Joanie's Shoes out at the mall. One of the Dead Girls takes the baby for me. Not a whole lot of money but something to call my own, I guess. Tommy pays the rent and stuff mostly on time. He drives a truck for Bert's Bakery—delivers bread and cakes and pies. Brings home whatever people don't want—smashed loaves and pies. Cakes with the frosting smeared mostly off. I know he hates the job because some mornings he sits at the table with this faraway look in his eyes. Looks like he's nailed to the seat. Guess me and the baby's the nails. He says he stays because what kind of man would he be if he left us. I know he stays because we're all he has—the only thing he can put his finger on and say, "I finished that."

The baby cries, "Mama, Mama," and I don't answer. The book says you have to let them cry and then they'll learn how to put themselves to sleep without somebody all the time getting up and going to them. He's almost twenty months now and I think it's time. Still taking the breast and I want to end that because they're starting to look like they belong to a thirty-year-old, not me. That's what Tommy first loved about me, but now he doesn't even look at them. Looks away when I go to put one in the baby's mouth. Not like I want him coming near me anyways, though. The house gets quiet again and I turn over. Close my eyes. It's almost light out and the baby's been calling most of the night. My eyes feel like they're made out of broken glass. My throat is burning and it's so damn cold in here.

Maybe sleep comes. I don't know. But I jump up when I hear the baby say, "Tommy, please. Please, Tommy," and it bust my heart wide open, him begging for Tommy like that and Tommy not even halfway loving him, so I go down the hall. The floors are cold and the walls are cold and there's that whistling sound of wind coming through the windows. They don't close all the way. I lift the baby out of his crib and he puts his cold cheek against mine. We sit down on the small rug in his room and I let him nurse. It's just me and him in almost-daylight. He sighs. Soon I hear his breath coming even and know he's asleep. Skin warm against my skin now. Hair soft against my arm. I named him Tommy Jr. but I just call him TJ mostly. Tommy tried to teach him how to say Dad but he never did, and after a while, Tommy just gave up trying.

It's December now and the house can't hold winter like rich people's houses can. Feels like we're living in a soup can most days—cold air and floors and walls. The small heater Tommy brought home from somewhere makes more noise than heat. It scares the baby. And since most days it's just him and me cuddling to stay warm, I leave the heater off and wrap more coats around us. He looks up at me and smiles some mornings. His smile ain't like nothing else in the world. It's like the sun coming out and the heat coming on and us living somewhere where the wind can't slip its cold head underneath every crack in the windows and walls.

The Dead Girls get to my house around one. Shanna brings bread and bologna and chips and cheese. I have some mayo and mustard in the fridge. Cleo brings salad greens and carrots and some frozen peas. Brandy has a box of cookies, some sodas, and a gallon of milk. It's the organic milk and we all look at her like she's lost her mind.

"That stuff costs about four dollars," Shanna says. She puts the meat and cheese on a plate. Opens the bread and takes out a bunch of slices.

I'm sitting with TJ on my lap and he's looking hard at the bologna, so I give him a small piece and for a while he works it with the twelve teeth he has in his mouth. I wait to see if he swallows or if it's gonna end up goo in my hand. He's the youngest of all our kids, the only one not in day care. The Dead Girls love coming over here after dropping their kids off. TJ's a good baby, easy to be around.

"It's supposed to be better for us," Brandy says. She's grown her hair out. It's red now. Used to be brown. She's still got the brown tips and roots. I like the way it looks. Her skin's clear as the milk she's pouring us and her body is long and skinny and beautiful. I run my hand over my stomach. It's still a bit round from my pregnancy days. All the Dead Girls' bodies bounced right back but mine is taking its time. Shanna said that's the good thing about having babies when you're sixteen—your body says, *Okay, I'm back and at it again in no time.* I tell her, "Well, then, that's the only good thing."

TJ says, "Yuck," and spits the pink goo of bologna out onto his chest. I pick it off with my hand and eat it. It don't taste like anything. A year ago, if I had seen someone doing that, I would have puked. But a year ago is a long time passed now.

TJ says, "Milk," and Brandy gives us a look like *I told you so.* She fills up his sippy cup and TJ says, "T'anks."

"The regular milk's all full of hormones and stuff," Brandy says. "Drink that and you'll be dead of cancer in no time. And I read how we shouldn't give it to our kids, either. Causes *precocious puberty*."

We all look at her, then at one another. Then we start laughing so hard it hurts. I hold TJ tight to keep from dropping him, but I'm laughing so hard it scares him and he starts to cry.

"Well, we may as well drink it," Cleo says. " 'Cause we already got that disease!"

Brandy shakes her head. She's smiling but the smile's kinda sad. She had college plans. Straight A's. Words and numbers come easy to her. Once she wanted to be a lawyer. She'd met one once at a conference she got picked to go to in eighth grade. The lawyer was a woman from Thedford. She'd told Brandy to go for it.

I look around the table. I'm the only one that's sixteen. Brandy and the others are all going on eighteen now. They treat me like their little sister some days, helping me figure out TJ's ways and how to stay living with Tommy, even though I'd rather be a hundred other places. Some days all the doors seem like they're slamming in my face. My mama was the first one to say, "You made your bed. . . ." Then her door closed behind me. Then school. Then the door to whatever little bit of love Tommy once had for me and me for him. Slam. Slam. Slam. The Dead Girls give me hugs and good words and let me know it's all gonna be all right. Most days, I need that kind of loving.

Outside, the sun's trying to come out. This part of Nebraska is so close to South Dakota, we get all of its light—and cold, too. Nebraska 99 takes you straight across, from one end of the state to the other. I've never driven it; Tommy keeps the car. But Brandy said she did once. Said if you start out looking west from Lincoln, it feels like you're looking at the whole world. "And the light is pink like dawn," Brandy said. "That's what I'll always remember—how that road glowed with my favorite color for miles and miles and miles."

We weren't always the Dead Girls. Once we were cheerleaders—them all in tenth grade and me in eighth but tall and loud enough to cheer Varsity. Shanna got pregnant first. Her belly started poking out and they kicked her out of school. Then Brandy. Then Cleo. TJ's the last of the babies. I met Tommy when he was twenty-two and I was fourteen. I lied and told him I was sixteen. Later on, he said he hadn't even believed me. "He's got those pretty eyes," Cleo had said, rocking her baby on her lap. "But if I was you, I'd stay away from him. You gonna be looking like me in no time flat."

But Tommy said he knew what he was doing. And even though I didn't believe him, I let him keep going.

I wipe snot away from TJ's nose, give him a piece of bread and cheese.

"T'anks," he says.

"How'd you get so polite?" Shanna says, smiling at him. She's wearing a new shirt. She's good at stealing from the Super Kmart, but I don't like to go with her. Bad luck and prison run in my family, and there ain't a soul I'd trust with TJ if something happened to me. I wait for things to go on sale at the Old Navy. End of season you can get nice stuff for three or four dollars.

We eat our sandwiches and drink our milk and talk about the good old days to come. Cleo's quiet mostly, looking off, daydreaming.

"One day, I'm not gonna be a teenager with a baby," Shanna says. "I mean, she's already a toddler, but one day . . ." She looks off, her sandwich halfway to her mouth. Shanna's the prettiest one if anyone asked. Pretty lips and high cheekbones. Dark hair that curls like crazy. Hazel eyes. Sad now but the color catches all kinds of light. "One day, me and my baby girl are just gonna take off. Not even look back at anything."

Cleo picks at the edge of the table. It's wood. I used to use lemon oil on it. Shine it up and have the tiny kitchen smelling nice. But that stuff ain't good for babies to be around. Now the table looks dull and chipped and like it wasn't ever new.

"Yeah," Cleo says. "Me, too. Soon as . . . soon as this one's grown."

Brandy squints at her. "This one? What's this one?"

Cleo's eyes get kinda watery, but she blinks and keeps staring down at the table. She points to her belly, then puts her head down on the table and moans.

"Fuck, Cleo!" Brandy says. "Fuck. Fuck. Fuck." She hits the table.

TJ hits the table, too. I want to tell them both to stop hitting my damn table but I don't. Instead, I pull TJ a little closer to me and swallow. The room feels tight now. Tight and hot and cold all at once.

It wasn't supposed to happen to any of us again. We were gonna get out. That's why we call ourselves the Dead Girls. As in dead and gone. Out of here! Us four and our grown kids driving west on Nebraska 99.

"Fuck, Cleo," I say.

"Tuck," TJ says. "Tuck, Cleo."

"Get rid of it," Shanna says.

Cleo holds up her fingers. "Five months," she moans. "I'm five months."

"How'd you let yourself get to be five months?" Shanna says. "Jeez, Cleo."

"Because for two of those months, I got my stupid period. And then when I didn't, I just figured it's 'cause I've been running so much."

"So much for the marathon," Shanna says. Cleo had bigger dreams than all of us. She'd been a cheerleader *and* a runner.

She'd said cheerleading was just for fun but running was gonna be her ticket.

She sits up now and covers her mouth with her hands. She's crying, tears coming down but no sound coming up.

"No cry," TJ says. He reaches out and touches her. Cleo lets out a little laugh.

We all get quiet. Our sandwiches half-eaten. Our expensive milk hardly even touched. There're chocolate chip cookies waiting. When we eat them, they'll probably taste like dust.

I don't love Tommy anymore. Cleo doesn't love Jake. Shanna doesn't love Alex. Brandy doesn't love Daniel. Feels like years and years ago we wrote our boyfriends' names inside hearts with our own. We love TJ and Shania and Alexandra and Jake Jr. We love these moments when we can sit around and talk about what's gonna happen in the future. We love television and fat love stories with shiny letters on the cover. We love what we dream and the smell of our children's hair and mouths. We love the promise of NE99—the pink light and the black road. Us burning it up and leaving everything we don't love anymore far, far behind.

"Maybe you'll get a girl this time," Shanna says. She gets up and puts her arms around Cleo's shoulders. "I'll give you all of Alexandra's pretty dresses."

Cleo smiles, a small, sad smile.

And all of us get quiet because none of us knows how to fit this into our dreams.

At night, Tommy turns toward me. Puts his arm across my belly.

"Remember the first time we kissed?" he says, pressing his lips to my cheek.

I nod in the darkness. It's late and the house is quiet. Tommy's brought home a down comforter from somewhere. I'm warm underneath it. His hand is soft and gentle on my belly. He moves closer to me, his lips moving all over me at once. I let him. Say a prayer that this is an okay time of the month to do this. And let him. Think about Cleo and the other Dead Girls. And let him.

South Dakota's a long, long ways away from here. And not even one of us has a car to start that trek across Nebraska 99. Tommy moans and I wrap my arms around him. Like he's that pretty pink sky Brandy told us about. Like he's some kinda promising future.

The Perfect Kiss

Sarah Mlynowski

My birthdays are jinxed. Some lowlights to prove I'm not being melodramatic:

On my sixth birthday the pipes in our basement froze and my parents were forced to cancel our trip to Disney World.

On my eighth birthday Sandy, my parakeet, flew smack into the kitchen window. He died.

On my twelfth birthday I discovered that my parents were getting a divorce. While brushing my teeth post-cake, I over-heard their secret discussion on the fun topics of alimony and joint custody through the bathroom door.

On my fifteenth birthday I slammed the car door on my middle finger. The nail turned green and then fell off. It still looks freakish.

Happy Birthday to me.

Unfortunately, my dread of January 2 now casts a haze of unpleasantness on winter vacation, thereby dampening my holiday cheer. Which is why I'm not exactly excited about the slumber birthday party that's currently taking place in my liv-ing room. I keep dozing off, even though it's not even eleven o'clock. My pillow and sleeping bag are cold and soft, like a swimming pool on a hot day. It's strangely refreshing, con-sidering it's twenty degrees outside.

Pressure. On. Stomach. Mandy is sitting on me. "Will you wake up?" she says.

I force a laugh and turn on my side, pushing Mandy onto the used-to-be-maroon-but-is-now-brown carpet. Valerie and Jane are in their sleeping bags, each on a leg of the L-shaped couch, deep into a bag of oversize salt-and-vinegar chips. They've already gone through two rows of Double Stuf Oreos, three bags of gummy bears, and two helpings of chocolate birthday cake, remnants of which litter the floor. My living room looks like a schoolyard after recess.

"I'm up, I'm up. It's been a long day." Our math and final winter exam was at nine this morning. I studied until three, woke up at six to review, then trekked forty minutes to school. I could barely keep my eyes open during the exam.

Mandy sticks her hand in the greasy bag, then changes her mind and pulls it out without a chip. "Yeah, for me, too. And I haven't even packed yet." She leaves for Miami tomorrow afternoon, which is why I'm having my sleepover party ten days before my actual birthday—if four girls eating Oreos in my living room can be classified as a party. The real party will be in Miami. Without me. Half of my high school does the southern migration with their families from Long Island to the Sunshine State for the holidays. Including my best friend, Mandy. And my boyfriend, Jordan.

But not me. Oh, no, my mother would never take me away from this snowy haven we call home.

"What am I going to do without you for two weeks?" I ask.

"I'll be here," Val says. Unfortunately, Val and I are more friends by association than actual buddies. So that won't help.

"Yeah, you'll hang out with Val," Mandy says. "And by the time I get back, you'll have the Cruisemobile!"

Cruisemobile is Mandy's pet name for the car we think my dad is buying me for the big birthday. She has all types of plans for my car, mostly involving us no longer having to take the bus to school.

I know that it sounds spoiled to get a car so young, but the way my father keeps bragging about how well he's doing at his new job in Manhattan, he can afford it. And he asked me what I wanted. So I told him a navy Jetta. But I'd take any vehicle—generous of me, isn't it?—that would help me escape the claustrophobia of my house. He said, "I'll see what I can do about getting you some wheels to get around." An "I'll see" from my dad is usually a green light. He has no problem saying no.

Last summer, after argument number 712 with my mother, this one over my missing her draconian eleven o'clock curfew, I begged my dad to let me live with him in the city. And he said no. *No, sorry, no room for you here, tough it out.*

One of my mother's other preposterous rules is no phone calls past eleven. To talk to Jordan at night, I turn off the ringers in the living room and my bedroom and put the answering machine on mute. The soft click of the machine makes my heart flutter—I know it's him. I pick it up, pull the duvet over my head, and whisper into the mouthpiece. Even though her room is slap next to mine, my mother never hears. I've clocked at least two hours a night of post-eleven phone calls with Jordan. Hah.

Once, as I breathed in the clean, hot smell of the duvet, the phone cradled between my ear and the mattress, I felt snowed under with happiness. After I whispered good night, I said the *L* word. "You, too," he said at full volume. "Sweet dreams."

I removed the covers from my head and hung up the phone. He could have pretended not to hear me if he didn't want to say it back. I wondered briefly if it was really Jordan I was in love with, or the forbidden excitement of hearing the clicking sound of the answering machine. Did it matter? I fell asleep smiling.

I know saying "I love you" doesn't mean a relationship will last. Mandy told Daryl she loved him, and they broke up two weeks later. Anyway, she's over him now that she has her Sweet Sixteen party to look forward to. It's on the Saturday after the break, four weeks before her actual birthday, since that's the only day she could reserve the golf club. My mother, who doesn't quite have the cash to compete with a car, offered to take me shopping on Monday for a dress. She teaches third grade and has two weeks off, and from the shopping bag full of crossword puzzle books in the kitchen, I'm guessing she's planned a week of mother-daughter activities. Since Mack, my stepfather, will be at work, my friends and boyfriend are deserting me, and my dad will be on a cruise with girlfriend number nineteen (or is that her age?), no one can save me from mother-daugher-bonding hell.

Val turns on the TV. "Emma, can we watch a movie? What did you rent?"

Perfect. While they watch, I can sleep. Why am I so tired? I motion to the Blockbuster bag. "*Titanic* and *Coyote Ugly,* and my mom rented her faves, *Grease* and *As Good as It Gets*." An integral part of her mother-daughter torture plan. I'm forced to watch them each at least once a month.

"*Grease! Grease! Grease!*" Mandy chants.

I catch Jane rolling her eyes at Val. Over the summer, Mandy won a *Seventeen*-sponsored clothing design competition, and ever since then she's been schmoozing with our high school's oh-so-cool crowd. Even though the four of us have been friends since fifth grade, since we perfected our French-kissing skills on carnival-won stuffed monkeys, Val and Jane now weigh everything Mandy says and does with measured suspicion.

I don't think she's the type to dump me for greener pastures. Although who knows? If I hadn't started dating Jordan, maybe eventually I would have been tossed in the trash, like a too-tight training bra.

Mandy changes out of one of her designs, a white shirt covered in squiggly red patterns, and into cotton pajamas. She covers her stomach as she does this. Being featured in *Seven-*

teen helped her social status, as well as her wardrobe (the prize was the actual dress of the design she entered—she's going to wear it to her Sweet), but not her body image. She thinks she's fat. She's not.

I open my mouth to tell them to put in anything but *Grease,* because I can't take hearing the songs again even in my sleep (my mother has the CD on replay in her car), when my line rings. My stomach jumps as I go to get the phone. I relax when I see it's only 10:58. I'm allowed to stay up all night because it's my sleepover, but I'm still not allowed to have calls past eleven. Yeah, that makes sense.

"Hi, Jordan!" Mandy croons in the background. Val gives Jane another look. Oh, grow up, I want to tell them. They're just jealous. Jordan is in the upper echelon of high-school society. I met him when I was out with Mandy one night, and suddenly I'm a coolio by association. Apparently I, too, am now worthy of suspicion.

"Hey," he says. "How's the party?"

I feel majorly pathetic for having a slumber party, but my mother insisted I do something to mark my birthday, and this is better than the bowling blowout she suggested. I wanted a real Sweet, with a DJ and everything, but I couldn't ask her to fork over that kind of money for one night. I'll get to party at Mandy's, anyway. That event will be over-the-top—catered, and with a caricaturist, magician, and DJ. She's also invited most of our grade, as well as the elite of the class above us. Including Jordan. I'm sure Val and Jane will be rolling their eyes all over the place at the extravagance and fakeness, but I can't wait. And I don't care if I'm being lame.

I wrap the phone wire around my thumb until it turns pink. "It's getting wild and crazy. We're about to start the pillow fight. Where are you?"

"Airport. On Ronnie's cell." Jordan and Ronnie are renting a room on South Beach. Jordan made the hotel reservations only a week after we started dating, so I can't be mad that he's missing my birthday and New Year's. Could be worse. If we weren't Jewish, he'd be missing Christmas, too.

I met him at the Mushroom Park. It's a too-cool hangout, and I'd never gone at night before, but since Mandy had achieved an elevated social status, she felt she had the right to check it out. I had told my mom I was going to keep Mandy company while she walked her dog, like I always do, which wasn't exactly a lie because sometimes she brings him, just not this time. She met me half a block down from my house, and when we could no longer see the glare from my living-room lights, she pulled out a cigarette hidden in her sleeve and sparked it. She'd read somewhere that smoking made you lose weight, which I didn't totally buy. We talked about Halloween, which was the following week, and Mandy complained that the candy was making her fat. She was also wondering if she should have sex with her then-boyfriend, Daryl. I thought Daryl was a jerk-off, but you can't tell that to your best friend.

The park, empty of little kids, was sprinkled with high-school students performing illicit activities. It got its name after some guys did magic mushrooms and puked all over the swing. Anyway, Mandy started telling me about the last time Daryl and she had hooked up, and how she had stopped before doing *it*, but had done everything else. "It was so gross," she said. "I think I would rather just do *it* so I never have to do *that* again." She bit her thumbnail, like she does whenever something is bothering her, and I slapped her hand away like I always do.

She reached in her sleeve for another cigarette, swearing under her breath as her matches dropped into a puddle. She started walking toward a group of guys from our high school to beg a light. Winning the competition, and now having a boyfriend, had made her brave. I wondered if they were doing mushrooms. As we got closer, I saw the four guys more clearly—Jordan Horris, Ronnie Michaels, Mike Nudisky, and

Zack Lodown, all juniors I knew by name and reputation. Each of them held a beer. Zack handed Mandy his Zippo and said, "Hey, Mandy, hey, Emma, why don't you join us?" I couldn't believe he knew my name. How did he know my name? Mandy sat right down, swoop, no problem, and I tried to appear calm. Then, suddenly, I was sitting with them. Jordan was beside me. He smelled like smoky shampoo and offered me his beer.

I hate the taste of beer, but I smiled and gulped it down, trying not to upchuck. Vile. Mandy swallowed hers no problem. These days she could swallow anything, apparently.

"You just made a bitter beer face," Jordan said.

Jordan Horris spoke. To me.

Great. I just looked like a tool in front of Jordan Horris. I took another gulp, hoping to appear poised and appealing, but it went down the wrong pipe, whatever pipe that is, and I started coughing and then quasi-choking, and Jordan Horris lifted my hands above my head.

I stopped coughing. "I'm not much of a beer drinker."

He raised a thick black eyebrow. "No?"

"No. I normally drink scotch."

He looked me over, maybe trying to decide if I was kidding. He said, "You're funny," and then laughed.

Jordan and I talked for forty minutes about the classes I was taking, teachers he thought were morons, and the new Jeep he'd just bought with his bar mitzvah money. We could have talked all night if Mandy hadn't nudged me when it was time to leave. He stood up with us and hugged me good-bye. We were almost the same height, and fit together perfectly. As we drifted home, Mandy was back to biting her thumb and talking about her weight, but I didn't care, I didn't care at all because I was plotting what I'd wear to school tomorrow, and what I'd say when Jordan passed me in the halls, and how I'd smile. . . .

I wish he wasn't at the airport. I wish he were here. Announcements and voices echo in the background. "I gotta go," he says. "Ronnie wants his cell back." I'm not a fan of Ronnie. At a party last week, he made fun of his ex-girlfriend's breasts. Mandy thinks he's hot. Since she broke up with Daryl, she's been on the prowl.

"Have fun. I'll speak to you soon?" I don't want to nag.

"I'll call you later in the week." *Click.*

I hang up the phone and feel swamped by exhaustion. I fall back into my makeshift bed. Mandy puts on *Grease* and jumps ahead to "Summer Nights."

As I fall asleep, the three of them are dancing in front of the screen, singing and waving their arms like they're trying to get someone's attention.

Throat. Hurts. Feels like hundreds of jalapeño peppers are marinating on my tongue.

"You're finally up," Mandy says. Their sleeping bags are rolled, and they're watching *Titanic.* "You okay?"

I nod. I might be eligible to win the Worst Slumber Party Hostess Ever award.

My mother cooks us waffles, and then the girls leave in a flutter of hugs and Happy Birthday!/Happy New Year!/Have a safe flight! That last one isn't to me obviously, since I'm not going anywhere. Except back to bed.

"Shopping day!" My mother storms into my room at nine Monday morning, a woman on a mission. The day after Christmas is my mother's favorite shopping day. She's Canadian, and up there today is Boxing Day, otherwise known as National Shopping Day. "Time to get up! Get up! Get up! Get up and beat the crowds."

I bet her students hate her in the morning.

In the car, I turn on the radio before "Greased Lightning"

assaults me. Then I secure my seat belt. My mother has serious signaling issues. As in she never does. She cuts off a Volvo, two Civics, a bus, and we're there.

Bloomingdale's is a mess in its post-Christmas glory. After an hour of searching, I find only one outfit I like. It's a satin, platinum two-piece dress, and it's a fortune. I take it, along with three other ugly ones, to the dressing room. I model the nasty ones first. My mother agrees that the first one makes me look like Santa Claus, the second like Tinkerbell, and the third like I'm in mourning. I've saved the expensive one for last. The bodice is strapless and fits snuggly across my 34B chest. The bottom of the skirt flares out and makes me feel like a mermaid. I don't mention the price.

She gasps. My mother is always gasping. When she's excited or upset she doesn't seem to get enough air. She motions for me to pivot. "It was made for you."

Glad she agrees. Jordan loves it when I go strapless. He says I have soft shoulders. "I love it, Mom. Love it. Can I have it?" I pretend to be studying the ceiling as she flips over the price tag.

She does another one of her gasps. "It's a fortune. I'm not your father. I don't have that kind of money."

"Please, Mom? Please? It's for my birthday. Please?" I use my most endearing voice.

She sighs. "All right. But no new dress for Jordan's prom."

My stomach somersaults at the mention of *prom*. I really, really want to go. I know it's months away, and that we've only been going out for a few months, but . . . I really want to go. "I doubt he'll ask me, Mom. He'll dump me for someone else way before then."

"Don't be crazy," she says, and pats my hair, which drives me nuts because if you pat curly hair, it gets flat. "Not all guys are jerks. And anyway, once he takes a look at you in that dress, he'll never leave you alone. But only if you don't slouch."

I stand up straight and assume the "jerks" comment was another dig at my dad. Whatever. Small price to pay for the dress.

I somehow convince my "I'm not your father" mother to buy me matching silver high heels and a back-to-school outfit.

"Where's your hat?" she asks, putting her arm around me on the way back to the car.

I hate the hat—a gray wool ski cap that is more functional than fashionable. She surprised me with it two months ago. "I must have forgotten it at home."

My mother wakes me up at nine every day this week with an ear-shattering "Good morning!"

On Thursday she thrusts a glass of juice in my face. "You've been looking a bit pasty."

I sip but stop mid-gulp when firecrackers detonate along my throat. "Ouch."

"What's wrong with you?"

"My throat hurts."

"Open your mouth."

I comply. She gasps. "You have strep. Again." She shakes her head with visible dismay.

What's her problem? It's not her throat that's on fire.

"I'm making you an appointment with Goldenblatt." Goldenblatt is my doctor. He weighs about four hundred pounds and smokes more than all the seniors in my high school put together. I have repeatedly alluded, to no avail, to the irony of an overweight doctor who smokes.

In the mirror, my throat looks like it's covered in whiteheads. I decide that it's in my best interest to resist the urge to pop them.

As I do up my jacket on the way to Doctor Hypocrite, my mother harasses me regarding the location of my hat.

"What hat?"

She sighs, her patience obviously dwindling. "You know what hat. It's cold out there. You can't walk into Goldenblatt's without a hat. He'll think I don't take care of you."

"Fine, okay? I'll put on the stupid hat." I shove the hat over my head and slam the front door behind me. The air numbs my face and hands. At least if I have strep, I can claim sickness to avoid crossword-puzzle-a-palooza.

It's been twenty-four hours and there's been no word from Doctor Hypocrite about my condition. I'm taking no news as good news, even though my throat feels like it was doused in gasoline and set on fire.

No news from Jordan, either. That, I take as bad news.

I'm lying on my stomach across the living-room couch. It's Friday night and I am not allowed out because I have a fever of 101. I've been flipping through the channels, alternating between the hockey game and the Home Shopping Network. Jordan is a hockey fan. The New York Islanders are playing the Toronto Maple Leafs. I memorized the names of all thirty hockey teams, in all six divisions, and can rattle them off in geographical order—a party trick I thought would impress Jordan. Secretly, I'm finding the Home Shopping Network more entertaining. During the commercials I brainstorm non-relationship-destroying reasons why Jordan hasn't called. I'm trying to convince myself that he doesn't have a calling card, but I'm losing the argument. Maybe he'll call tomorrow—New Year's Eve. Most likely he's met and hooked up with some tanned, vacationing hoochie.

I wonder if sleeping with him would have increased my chances of a phone call.

I dial Mandy's cell to ask if she's seen him, but she doesn't answer.

"Five! Four! Three! Two! One! Happy New Year!"

The ball drops on TV and my mother and stepfather start

making out. Yeah. It's a wild and crazy New Year's for me, in my pajamas, lying on the carpet. My mother and stepfather are cuddling on the couch. Val invited me to a party, but my mother refused to let me go because of my fever.

Oh, well. At least I'm resting up for Mandy's Sweet.

The parental units behind me are still lip-locked.

Jordan and I first kissed outside a movie theater. I wasn't ready for it. I mean, I was *ready* for it, but I wasn't expecting it. It was our first date, and the new James Bond movie had just let out. I was squishing my curls to give them some body, when suddenly we were kissing.

I'd kissed two guys before, one random classmate at a sixth-grade game of Spin the Bottle, and later my eighth-grade boyfriend, Daniel. But I'd never kissed anyone like Jordan Horris. At first, I just stood there, too stunned to move, feeling his thin tongue inside my mouth. He tasted salty like popcorn, and when I unfroze, I licked the inside of his lips even though I knew I wasn't supposed to. His mouth was dry. We stood outside for at least twenty minutes, until the theater had emptied out entirely. Then we kissed for another half hour in his car. And another half hour outside my house.

The next day during recess, when we were sitting by his locker, he referred to me as his girlfriend. I melted into the floor, like ice on my now-fevered forehead.

My mother leans off the couch to kiss me. "Happy New Year, honey."

"Don't touch me; you'll get sick."

She kisses me anyway. I'm afraid this is the only lovin' I'll be getting for a long, long time. Jordan is still MIA. My elaborate theory on why he hasn't called: Ronnie has forbidden Jordan from using up his long-distance minutes. He told Jordan he could only call once. Jordan is planning on calling on Monday. My birthday. Sure, he could call me directly from the hotel, but that's expensive. Not as expensive as a trip to Miami, but who's counting?

Mack pats my head. "Happy New Year, kiddo." Mack is fifteen years older than my mother. His head is as bald as a peeled soft-boiled egg, and his stringy gray beard hangs over his neck. He looks like a hippy Mr. Potato Head. He doesn't talk to me much, but I don't take it personally. I'm like a lamp, or the sofa. I came with the house.

He pulls my mom to him for another go. Ew. I think I just saw tongue.

I wake at nine-thirty to the ringing doorbell.

Happy Birthday to me; Happy Birthday to me. Maybe Jordan sent me flowers? Dozens of long-stemmed glorious roses? He didn't call because he wanted to wow me. Like how your friends ignore you before they throw you a surprise party?

"Birthday girl, come downstairs!" my mother hollers. "Your father sent you a present!"

My father? My father! My car! I skip down the stairs two at a time. The deliveryman has left a huge cardboard box in the hallway. Any chance tires come separately?

Holding my breath, I slash the box open with the kitchen scissors. And it's a—

Bike.

A metallic blue bike.

There is a metallic blue bike in my hallway.

I spin the wheel with my big toe. This is not a Jetta. It's not even navy. This is what my father promised would get me around? Should I drive it through the snow? True, I did want a bike for my birthday—when I was eleven. These days I don't want the wind in my hair, unless I'm in a convertible. And I already have a bike. It's in the garage behind the stuff-to-be-donated-to-charity pile.

I park my deflated self on the bottom stair. "This sucks."

My mother does her gasp. "What kind of a thing is that to say?"

"I wanted a car."

"Stop being so spoiled. What do you need a car for? A bike will be wonderful for you. For your posture."

My posture? How does it help my posture? My head pounds. "Yeah, right, wonderful. Maybe I'll take it out now. It's at least eleven degrees." No car and no roses. Happy Birthday to me.

As I slink up the stairs in defeat, a phone rings. For a split second I wonder if it's Jordan, but then I realize it's only nine-thirty. I doubt Party Man is up at this absurd hour. Anyway, it's my mother's line.

"Hello, Doctor Goldenblatt! So what's the diagnosis?" Pause. "But I'm her mother!" She grumbles. "All right, hold on. Emma! Pick up the phone! It's the doctor!"

Nice of him to call, finally. I thought he might have taken off for Miami, too.

"Hi, Emma, how are you feeling?"

"I've been better."

"Yes, well, that's understandable. You have mononucleosis."

What? "What?"

"Mono. I got your blood test back."

"But . . . mono? I have mono? How did I get mono? How do I get rid of mono?"

"It's a virus, passed on through direct contact with infected saliva—sharing a straw or an eating utensil with someone who recently had mono could have exposed you to the virus. Or kissing someone who's infected. You need to rest and drink plenty of fluids. Try eating anything cold. You also might want to take Tylenol."

Oh. My. God. "How long does it last?"

"That depends on how well you take care of yourself."

Blah, blah, blah. "I need a time frame, Doctor. Give it to me cold. In weeks."

"Anywhere from ten days to a few months."

A few months? I could be out of commission for a few months? I hand my mother the phone and mope my way back to my room. See? I have the worst birthdays. I'm still sulking when the answering machine clicks. I forgot to turn my bedroom phone volume back on. Jordan?

Nope. "Happy Birthday, Emma!"

"Hi, Dad. Thanks. And thanks for the bike." I try to muster up the appropriate amount of enthusiasm for the gift that skewered my dreams of freedom.

"Oh, good, I'm glad you like it. I was going to get that Jetta we talked about, but your mom thinks you're too young to have your own car. She suggested a bicycle. Says the one you have is too small for you and is bad for your posture."

"She *what*?"

"You know how she is. I didn't want to start."

I don't believe this. And why is she obsessed with my freakin' posture? I chitchat about fun things like mono and how maybe we can take a vacation together at spring break (yeah, thanks, I've heard that before). Then I stomp into the kitchen, where my mother is sitting at the table, tapping the bitten end of her pencil against the Formica.

She looks up from her crossword puzzle book. "Do you want pancakes for breakfast?"

How is she so oblivious? "I can barely swallow; do you think I want pancakes?"

"Hmm, I can make you—"

"How could you not let Daddy buy me a car?"

She's momentarily confused, then says, "You're too young."

"No, I'm not!"

"When I think you're ready, I'll teach you to drive my car."

Right, because who needs turn signals? "I'd be better off doing my road test blindfolded."

She shakes her head. "You're close to crossing the line, Emma. And until you learn to take care of yourself, you can't take care of a car. It's a big responsibility."

"What do you mean I can't take care of myself?"

"Your room is a mess. Your clothes are all over the place."

You'd think she'd be willing to cut me a wee bit of slack considering the situation. "Uh, hello? I have mono."

"Exactly." She nods as though I've proven her point. "You can't take care of your own body."

She's nuts. Totally nuts. "You're insane. No wonder he left you."

Oops. I think I've just cartwheeled right over the line.

I expect a gasp, but instead she looks away. And closes her eyes. "I don't want to talk to you right now."

"Fine. I don't want to talk to you, either." As I walk back up the stairs I listen for the tapping of her pencil on the table, but the house is quiet. I close my door and try to take a nap, but for the first time in over a week, I can't sleep.

Phone rings. Jordan? No, Mandy's cell.

"Hiya!" she says.

"Hi," I croak.

"Happy Birthday to you! Happy Birthday to you! Happy Birthday, dear Emma, Happy Birthday to you!"

So not in the mood. "Thanks."

"What's wrong with your voice?"

"The birthday curse has struck again. I have mono."

"No!"

"Yup."

"But you have to get better. Doesn't that last for months? You can't miss my Sweet!"

I get a little choked up.

"Are you crying?" she asks. "Don't cry. Don't worry, you won't miss it. You just won't, okay? We'll figure it out. You won't miss it, I promise."

Sniff. "Thanks."

"I wish I were the one with mono. That's the weight-loss disease, right? I need to lose ten pounds to fit into *the* dress."

"Do you realize what a sick thing to say that is?"

She sighs. "Kind of. Did you get the Cruisemobile, at least?"

The tears start rolling again. "He got me a bike."

"No!" She sounds as horrified as I feel. Then she starts laughing. "We can still cruise. I'll just have to sit on the handlebars."

I laugh. A little. "What a bad, bad day."

"I know something that will cheer you up. I saw Jordan on New Year's Eve."

My heart thumps. "You did? What did he say?"

"He said he missed you a lot."

"He did?" Then why hasn't he called? "Who was he with?"

"I think, um, Amber and Lena."

Amber and Lena? He was with Amber and Lena? Two senior hobags? "Where was Ronnie?"

She takes a deep breath. "Hooking up with me! But nothing's going on, because I heard he hooked up with someone else the next night. Whatever. I'm not looking for another relationship right now."

I try to fake the appropriate best-friend empathy, but all I can think is Amber and Lena, Amber and Lena, Amber and Lena. But he said he missed me. Doesn't that count for something?

After the conversation with Mandy, I return to the kitchen to squelch my burning throat. My mother is still sitting at the table. I feel bad about my earlier comment. "Sorry about before."

"It's okay," she says, but doesn't look up. Definite bad sign.

"You can't be mad at me on my birthday. You know I always have bad birthdays."

"I'm not mad." She sighs loudly, so I think she might be lying, but then she says, "I bought you some frozen yogurt. Thought it would help your throat."

"Thanks, I'll try." I scoop a small amount into a bowl and return upstairs, to read and wait for Jordan to call.

By eight that night the yogurt is a melted mess in the bowl, and he still hasn't called. My mother tries to force-feed me chocolate birthday cake number two, but I can't swallow it.

At ten my mother gives up on making me eat, and I give up on telepathically telling Jordan to call. He doesn't remember my birthday. Too busy with Amber and Lena. At eleven I unplug my line downstairs and turn off the sound in my bedroom. In case. By 11:52 I am convinced that he must have forgotten my number. He has it on speed dial at home, so maybe he never memorized it.

I search for Ronnie's cell on my Caller ID, and dial before I feel like a dumb-ass.

"Hello?" There's static in the background. I hear laughter.

"Hi, Ronnie. Is Jordan there?" I whisper.

"Hey, Emma, baby! Whassup?"

"Can I talk to Jordan?"

I hear a shuffle, and then a muffle. "Hello?"

My heart is hammering loud enough to wake my mother. I pull the duvet over my head. "Hi. It's me."

Pause. "Hi." Where's his joy at the sound of my hushed voice?

"Happy New Year," I whisper.

"Yeah, you, too." I wait to see if he remembers. And wait. Instead he says, "I've been meaning to call you. We have to talk." We have to talk? Did he just say we have to talk? On my birthday? No, no, no. "I've been thinking we should see other people."

What? No. "Okay."

Pause. "I'm sorry, Em."

"Okay. I, uh, I have to go." I hang up the phone before I start to cry. Why am I so pathetic?

I throw off my duvet in time to see the clock change from 11:59 to twelve.

Can't wait for my seventeenth birthday. Maybe I'll get run over by a car. Perhaps a navy Jetta.

■ ■ ■

Mandy comes over as soon as she gets home from Florida. The doctor said she can't catch mono unless I cough on her or we exchange saliva.

We watch TV. I flip over an Islanders game without stopping. Hah. That'll show him. I stop Mandy from "accidentally" drinking from my glass. "It's not Weight Watchers, you moron."

"I know, I know. But how did you get it? And why do you look like a chipmunk?"

My mother sticks her head into the living room. "Do you girls want something to drink?"

My throat is still killing, so I nod. "My glands are swollen," I explain to Mandy. I know I look ridiculous, like I swallowed hormone-infused marbles. "And I must have drank from someone's infested water bottle or something. Obviously I didn't get it from Jordan."

Mandy starts picking her fingers.

My mom sets two glasses of water on two matching pink coasters. "How are you feeling?"

"Much better," I lie. "I'm cured. Can I go to Mandy's Sweet?"

On her way out she puts her hand on my forehead. "You still have a fever, so no."

I push Mandy's hand away from her mouth with my socked foot. "Why are you picking? What's wrong?"

"There's something I have to tell you about Jordan. Do you want to know?"

Despite the fact that my stomach just sunk *Titanic*-style, I nod. "What?"

"I heard that he cheated on you on New Year's, and he broke up with you because he felt guilty."

My legs become weights, as though all the blood in my body just fell to my feet. "With Amber or Lena?"

She inserts her thumbnail back into her mouth. "Amber *and* Lena."

"What? He cheated on me twice? He hooked up with both of them on the same night?"

She flushes. "No. At the same time."

Oh. My. God. Good thing I'm only eating liquids these days.

School started today. Without me. My back-to-school outfit is collecting dust in the closet. I missed the white-shirt-to-show-off-the-tan parade and the excitement of new classes, new classrooms, new classmates. I missed Jordan.

I miss Jordan. I wrap my covers around me tightly to warm me up. I know I'm supposed to hate him, and I do, a little. But I think if he called and apologized, I might be persuaded to forgive him. He did say he loved me. Who else will listen to me whisper every night, tell me I'm funny, and think I have soft shoulders? If he said he was sorry, I'd tell him I'd have to think about it, but then I'd forgive him. Mandy said she heard that it was Amber and Lena who hit on him. Not the other way around. What guy would say no to two seniors?

He felt bad. He might still like me.

This horrible day is finally coming to an end. It's eleven, but I don't bother turning off my phone. No one's calling. No calls, no prom, and since I'm still sick, no Mandy's Sweet.

Sell self-pity somewhere else. I'm all stocked up.

On Tuesday when my mother returns from school, she finds me doing a crossword puzzle at the kitchen table. "And how is the patient feeling today?"

"Better." Surprisingly, I am feeling better. But that might be because of the two Tylenols I took an hour ago.

She places her hand on my forehead. "You're cool."

"I am? Really?"

She takes my temperature and reads it against the light. Can you say, Time to get a Digital One? "Normal."

Normal? "I'm healed! I can go!"

She shakes her finger at me. "Not so fast. The doctor wants your temperature to stay down for at least three days before you go out."

I call Mandy to share the news. Then I take my perfect dress out of the garment bag, put it on, and start zipping it up. Jordan will see me in my fabulous dress and fall for me again. He'll ask me to dance, and I'll sigh but say yes, and I'll snuggle against his chest, and he'll tell me he made the biggest mistake of his life and that he wants me back—

Huh? The top of my dress has slid down to my waist. At least an inch of material sags on each side. It's too big. I hate mono.

I stuff myself with dinner in an attempt to re-fit into my dress.

"You certainly have your appetite back," my mother says.

"Uh-huh," I say between bites of mashed potatoes. "Feeling much better."

"Why don't I take your temperature tomorrow before I leave for school, okay? And we'll see how you do."

I call Mandy at eleven-thirty from under my covers. "Cross your fingers. My mother is taking my temperature in the morning. She wants to make sure it's not just because of the Tylenol that I have no fever."

"Why don't you take it an hour before she checks? You know. In case."

Pause. "That's a brilliant idea. But if I set my alarm, she'll hear."

"So I'll set my alarm. Turn off your ringer and I'll call you."

"You're a genius!"

I whisper to her from under the covers for another hour, then fill a glass with water and hide two pills from the bathroom under my bed in a folded tissue.

I wake up to the click of the answering machine. The clock says 6:45.

I giggle into the phone. "Hi."

"Morning," Mandy says. "Time for you to take your pills."

"Thanks. Have a good day at school."

I feel for the pills and swallow them. And right before I fall back asleep, I think about how fortunate I am to have a friend so willing to participate in parental deception.

At 7:15 my mother opens my door, in her bathrobe and tights, brushing her teeth. "Hi, hon," she mumbles, toothpaste foaming. She inserts the thermometer into my mouth. Three minutes later, she returns with her lipstick and clothing intact.

"Normal," she says, and kisses me on the forehead. "Have a good day and call me if you need anything."

I feel perversely devious. It's like sticking the thermometer under a lightbulb in reverse.

The next day we do the same routine.

Me: "Morning."

Mandy: "It's time."

Me: "Thanks! Have a good day." *(Reach under bed, swallow.)*

My mother opens my door, inserts, removes. Normal. I spend the rest of the day taking naps and stuffing myself with leftover chocolate cake.

On the third day, my mother says, "I hereby declare you healthy!"

Hurrah! Mandy calls me at lunch for the news. "I can come!" I scream.

She shrieks the news to anyone who will listen.

Sweet day! I spend the afternoon washing and straightening my hair, doing my nails, and eating whatever I can stomach without making myself sick. My glands seem to have morphed back to their nonmonstrous size.

At seven that evening I zip up the dress. It fits! Sort of.

My mother gives me a gasp. I twirl. "Don't you look beautiful," she says. "How do you feel?"

"Good." And I mean it. "Do you mind taking me?"

"Jordan isn't picking you up?"

She is clueless about what went down with Jordan. I couldn't find the Mom-appropriate words to explain his threesome. I shake my head, stepping into my heels and coat.

"Put your hat on," she says.

I'm about to argue, but I stop myself. I slide it on my head. Whatever. At least my hair is straight.

"And no glass sharing, and no kissing. In case you're still contagious."

I'm one of the first to arrive at the party. Mandy grabs me in a hug. "Happy Birthday," she sings.

"You, too. Your dress looks amazing." It's red with lace and a sweetheart neck, and is honestly the most gorgeous dress I've ever seen in my life.

I get my caricature done and watch the magician pull an eight of clubs from Val's ear. I spend most of the night heaving up my top to avoid flashing my class, and gazing around the room, wondering if Jordan will show up.

When he finally does, at eleven, my body heats up fast and I wonder if I'm having a relapse. He scans the room and stops on me.

"Ignore him," Mandy tells me. "Brush him off."

But he's still looking at me. He wouldn't have come if he didn't want to see me, right?

"I'll be back in a sec." I walk away before she can block me.

He smiles as I approach. "Hey."

"Hey." The new Britney song starts playing in the background, and I cross my arms in front of my chest, not only to appear in control, but to keep my top up.

His eyes feverishly check out my outfit. "You look amazing."

Damn straight. "Thanks."

He raises one of his thick black eyebrows until it looks like a question mark. "I, uh, I guess you heard about New Year's."

It might have come up. "Yeah."

His forehead is peeling. Florida action too hot for him? "I never meant to do it, you know? They kind of— Well, I, uh, still have feelings for you."

He still has feelings for me. Isn't that what I've waited all week to hear? He wraps his arms around me and hugs me tightly, like he did on the first night at the park. His freshly washed yet dirty smell is familiar. Did he shrink? In my heels I have a view of the top of his head.

Across the room, I spot Mandy shaking her head with disapproval.

"Emma, I'm sorry." Sorry? For cheating, for not calling, or for breaking up with me on my birthday? And why is he so sorry, all of a sudden? Because I'm dressed up? "I miss you," he says.

He told Mandy he missed me on New Year's. And look how much it meant to him then. Jerk. Who does Jordan Horris think he is?

And then, just as he'd done on our first date, he surprises me with a kiss. Our lips touch, and I just stand there, stunned. Then he opens his mouth, and his tongue zips around my teeth.

The song ends, and I pull back. And smile to myself. "You know what, Jordan? I don't want to forgive you." Before he responds, I turn around and march back to my friends.

Mandy's mouth is hanging open. "What just happened? Are you back together?"

Truth is, he's not that good a kisser. He has a sandpaper tongue. I shrug and tug up my top. "He isn't worth it."

"Oh. My. God. He looks so confused. But why'd you kiss him? He's going to get sick for sure."

"I didn't kiss him, he kissed me."

Somehow I bet even my mom would approve. Or not.

Mandy covers her mouth and laughs. The DJ puts on the oh-so-popular Sweet Sixteen *Grease* remix, and I can't help but roll my eyes.

"Come celebrate with me," Mandy says, pulling me toward the already-dancing Val and Jane. And I do.

Cowgirls & Indie Boys

Tanuja Desai Hidier

On Saturday, May 22, at 11:14 A.M. in her birthplace, India (though 12:44 EST here out West), Sulekha Madhav Shahane would turn sweet sixteen and never been kissed. This was something her best friend, Gemma Nicks—who by sixteen, it seemed, had *never* never been kissed—decided to set straight once and for all.

Thursday at lunch, Gemma spoke with surprising urgency to Marisa Salerno, who convened with Poppy Shea and Carmen Roncevic, who was going with Sledge Davies, who was tight with both the baseball and brainy boys due to his left hook and right-hand-man ease with rotating solids around the Y axis. Sledge could swiftly find the boyman for the job.

And so a plan was hatched: They would gather Friday evening at Carmen's. A stroke before midnight (for more nick-of-time dramatic effect), Sulekha would cross the street and head uphill into the woodland cove that split Carmen and Gemma's neighborhood from the middle-school sports field. This evergreen enclave was called the Saloon. By Sulk and Gem, that was. Rumor had it the football team had buried a galleon of whiskey bottles under the knottiest oak for deep forest forays with females; there were other F's involved in that as well. So it was an apt place for Sulekha to meet the chosen boy and get the first, the French, deed done.

As Carmen explained, Sulk fidgeted her booted foot in and

out of the baby-blue hopscotch square. It all sounded complicated, but the Bees liked complicating things. They thrived on rites of passage. Personally, Sulekha wondered when these initiations would end, when where she was would be where she was trying to get to.

Maybe after this midnight kiss, she thought, Gem'd be back in boots again.

Gazing down at the array of girlfeet, Sulk saw her former Wild West pardner donned army green platform sneaks, the ones she'd gotten en masse with her employee discount. They'd gotten close with their part-time jobs, the Bees—Carmen in the drugstore (replenishing her condom stock), Marisa and Poppy steaming at Starbucks, and Gemma in shoes. And when their hours upped with summertime, this mall bonding could only intensify. Sulekha had wanted to join in on all the fun, but her parents wouldn't hear of it.

—Part-time job! her father nearly guffawed, patting his belly after a particularly large bowl of pista kulfi. —What are you needing part-time job for? You have a roof over your head.

—People will begin to speak, her mother whispered, as if the world had been mute until then. —You need to focus on your studies, Baby, so you can go to a good university, earn a fine degree. . . .

—And give it all up for a suitable CKP Indian boy, her sister, Reshem, who was home for Thanksgiving, had interjected with her new higher-learning snort.

And so the rest of the Bees had gone on to punch in and out and Sulekha not.

Gemma was standing farther from Sulekha than usual today, leaning in with Carmen. A wistful view, but it afforded Sulk a glimpse she normally never had when they were all whispering ears and eyelock, fingertwined and braidmaking. Gemma afar was nearly as beautiful as she was up close. A lotus from a muddy bank, she was growing into her wildness with a savage grace: long, weedy tangles of dirty blond hair, the big beauty mark the blush of cinnamon under her left lower lid, and the cat-slant eyes, flecked yellow as if gold were there for the panning just below. Her faded jeans dragged too long on the ground, running under the backs of her squashy heels, and the knit violet halter dress barely covered her womanchest. But that was the point, wasn't it?

—We've gotta take care of this pronto, she was saying. Her back was decked in freckles, an arched map of Little Dippers, stolen sun, and wish-upons.

Sulekha knew the inflections in Gemma's voice as if she'd lain in them till they molded her own body. All her voices: her mother-on-the-phone-from-L.A. monotone, father-may-I sing-sing, dog-ate-my-homework sugarcoat, can-I-help-you brisk beat, mmm-like-what-I-see meadowy melt. But this was a new voice. A We voice, not as in she and Gemma, but as in Us— and then there's You.

Sulk sucked in the dip of her upper lip. She hovered with one foot sinking in the pliant spring grass, the other on the edge, where it abruptly capitulated to concrete. Forever on the edge of things, it seemed. Of this conversation, for example. Her family was always going on about borders, the ones they'd traversed and the generations before: Pakistan and India, village to city. America for them marked the end of this perpetual crossing over. But what no one had told Sulekha was there were just as many invisible frontiers once you got there.

Take sixteen. Sixteen itself was a borderline: neither here nor there yet everywhere. The age of the kiss, of the never-been-kissed. If you didn't have your period, you were late, as the doctor had informed Sulk, alarming her mother by diagnosing stress as serenely as possible. And if you *were* getting it, you prayed to gods you wouldn't be late, as Carmen had been, despite all the rounds of rosaries. Legal for some things, illegal for others; just barely consensual. The driver's permit, which Sulekha would be eligible for soon, summed it up: You had the basics, a beginning ability to take on new roads, but you didn't have the grace yet, the map yet, and if you did, the keys were someone else's. You couldn't be you without surveillance.

At sixteen, everyone was watching you—especially you. And the boys were watching, too, sometimes looking right through you, sometimes not getting past the skin of you.

—Well, Sulekha said now. She couldn't feel the sunstuck tar through her sturdy sole. —Who will it be, then?

—Could be anyone, couldn't it? Poppy mused into a tangerine-sheen bubble of Bazooka.

—Danny Kinsley, Marisa offered kindly.

—Joel Macero, Poppy counterpopped.

—Sledge Davies, Carmen suggested, smiling mischievously. (She wouldn't!)

They began to rattle off the Wanted Alive list, more for their own pleasure. They were in the part of the parking lot where the burnout girls leaned on wine-colored car hoods smoking reds and letting rocker boys slip sure hands under their low-rider waistbands. The Honors girls (minus Sulekha) collected in beige cropped chinos in the mottled shade, simmering strands of sunshine filtering through leaf and lighting them up like a group of laptopped angels. Gemma had been Sulk's way in to this group of in-betweens, these Bees; they hung about on the chalky lines of four-squares that were still around from when this school had been for kids. But recently this in-between had begun to seem like a somewhere.

The Bees efficiently used the twenty-minute break to digest iceberg lettuce and update one another on the expanding constellations of fingerprints on their flesh. As such, Gemma's affair with a much older boyman, a manboy, in fact, had been her ticket to hive entry. Sulk had nil to add, though her own hands had taken on an astronomical tendency to chart out new ports of call on her own body of late. There were terms for this pastime, the more technical M-word sounding like a medical condition, and "jerking off" making *you* seem like the jerk. Sulk thought of it more as a melting pot, a clay unmaking—the reverse rendering of an earthen bowl whirring into being on a potter's wheel. It was the only moment when no words pressed against the inner screen of her forehead.

But other than boymen brushing inadvertently against her in the crammed corridors, or the brief thrill of knucklebrush while passing a lunch tray, no Big, no Little Dippers could be found on Sulekha's own unfreckled skin. She envied the Bees, especially rosy-cheeked, licorice-locked Carmen, who took an exuberant, almost malicious joy in the power of her swooshingly blossoming body, wielded it like a tool to navigate the uncharted territory that lay ahead. That they were already in.

—We'll arrange it all for you, Suzy, Carmen assured her now. That's what they called her, a taste their tongues knew. Carmen wore a stick-on bindi from one of the many fashion magazines she subscribed to. It was last year's issue but it'd been a good one—complete with a foldout of Justin Timberlake, creasing him cleanly, excruciatingly down the crotch. —We'll choose the boy. You'll see him when the time is right—when the stars are in place and all that. That's how it works for you people, anyways, no?

Sulk hadn't been "you people" before. But she was glad Carmen was at least talking to her.

—Oh right, that arranged-marriage business, said Poppy. —I read an article on that in *Radolescence*. About how all these Indian women are suppressed and have no choices in life.

—But they've had so many Miss Universes, Marisa sighed dreamily. —That doesn't sound so oppressed. . . .

—Don't get off the subject, Carmen cut in. —Listen, Suze, consider it an emergency birthday present.

—I know, but it's just my parents. You know how they are.

—Who's about to turn sixteen? You or them? said Carmen, eyes smirking. —You know, Suzy, I've about had it with these excuses. There's always something with you. You've been getting a little too big for your boots lately is the feeling I'm getting. I know your 'rents don't want you to be like us. But what's wrong with us?

Sulk bit her tongue tip. It was true, about her parents. That's why she never invited the posse over, only Gemma on her own. And if her parents knew the half of it, it'd be doubly true. Already she couldn't attend the same parties, where they were convinced sperm could cantor across carpet, hurdle a TV screen, and up-wriggle a pair of boot-cuts to impregnate a girl. (That's why it's called a *shag* rug, Gemma had snickered, employing a bit of the British slang she'd brought over from her own motherland.) Where boys were certainly slipping pills in these girls' drinks and making promises that had always been broken.

—Or, actually, what's wrong with *you*? Carmen challenged now, her words glinting as if rubbed on stone. —Don't *you* want it?

Of course Sulk wanted. But she didn't know what, or where. She knew she lay awake at night with this wanting, like a new tensely wound organ, hands pressed to lower belly to keep it from rupturing skin. Her belly had been aching for days now, around the button, like a cord yanking her out of herself. Too many boys, boys. What to do with them? They made her feel breathlessly cloddy when she had to interact with them, especially the ones who ran around chasing balls on fields as if engaged in some primordial dance with the Nerf god. Their voices were like the bottom of boats. Their throats bobbed when they talked as if they couldn't get out what they really wanted to say. They looked like they knew different things.

Take *Lane Hallestorm*, the one the Bees were eyeing at the moment, even Carmen, who was with Sledge but always stocking up for the winter. He was one of the ones who looked like he could break you and you should be grateful he hadn't already. His face was all carved ice. The one who swept you in his view for a second and made you feel he'd held you an eternity. *Lane Hallestorm*, the Bees swooned, always first-name-last. Not like Gem's ex Ryder, who was out of school and therefore had only one name. Nor Abhijit, who also went by one name—Abe, just like Sulekha was Suzy—because as the only other Indian at Royal Oak, he was too contexted.

—*Lane Hallestorm.* Sulekha swooned now. Not so much because of the boyman himself, but because swooning felt so good, a sheer relief to hear how her voice took on the swooping frequencies and flavor of theirs when she did.

Carmen relaxed a notch, even as she said, —I know it's your birthday, but we can't promise a miracle, Suzy. We've only got twenty-four hours.

—It doesn't really matter who it is, Poppy said, shrugging, sucking her words out a deflating bubble. Sulk imagined them floating around in there, a cartoon caption. —Just get it out of the way.

—You can't be a baby forever, whatever your parents think, Gemma agreed in her new hive voice. —It's only a kiss. No rubber, no pill. You don't even need your nappies.

That was a new-old development; Gemma had forcepped from her vocabulary most of the British English terms that had set her apart as a kid in this town. It'd been part of Sulk and Gem's Wild West pact. But that pact was cracking, and Gemma's kind of different now held its charm, while Sulk's just slowed the posse down.

—Yeah, Suze. You kiss him, diss him, then text in.

That she had to be with a boy to be one of the girls seemed ironic but incontestable. Sulekha could read Carmen's unspoken thought as if she were subtitled:

Do this and you can buzz with the Bees.

They called themselves the Bees 'cause they could make honey and sting. Honey with their smiles and sting with their tongues. Sometimes they honeyuttered and glance-stung. Rarely did they honey-honey sting-sting.

At first Sulekha had thought the name was because of their grades. Sulk had never seen a B on her own report card. But sometimes she longed for one, voluptuous. She sometimes longed to make a mistake. What might happen then?

The bell *dddrrringed*. The Bees headed off in one direction, Sulk in the other.

Later, when she got on the bus, Sulekha took the window seat, leaving room just in case. But Gemma sat behind her, silent. So Sulk was surprised when she descended at her stop, even though her own was still four away.

When the bus was out of view, Gemma grabbed Sulk's elbow.

—Damsel, I'm distressed, she said.

That was cowgirl code for sorry and Sulekha softened. Gemma rarely used their lingo in posse mode anymore, or even one-on-one.

—About the nappies. I know you're not a baby. I don't know why I say those things sometimes. It's like someone else's words are coming out of my mouth.

—I know what you mean, said Sulekha, and she did. —Like a bandit ventriloquist.

—Sounds like our next song, Gemma said, smiling sadly.

She hadn't talked about the songs in ages. Sulk felt a tug of hope.

—Gem, I know they don't really like me. I'm sorry, too. I know it's hard for you.

—We just need to all get along, said Gemma too earnestly. She squeezed Sulk's hand, then dropped it as if it were too hot. —I want them to see the damsel I see. But you've got to buzz with the Bees. Don't make me choose—stick with me.

Sulekha looked at Gemma and the goldrush eyes that were so familiar when no one else was watching. She knew she wouldn't make her choose. Because now the choice Gemma would make was clear.

—After tomorrow, said Gemma, closing her eyes. —We'll all be the same.

—I'll be there, said Sulk. And then, to remind Gem who they were: —You know I love you, lonestar.

—We can't keep talking like that, Suzy, Gemma said, and the name made a funny-mirror sound coming from her mouth. —Especially not in front of the Bees. I'm sixteen now, you know.

Gemma got her period first; Gemma wore a bra first and took it off first, and now, though they were only months apart, it seemed as if mysteriously dense and ambiguous years were accumulating between them.

—I know, Sulekha said.

Gemma tapped her shades off head and over eyes and Sulk popped up double in the glassy lenses. She looked redundant. Gemma waved, turned, and walked away.

At home Sulekha kicked off her clogs in the foyer. She'd stashed the boots safely in her locker. Her mother had just shaken her head, with a funny little illegible expression, when she'd first worn the lime-and-sage cowkicks home two Septembers ago. She'd told Sulekha they were meant for a boy, and later turned back to the kitchen temple, the low candle glowing and the small ultrasound beside it, its speck of bright, brief life petaled from view by the curling edges. Sticks and stones; the unspoken in that was enough to make Sulk start sneaking them on at school instead, and it was strangely sweet turning secret, breathtakingly boundless going outlaw.

Unbaby was the unspoken. And since his unarrival, Sulk's mother had begun to cast her eyes around this house they'd lived in for a decade as if startled to find herself in it. When Sulekha first heard the word *stillborn*, she thought it meant that despite everything, he'd still come through, was *still born*, this little one she already loved. She didn't realize that that everything included his negation until she saw how her mother's eyes chasmed after, how even she and Reshem no longer seemed to shine in them.

The house as usual was unbearably quiet without Reshem home. Long nights with only the thud of the dishwasher tablet releasing, the train-track spin cycle, a hiss of eraser to page. Television tuned low, an occasional uprising of programmed laughter; thick, silky rugs muffling footfall. *Shh, Baby is studying.* So silent the swirling dust motes hovering in the paned light ached her ears.

Reshem was in New York. Before she left, she chopped her hair, streaked it sunflower and satsuma and still blacker between. She began to look like a boy and the boys began to look at her: the Big Y baggers, the fertilizer company kids who came to lay the mulch, the paperboy with his topply twelve-speed, even her father's whiskey-grinned colleague. But mostly the Radio Shack manboy with the dyed-blond dreadlocks; in this case Reshem had gazed right back, all summer long.

Sulekha recalled watching through the family-room window that week before Reshem left home, how her sister had huddled on her haunches and wept alone in the driveway, a staticky silence when that dyed-blond boy stormed off, just as tired of being hidden from her parents as they were of their true daughter being withheld from them.

That night, contemplating Reshem in her carefully ripped jeans and CBGBs T-shirt, her hair scuffed and face the most visible part of her, as if she were floating neck-deep in the black lake of the driveway, Sulekha remembered another Reshem: Monsoon Reshem, how she'd always prayed extra-hard for the rains, and when they came, ran from the swinging bed in Smita Villa out into the gray embrace of it all, spinning sun and moon, Surya and Soma, from her sari silk, her hair so long and even longer wet, her eyes so bright and even brighter then.

Her heart went out to Reshem. But what Reshem didn't know was that inside her mother was weeping as well, before the goddess Laxmi, her father watching as well, from another darkened window. And caught between them, Sulekha fell mute, could not cross over to either side, straddle their pain and bring them together.

They seemed so confused by their children lately. Almost afraid of these creatures they'd birthed and fed and who were now sinking roots in foreign soil, flourishing like exotic plants and branching out in unforeseen directions.

Sulk switched on the computer and was grateful for its noisy hum. Half-smiling at the cheery face signaling the system was ready to go, she spelled in her password: Gem4Ever. It seemed unlikely Gem's was still SulkOnly.

Like a bandit ventriloquist, Sulk thought to herself. It would be their next song if only Gemma let it. *Tongue-tied, you've twisted / The words from my mouth / And oh, now I miss them.*

A missing period. But Sulekha knew those were unspoken words bundled at the bottom of her belly. She felt like some of them got said unspokenly when she was around Gemma, even now. But she missed the days they were sung.

Sulekha wrote the words and Gemma sang them into the air like a paper airplane with a message that reached everyone. Gem strummed Sulk to new places; Sulekha's words meant something else on her friend's tongue, sunk in another salt and sweet. Or maybe they found their true meaning in Gemma's mouth: She made sad things ring joyful; if you said you were blue, she made blue sound like the most beautiful hue to behold, the stroke to paint the world with.

—Cowgirls and indie boys, Gem rambled that last time.

—Give us another choice, Sulekha inked.

—Cowgirls and indie boys.

—Sing in another voice.

Sulekha loved Gemma. She loved her so much she wished

she could have cried the tears Gemma left on Sulk's pillow for days after Ryder rode off with her innocence. Sulekha knew every shift of her face, every flick and nail-pick of her fingers. She didn't know how to play the guitar herself, but she memorized the shapes of Gemma's hands on the frets, a sign-language counterpart to the voice that glowed like hot stones.

She loved her so much it broke her heart when Gemma frosted her words around the other girls, ice not to skate on; alone, they'd always been summerfield tones.

But on IM it was reassuringly different. She saw lonestar was online and shot off a *Howdy, pardner*. Moments later, the comforting tinkerbell ring:

lonestar: u doin ur xoxos?

Damsel: How will I know what to do?

lonestar: nuttin 2 do m8.

Damsel: But what will it be like?

lonestar: like rollng ur tung bk on itslf. try.

lonestar: u try?

Damsel: Yes. Two cavities.

lonestar: like som1 talk in ur mouth som1 put words in ur mouth.

lonestar: got it?

Damsel: Got it.

lonestar: gr8.

lonestar: feel ur way.

Damsel: I feel your way.

Damsel: Lone?

Damsel: Miss you.

lonestar: missu2.

lonestar: go west.

Damsel: But I have so many questions.

Damsel: ??

No reply, and when she glanced at the box she could see *charmincarmen* now up and online. For a while she stared at the two names fixed in the upper-right corner of her screen, as if waiting for them to do something. She felt she was spying somehow, and clicked the corner X to close the box. A half hour later, after finishing *The Scarlet Letter,* she fired out another question mark.

lonestar is not currently signed on.

Go West. That's all Sulekha had been doing for the decade since coming to America. For a moment, her classmates were fascinated with her culture: There was a brief hip wink when they turned expectant faces to her over desktops and under monkey bars and looked for kamasutronic elucidation to shoot out from the space between her brows and zap them enlightened. Madonna was doing yoga. But Madonna was also having sex (which, it occurred to Sulekha, must have been pretty good with all that yoga). A few indie movies with Indie themes came out and played at the art-house cinemas near college campuses. Movies with Indians playing—Indians! And Indians—having sex!

None did yoga.

At first her parents had been excited about this focus on the motherland, but subsequently didn't know quite what to make of it when it came packaged for America. Sulekha was not one of the new harmoniously whole South Asians, like her sister was determined to be in her new interdisciplinary life. She didn't like bindis—she had enough to contend with in the form of round red facial explosions that occasionally, irreverently, appeared left of center, like one of Carmen's stick-ons with faulty adhesive. Sulk begged for a nose ring in India, but no longer wanted it in East River, ever since she'd been asked on the seesaw if it was a perma-booger (a thump as she slid off and bumped her gnomelike interrogator to the sandy ground). Her parents refused to let the hole close, insisting it looked lovely on her. But then, years later, when they saw that half the girls at Royal Oak sported a nasal stud, they urged Sulekha to take it out.

—Why now? Sulk had asked, joining the tiny diamond with its pair in her ballerina box.

—Because we can't make *them* take it off, her mother replied.

The hole didn't close. Sulekha's tongue weakened. She found asafetida disturbing and cayenne too hot. She had to spoon sugar in her mouth to stop the burning.

—You had no trouble with that in India, her mother worried.

But the same tongue in a new American context tasted things differently. Sulekha longed for the spaghetti and meatballs at Carmen's, the twinklingly lenient TV dinners at Gemma's, doughnuts that left your fingers shiny and sticky and salaciously oozed yellow cream.

So no yoga, no bindis, no nose ring (but a nose hole); no Bharat Nãtyam, no vegetarianism, better Spanish than Marathi. The Bees were tongue-cluckingly disappointed; it had been an opportunity for Sulekha to redeem herself for her difference, to exoticize it, and she'd failed miserably. To make matters worse, Sulk didn't drink, didn't smoke, didn't party, and she certainly didn't kiss. She did study; she did get good grades. She did think about drinking, smoking, and kissing.

Still she couldn't actually see *herself* engaging in these activities. It would be like picturing her parents. But she could imagine Carmen and Sledge, Carmen and Lane, Marisa and Ethan, and, mostly, Gemma. She didn't have to conjure much with Carmen, who thrived on sharing technique in the gym at school dances. Or Marisa, who spilled all the d's for the Bees and seemed to enjoy that more than doing it, even. That was all they ever talked about, in fact. They were on to more advanced forms of kissing these days—capital K, with other body parts— but it was all the same set of hieroglyphics to Sulk.

Envisioning herself with one of the boymen was tough; she was always invisible in these equations, the boys even more delineated in her mind than they were in the lockered halls before her. With Gemma it was just the opposite. Gemma kissed invisible boys in Sulekha's mind. Sometimes the boys shape-shifted, from Lane to strangers to Omar Sharif. But always at the meltiest end of Sulk's imaginings they vanished again.

Now she recalled an image from a movie she'd once seen: a woman stripped to skin on a wild horse at a hacienda, doubly bareback. She couldn't remember much else about the film. But she could hear the hooves strike dust, see the surrender of flesh on flesh, human hip on horse's haunch, and that flying, fiery hair, like a flag to somewhere else.

Her hands worked a swirling script between her legs till the ache spasmed, left her throbbingly boneless in the swivel chair. She lay back panting gently, feeling ashamed and amazed.

Sulekha finished her homework. She helped her mother with the rest of the meal, chopping up onions under cold water, crushing cardamom with mortar and pestle. She cleaned up after, careful to twist-tie the excess oil into double plastic bags so as not to clog the drain, wiping the floury countertops back to peach. She poured iceless water into stainless-steel cups, folded paper-towel triangles, and laid it all out: fresh saag studded with garlic cloves, sweet thick dahl and rice, okra.

Her father was home early, whistling as he entered as if a golden retriever might be waggingly waiting around the corner. He washed his hands, Sulk's mother washed hers, and then Sulekha did, too, at the kitchen tap. At the table, which was square, her sister's spot, as usual, gaped.

—So Reshem cannot come until Sunday, Daddy, her mother told her father. —Too much busy-busy college business. She has to *think*.

—About what? She can think here, can't she? her father wondered.

—Apparently not.

—Baby, beta, I hope you're not too disappointed, he said, turning anxious eyes to Sulekha. —I know you're missing your sister these days.

Sulekha sensed an opportunity.

—Well, I *do* miss having a sister around, she said slowly.

Her parents exchanged pained glances. Sulekha cleared her unimpeded throat.

—You know, Aai, Baba—the girls from school wanted to have a party for me tomorrow night. At Carmen Roncevic's, just across the town line by Gemma's.

They stared as if she'd just announced she was joining a traveling circus.

—Not even a party really. Just to, you know, celebrate my . . . sweet sixteen.

Sulekha felt a near-hysterical giggle hiccup up when she said it. Sweet sixteens were for SPF 15 girls with slim hips and Little Dippered skin. Not her.

—What is so sweet about sixteen in this country? her father wondered aloud, chewing slowly, perplexed. —Why not fifteen?

—Baby is very sweet, her mother said, arrowing a glance at her father.

—Why not eleven?

—Alliteration, probably, said Sulk.

That last word seemed to frighten her mother.

—Baby, do not stress, she nearly pleaded. —But why you can't invite your friends here? I will make puran poli—just the way you like!—and we will all do the pooja together. Kaka and Kaki might even come from Hartford.

Sulekha considered this incongruous image of the Bees mingling cross-leggedly with her family before the floored Ganesha, with her uncle, who was unabashedly prone to a vigorous belch after meals, and her aunt, whose regurgitative release was shallower but still Richter-registerable; even though Reshem couldn't make it, Sulk still pictured her, lobbing about looks of disgust, taking solace in the fact that they weren't her real uncle and aunt, just called that the way all your parents' friends were in India.

It didn't seem very sweet.

—They can't come Saturday, said Sulekha. —They go to church.

—On Saturday? I thought church was Sunday.

—Right. To practice. For Sunday.

—Good girls, her father said, nodding with surprising seriousness.

—I'd be back in time to help get everything ready for Kaka and Kaki.

—Oh, Baby, I don't—

—It's just the girls, she added. —It's just one night. It's not even my actual birthday.

When there was no response, she played the missing-period factor.

—It would really de-stress me.

—Well, her mother sighed. —I suppose it can't hurt. And Gemma will be there to keep an eye on you.

—Ah, Mummy, it's okay, her father said, smiling, patting her hand, gently, clumsily. —What kind of trouble can she get into with the girls?

Sulekha's mother and father had really taken to Gemma ever since she'd dissed Winston Churchill for allegedly calling Gandhi "that little man in a loincloth," which made them instantly forgive her burgundy passport. They might have appreciated her sooner had they realized that until Gemma arrived, Sulekha's first year in America had been the loneliest of her short but deeply felt life.

That first day of school in the U.S.A. felt like a birthday.

Not in the sense of a celebration, but in that it felt like no matter how far she'd come in her six adventure-studded jamrukh-slaked years, she'd have to start all over as if they'd never happened at all. Sulekha was dressed in her Catholic-school uniform from India (she was Hindu but that's how it worked if you wanted a proper British education there): starched white short-sleeved shirt, denim-blue skirt to the knees, and chappals, her hair tightened in two coconut-oiled braids with even longer ribbons (red, white, and blue; her mother thought it would be a nice touch). She stood out like a small brown pilgrim awash in a sea of scintillating pinks and iron-ons. This was not an auspicious start. So many of the American mother-daughters were dressed nearly identically; a number were in tracksuits, which made Sulekha worry they'd be asked to run or climb soon.

—Aai, Mummy, what will I say? little Sulekha had panicked when it was time for the children to leave their parents.

—Do not worry, Baby, her mother murmured. —It's the English, it's the same. It is your second language.

That wasn't what Sulekha had meant. And in any case, it wasn't the same language. The English she'd learned in India, British English taught by Indian nuns with its tea blend of chiseled stone and hilly sky, was not the highway slur and blurry blue windows of American English. And this distinction was made plain right away, at roll call.

—Sue . . . Sue Lake Shayne?

She hadn't recognized it as her name at first. Then it clicked.

—Uh . . . heeyuh, she'd said. *Here.*

—Hee haw? someone chortled.

They giggled at her *shalls* and *shan'ts* and *lorries,* her *queues* and *jolly goods.* Sulekha didn't share with them the *bloody hells* that marqueed resoundingly in fantastic fonts across the backs of her eyes. They wrinkled their eyebrow-noses at her saran-wrapped samosas and asked if she was

Cherokee (her art teacher had been to a reservation once! It had changed her life!).

Until Gemma arrived.

Gem then looked a miniature version of Gem now, the longly tangled hair, and something like a patchwork quilt for a skirt and camisole top. Blue and fuchsia rubber bands wound round her wrist, the same way Sulk wore seven gold bangles. She had an utterly serious expression on her face.

—Class. This is Gemma Nicks, they'd announced. —She has arrived to Royal Oak from London . . . *England!*

A collective intake of breath.

—I shan't be late again, Gemma had said in a crisp, controlled accent that trimmed the air of all its excess fat. Sulk's heart leaped: *Shan't.*

At recess, scores of seven-year-olds thronged around the mysterious girl, not least because of this accent that evoked little princesses and single princes, powdery queens and page-turning Dickens, but, more important, the Spice Girls. Sulekha, however, was drawn to it for another reason: It was just like her own with the soft parts pared off, the core of an overripe apple. She began to sense the pulse of vindication on a nearing horizon. And at lunch that day, as she fiddled with her brown paper bag at a corner table, it was confirmed when, in front of absolutely everyone and their dog, Gemma Nicks set her tray down next to hers, and for a brief rapturous moment made Sulekha Madhav Shahane *good* visible.

—Papadum! I simply adore papadum! Gemma exclaimed, cat eyes tipping higher. —I don't reckon you've got another, Sulekha?

Sulekha: sung like a sigh. It had been ages.

—I'll trade you, she'd added, rummaging in her rucksack.

India, it turned out, was nothing new to Gemma Nicks: India was well tucked into London with its curry houses and supermarket spices, its imported marble temples and the Brick Lane she spoke of that seemed a kind of Yellow Brick

Road but red, but blue, but many-hued. Sulekha couldn't believe her ears. And when Gemma produced a luridly wonderfully large Toblerone bar, she couldn't believe her eyes.

—Chocolate? she offered, and it sounded like *chalk lit*. As the nougat emerged on her tongue, Sulekha imagined glow-in-the-dark blackboards scripted in luminous cursives that spoke to her alone.

They chose Gemma. But Gemma chose Sulekha.

Over the years they teamed up, the British-born and the Indian, in a quest to become American as quickly as possible. Together, as if they were performing the most exacting surgery, they learned to extract the *l* from *travelling,* the *u* from *colour.* They shifted "shan't" to "won't" and "a bit" to "a little." They never, ever engaged in "dreadfully frightful rows." And, word by word, it worked. It didn't feel so much a surrender as a fantastic linguistic heist, a game of dress-up of audible proportions. What was lonely as one was lovely with tea for two.

And, as seemed only fitting, along the way they created a new language for this young map:

A stirrup was when something moved your heart. A hodeo was a bunch of fooled-around girls getting together and spelling out the d's. Bullfight: when someone was lying to you. Giddyup—noun, singular—an outfit that made you feel particularly gorgeous. The good, the rad, and the snoggly was an irresistible boy; the hood, the bad, and the ugly, a nasty one—increasingly, the line between the two thinned for Gemma and solidified for Sulekha. Holster was gimme-a-hug, saddled was bummed out. Bareback: being caught in your birthday suit. *Riding* bareback involved entanglements in other people's birthday suits. Ghost town? A dead party—that's how Gemma usually described the ones Sulekha couldn't attend.

A goldrush was how they felt around one another.

—Do you speak Indian? the creamy-skinned children had asked.

Now she spoke cowgirl.

—Don't forget your mother tongue, the umber ones in India had warned.

Now, with Gemma, she remembered herself.

The September before embarking on high school, with Gemma's Christmas checks and Sulekha's odd-figure Diwali dollars, they gifted each other their most prized possessions ever: a pair of bona fide cowboy boots. Sulk's were pull-on lizardskin, green as limes. Gemma's were crisscross lace-ups, purple with suede fringe. Gazing in the floorbound mirrors that made the world seem a swiftly tilting planet, Sulekha was mesmerized.

—We made it, Damsel, Gemma had said. —We've conquered the Wild West.

They were a size too big so the girls could grow into them. Sulekha's feet slipped around a little on their slopes, but they were magnificent. In these cowgirl shoes, she felt like a different person. Or the one she actually was. A pioneer, a buccaneer. A pardner.

—Lonestar, Sulk said with a twang that lay somewhere shot through the middle of a pile of maps. —Let's ride.

Fourteen and this turf was just big enough for the two of them. But that was all before the indie boys rode into town with their caravan of stick-shift cars and dusty grins. Fifteen, and the playing field was replete with damsels in distress. It didn't pay to be a lonestar—you wanted to be part of a constellation. Nearing sixteen, bitterstung bee-sweet: Gemma stopped wearing the boots.

—It's getting childish to match like that, she explained, in kitten heels identical to the ones the Bees were wearing that week.

A kick, invisible, in Sulekha's belly.

Last September, in the sweltering season of Ryder, Gemma grew shy about her body. One afternoon, when they were last in the group shower stall for the required pre-pool rinse, Sulekha was astonished to see Gem'd come up with fresh prep choreography: She curled over herself fetuslike, rolling over the shifting landscape of her chest and Down There— jealously, possessively, shyly, as if she were cupping her hands over a particularly important exam answer. And Sulekha tried not to cheat but couldn't help herself: Off the edge of her eye, as Gemma unfurled for an instant to shave her underarms, Sulk was amazed at how the lush, unruly undergrowth below her belly button had condensed to a tamed slim strip, more of her baby shape visible than had been in four summers. Sulekha felt a strange sense of nostalgia and revulsion, was suddenly conscious of her own nakedness in a way she'd never been with Gemma before. She felt shy, and sad to feel shy.

—What are you looking at? Gemma snapped, rapidly pulling on a one-piece, but not before Sulk had seen the double blues of bitemarks running down her inner thigh flesh.

—I dunno.

—Boys like this.

—It's just . . . different.

—Well, if you want it to be the same, Gemma said then, curtly handing the razor over. —Make it the same.

Sulk stood stupidly holding the pink plastic handle until she realized what Gemma meant.

—Go on.

She sudsed up, feeling absurdly frothy Down There. She took the razor with one hand, stretched her skin back tight with the other, stroking upward. She was surprised at the thickness and curliness of the hair that coated the razor with that single stroke. She glanced up. Gemma stood with her arms crossed and nodded at her to continue. Sulk shaved off one more strip from the outer edge, a little too hard. She sucked in her upper lip as a single drop of rose reddened up on that previously untouched flesh.

And then Gemma was kneeling before her. She took the razor from her hand.

—Here, you'll hurt yourself, she said gently. —Let me do it.

She felt frozen looking down at Gemma's head, the hair so dark when it was wet, almost like Sulk's own. Her heart dropped to the base of her belly, swelling.

Gemma slipped the blade up so easily she didn't feel a thing. And when she was done, Sulekha looked just like her. There.

—Let me see, Gemma had said, standing. It felt strange, being examined by her. They'd shared this space before, but that day it was different. That day Gemma perused her with a stranger's eyes. And there was a little sad something in those eyes, and a little something Sulk had never seen there before, like hunger and fear combined; hunger for fear? But in an instant it was business as usual. Gemma rinsed the razor and turned her back.

—Join the club, she said, and stepped out of the stall.

From that day forward, they stopped walking with their schoolgirl arms around each other. They knew what was happening inside each other's clothes, and though they did not touch, they held on even more tightly in their exchanged glances, their averted eyes, in what they didn't say.

On Friday morning, from the pre-homeroom moment Sulk coaxed on her lizardskin boots, Royal Oak Regional High School resonated with new meaning. No one but the Bees knew who the midnight boyman would be, but it felt like everyone—from the custodian to passing upperclassmen—was giving Sulk looks loaded with meaning.

It was a different world in which anyone could be The One. The rowdy boys, the brainy boys, the alt boys with MP3s dreaming moody music, the skater boys and their proudly displayed bruises. It was a more hopeful world. The boys began to look less and less like parts of their various groups, and more just like boys. Independent. Even Lane Hallestorm (would it be? had he given her a glance just now? how could it be?): Once you zoned in on him and not the posse he posed in, he cocooned nearly human.

All day Sulekha gazed with an intensity at the mouths of her classmates—Carmen's carefully applied, Joel Macero's pensively chewed, Patrick Trainor's brazenly toothed, Gemma's own bare heart-shaped lips—until it seemed the whole room was awash in a sea of tongue steeped, a chorus of openings.

Her family seemed joyfully far.

And the Bees seemed satisfied. They were laughing at her as they went through a round of puckering exercises in the parking lot, but they were also closer than they'd ever been, and that meant something. And most important, Gemma was nearly being Gemma again. Sending her secret shimmering winks that made the butterflies flutter by in the pit of Sulk's queasy stomach. *We made it across,* the smiles seemed to say. *Nearly there. Nearly together again.* In spite of herself, anticipation began to mount. Sulekha's lower belly was in twirling cramps, like springs longing to shoot into the world, unspiral, straighten out a truth.

Last period put an end to the ellipses. In Honors American History, she turned around to pass the assignment back to Abhijit, today wearing a bandanna over his forehead that she'd seen him tying on by his locker. He mumbled:

—Got your phone?

She nodded, confused.

Moments later, she felt it vibrate through her bag, against her boot. Peering down, she saw the tiny envelope symbol and clicked.

xo + folks = kill. 210 at nth-sth

She understood.

At a little before two P.M., Abhijit raised his hand and asked to go to the boys' room. A smidge after, Sulekha waved and requested the girls'.

At the junction of North and South Halls, by the handicapped toilet, she found him.

—Abe, she said, just in case anyone was around, and then, closer up. —Abhijit.

Despite the brazenly patterned headwrap, he looked sheepish.

—I'm really sorry, he said.

—So it's you.

So this was the suitable boy they'd sorted for her? Abhijit. No alt, no rowdy, no jock, no skater, no brain, and of course, no Lane. But Abhijit Joshi, the only other desi (however American born) in school. How uncreative. Or actually, perhaps how creative, nearly doing her parents' work for them— though the Bees probably didn't realize that joint outcastedness at Royal Oak Regional High did not undo the biases their families had long ago packed in their luggage just in case and later casually unfolded before the eyes of their U.S.-bred children. Though both were Marathi, the Joshis were Brahmin, the religious caste, and more important, a higher caste than the Shahanes' warrior one Kshatriya, which made them a little too uppity in Sulk's mother's opinion. Mrs. Joshi was always going on (in front of her) about how *their* bodies ran with pundit blood. And Sulekha's mother was constantly proclaiming (behind her back) about how it was the Kshatriyas, the caste of kings, who'd protected these supposed pundits during all the great wars.

They stared at each other a moment, then simultaneously began to laugh.

—Look at us, said Abhijit, shaking his head. —My parents would kill me—with a CKP NRI like you.

—Nonresident immigrant? Excuse me, we live here, Sulekha said, smiling. —And imagine mine, with a pseudo-pundit ABCD like you.

—Look, I'm not gonna be able to escape so late without my folks sending out a SWAT team, Abhijit said, lowering his voice. —But can you act like it happened? You only have to go for a few. You don't even have to do the woods; they won't know.

—Don't worry, said Sulekha. —I'm kind of in the same situation.

Of course, she couldn't call his bluff. It was in both their interests, whatever the stakes were on his end, to just say they'd gone through with it.

She presented her hand. After a moment he took it and shook. His palm was warm and his grip surprisingly firm.

—Thanks, Sulekha, I owe you, he said, and grinned. His mouth wasn't so outcaste then, though it was still hard to imagine kissing it. —I hope it was good for you.

—The sweetest sixteen I never had, she said.

She almost liked this boy she'd called an American Born Confused Desi, with his earnest eyes and eager bandanna. She expected to feel winded, a tangible disappointment. But instead relief pumped her body bright. And when she looked around at her classmates running for the buses, clustering with friends in the sidewalk light, the sun still shone, stored with gold across a nearing frontier.

That night after dinner, Sulk brushed and even flossed. She had to get decked enough so the Bees wouldn't suspect nothing was going to happen, but not so much so that her parents thought something would. She settled for flared jeans and a fitted button-down lilac shirt. She butterfly-clipped her hair, carefully pulling a few waves out to twirl around her face. Bangles and, finally, boots. The girl in the mirror was glowing, she was startled to see. Eyes the shade of gingerroot and shine of night rain. She was all dressed up with someplace to go.

Her parents both drove her to Carmen's. They climbed partially up the drive, but not too far, and even stopped the engine. Inside the den window, Sulk could see shadowy figures drifting about on a soft swell of music. She hoisted the duffel she'd packed and opened the back door.

—Now, don't forget to phone as soon as you're up so we can come get you, her father said.

—I won't forget.

—And call if you change location, her mother added. —Even for a half hour.

—Mummy, Daddy, said Sulk, trying on a reassuring smile. —Nothing's going to happen here.

She got out, slinging the sack on her shoulder as she headed off. Out of habit she turned back, and they were still there, the engine now running but the car most probably in park; nevertheless, her father gripped the wheel as if it were moving, and her mother remained belted down, looking squashed under the straps she never lengthened after Sulekha had last been in the passenger seat. Sulk was reminded of that first day of school in America and her mother's split-end braid, the salwar pants that billowed like pajamas out from under her coat. Today her mother's hair was layered short, based on a photo she'd clipped from *Redbook*. She was watching her daughter fearfully through the windshield. Sulekha couldn't help but go back and lean in the unrolling window.

—Don't worry, Aai, she whispered, laying her hand on her mother's cheek. —It's going to be all right.

This time when Sulekha walked away, she didn't turn back. But she could feel their eyes all candle on her until Carmen's front door opened and they knew she was safely inside, felt the swing of headlights scan her back as they reversed and left.

The first thing she noticed when she entered: Gem in braids and boots! This was an auspicious start.

—Facesucker!

—Liplocker!

—Tongue-twister!

Marisa and Poppy and Carmen seemed far more excited than Gemma, though, who stood back almost shyly as they group-hugged Sulk.

—Snogger, she finally, quietly, said when Sulekha was released.

The room was a lively mess of magazines and makeup boxes, CDs strewn in silver spinning heaps. Missy Elliott was playing, and juice spilled off a speaker top, a drop off the beat. Carmen nabbed the plastic cup and pressed it into Sulk's hands.

—Bottoms up, honeybee.

It was a well-sweetened command, and the contents of the cup were much paler than calcium-enriched Tropicana OJ usually was. That's when Sulk noted the unscrewed bottle of Absolut on the coffee table. She tipped the cup to make Carmen happy, and her dipped lip immediately hummed.

—Come on, Suzy! yelped Poppy, turning up the volume. She began to sing along. —You gotta *work* it, lemme *work* it . . .

—Now, we don't have time to waste on prehistoric tunes, Carmen announced, slamming her hands together. —We gotta get on Project SMS.

—Project SMS? Sulk and Gem said at the same time. They looked at each other, and Gemma half-smiled.

—We are gonna doll, you, up, Suzy M. Shahane, Carmen proclaimed.

—What do you mean?

This is what she meant (Carmen gestured like an airline hostess): a facial (self-heating), a manicure (aqua), a pedicure (violet), straight-ironing Sulekha's hair (old-*Friends* Rachel). A trio of eyeshadows (on the brow bone, lid, and rim), a trinity of lip products (liner, lipstick, and gloss, all the same shade-too-cherry for Sulk's taste), and a stroke of blush up the cheeks. They went to it, Marisa reading aloud from the prom issue they were using as a guide.

Poppy unbuttoned Sulekha's top two buttons. Marisa undid the bottom four and knotted her shirt ends together just below the bra line. Carmen tugged the jeans a lick lower and lent her a double-looped rhinestone belt to create a sort of cowgirl-popstar midriff expose. A spritz of J Lo Glow hot off Carmen's vanity table, and, at a little after 11:30 P.M. EST, Friday, May 21, Sulekha was ready to go.

—How do I look? she asked Gemma, who she saw then was sitting a small distance away, nursing her plastic cup.

—Who *are* you? said Gemma, barely looking up. The contents of her cup were translucent as a goldfish fin. —You're hardly recognizable.

—Exactly! cried Carmen triumphantly. She unpeeled the bindi from her own forehead and stuck it on Sulekha's.

—You might need this, she added with exaggerated mystery.

Sulk tried to look confused, as if she had no idea how the bindi could apply. Actually it wasn't so hard with the way Gemma was acting—maybe she'd had a little too much? It seemed the same cup she turned slowly in her hands, but perhaps Sulekha had missed the transitional refill.

—Now, if he gets stuck on your bra straps, just undo them yourself, Marisa advised. —It is *so* cringeworthy watching a guy go through that. Kills all the atmosphere.

—Are your jeans button-fly or zip? Poppy interjected, chompingly cocking her head. She sucked in a snapped bubble. —Okay, cool thinking—zip's easier.

—But that between-the-buttons move can be totally hot, too. . . .

—Keep your cell on in case, was Gemma's only contribution to the conversation. She leaned her head against the wall as if it hurt and peered up at them from under a curtain of dirty-blond hair.

—Yeah, in case you don't know what to do—

—Or he knows too much—

—Or you just can't stop!

—I thought it was just a kiss, exclaimed Sulekha, mock-shocked; she was safe in her secret. She and Abhijit had shaken on it, after all. Maybe they *were* a great match.

—A kiss is never just a kiss, Poppy said, grinning, breath redolent of grape and turpentine this close. —Don't believe those black-and-white movies.

The Bees seemed to be growing very fond of her the more they dispensed this advice, or at least of their own voices, clamoring in close, buzzing into her ears, making honey-honey.

—This is stupid, Gemma suddenly snapped. All heads swiveled. Sulk could see her trying to rein in her flexed brow and furrowed mouth. Gemma wasn't looking at her, though, but at Carmen. —She doesn't need your advice. She knows what she's doing.

—Really? said Carmen coolly. —Since when?

—Since now. She's sixteen, bloody hell. What is *wrong* with you all?

—What's wrong with *you*? Carmen challenged. It felt funny seeing the words she'd used on Sulekha just yesterday doing a spin and shooting out Gemwards.

—I'm going home, said Gemma, rising in one swoop as if strings had jerked her up marionette-like. —I've got things to do.

She was at the door. The Bees stared, stunned.

—Whatever, Carmen said, rolling her eyes. —You've been acting weird all night.

—PMS, honey? slurred Poppy, gazing, fascinated, into her empty cup. But Gemma was already out the door.

—She'll be back, Carmen said, nodding. —Got to buzz with the Bees.

She tapped her watch.

—You better go, too, Suzy. You don't want to blitz all these hours of prepping.

Sulekha already had her hand on the latch.

She sped down the driveway, boots tock-tocking as she caught up to Gemma. Gemma glanced at her, then quickened her pace.

—I thought you wanted this, said Sulk, quietly breathless.

—I do want it.

—I'm doing it for you.

Gemma stopped short and her eyes were mesmerizing and cold as a doll's.

—Why don't you do something for yourself for a change? she hissed.

—Well, I will, then, said Sulekha, but her heart wasn't in it.

She stood a moment watching Gemma go, turn into darkness, return in the lamplight, and vanish, as if someone were flicking on and off a switch.

Sulekha knew the Saloon so well she could find her way there even in the dark. True that new shoots had sprung, a few branches snapped down with the spring's thunderstorms. But she read the forest with her fingers until she was securely in the star-mossed cove. She could feel it from the way her boot heels dug plushed as if on living-room carpet. She could tell from the angle of moon slipping between the branches and down.

She wasn't sure what to do. She didn't know how long she'd have to wait to make it convincing, or if she even wanted to go back to Carmen's—lying by withholding was doable, but without keyboard or pen and paper, how would she create a convincing tale of the passionate exchanges that would not take place this evening by the roots of the knottiest oak?

An owl's persistent who.

Dropping to her haunches, she ran her fingers along the tangle of roots at the trunk's base. What other secrets does this tree have to tell? she wondered. How many times had they lain here as kids, right here, talking cowgirls and indie boys? How many times had the others come, had skin transformed skin and frontiers been crossed? She was peering so closely at the rugged landscape of broken bark, at first she didn't realize what she took for a variation in its layered texture was in fact someone separating from trunk, stepping out from behind as if from within it. She knew that silhouette, that wrangler stance, and rolled slowly up off her hips to stand face-to-face with Gemma.

—Hi, she said warily.

—Hey.

Gemma's voice sounded disembodied in the woods: vulnerable. She was braidless now, and the dirty-blond hair wavier still, rippling to her waist, nearly. Sulekha could tell she was uncomfortable from the way she shifted from balls to heels of her fringed purple boots, rocking in a puddle of twig-latticed moon.

—What are you doing here?

—So he didn't come.

It wasn't an answer. Was it.

—How do you know?

—I know, Gemma said. She jolted to her toes and lingered a moment before coming down. —I called him.

—Why would you do that?

Sulk moved back a step, annoyed for some reason.

—I'm sorry, Suzy. I got a little worried when all that button-fly this and that came up just now.

—Great, Sulekha sighed, leaning against the oak. —And what do the Bees think of all this?

Gemma looked confused.

—How should I know? she said. —I just came straight here.

Gemma stepped farther out from behind the trunk and came to stand beside her.

—So . . . you're not too disappointed?

—No, Sulk said, shrugging and turning away a little. She turned back again. —You know, I am curious, though. Who would pick a boy I would never kiss?

Gemma stood half in shadow, a stunningly melancholy half-moon; it took Sulekha's breath away. Like that, both of them partly veiled, it could have been all those years ago, their nearly far childhood, right here and now.

—I would, she said. Her words swayed but held.

—Why? Sulekha said softly. But somehow she could taste Gemma's words in her mouth, and in this childed darkness, was beginning to know where they came from.

—I don't know. I couldn't stand the thought of another Ryder in here with you—someone treating it like a game. I went along but then I was sorry. Someone doing that with my Damsel.

Sulekha's heart start-and-stopped.

—What? Gemma said, the illuminated side of her face worrying the moon riven.

—I'm just surprised you called me that.

Gemma looked down and tested the moss with her boot toe as if searching for a weak floorboard.

—I didn't want you to get your heart broken, she said.

—Only heartbreak I've ever had is you, Sulekha replied, and immediately regretted it until she saw Gemma's sad smile.

—Sounds like a song, she said.

They both slid down to the base of the trunk and sat, knees up, arms wrapped around in separate self-hugs.

It was so quiet suddenly that Sulekha could hear loud and clear. She could hear the whiskey bottles glittering in the soil just a foot below their bottoms. She could hear crickets, distant traffic, the stitching hum of people far, far above, flying from one place to another.

—I . . . Gemma said softly, trailing off.

Childheart beating in womanchest.

The past, the present, the future all mixed up in this moment.

Sulekha can hear midnight come and go.

They are watching each other unspokenly now. Sulekha can

see herself in Gemma's pupils, wide as oceans from a night airplane, the all-those-years-ago night they left India behind to come here, now.

But Gemma keeps arriving.

And then she is so close Sulk can't see her anymore. A faint scent of orange, and the world Sulekha knows begins to crumble away like dry earth.

Inside, something sparkles.

It isn't like rolling your tongue back on itself. No—rather, a slow unfurling, an unsuspected blossom, and a thrill deep as root insisting its way through earth. This dark push fills her.

This is me, I am doing this.

Sulekha's belly gives; autumn between her legs already, an early turning. A sound of ink sliding from broken pen, seeping unnamed into the roots of the knottiest oak, sucking up into trunk and branch: red leaves, green sky, blue grass.

Gemma begins to laugh and cry at the same time, and she smells like a little girl.

—Sulekha, Gemma whispers.

—Gemma, Sulekha sighs.

The Mud and Fever Dialogues

M. T. Anderson

i

When Pyrrho had his fever the summer of our sixteenth year, something in him changed. His forehead grew hot. He lay in bed and watched the walls pimple and scar. He saw world-mothers as large and as sagging as elephants sitting on dirty benches. They held out a basin to him, but he would not take it, because he knew it was brimful of death. He struggled so much, his father and sister had to hold him down.

They poured water on his face to cool him.

The rest of us had already gotten over the fever, so we sat outside in the summer heat. We watched our goats wander through the fallen pillars on the hilltops. We sat in the atria of ruined villas, cross-legged on the broken tile, and argued about Truth, the Good, and Beauty. That month, I was going out with a discus-thrower who was missing an ear.

At sunset, we all would go up to the fallen temple and stand there in beautiful poses. People went by on the dirt road and looked up at us. A real victory for us was a day when one said, "Those can't be real boys. Those must be boys of stone."

One evening we were standing there motionless when we saw Pyrrho coming up the hill. We had not seen him for a week. He was still looking pale and greasy.

He came up to our side and said, "I guess I'm better."

We did not move.

He poked Alex with his finger. "Hey," he said.

Alex didn't move. "I'm a statue," said Alex, without moving his jaw.

Pyrrho punched him in the stomach. Alex fell off his mount.

"Ow!" said Alex. "Damn!"

Pyrrho said, "Thus I refute you."

ii

We sat around the fire, eating mutton we had cooked on the flames. We watched gods and crustaceans in the stars; they circled Earth for a glimpse of its crevasses.

"We can't trust what we see or hear," said Pyrrho. "When I was sick, I saw the walls grow a scaly hide. I could hear people order me to run up and down stairs. All we have to judge the world are our senses, and them, we can't trust."

"I'm color-blind," agreed Menalcus glumly. "People tell me something is green, and I have to believe them."

"It's all a big joke," I whispered to Menalcus, hoping to confuse him. "There is no green. Your parents just told us to play along."

"I saw the most amazing thing in my delirium," said Pyrrho. "I saw all of time and space unwrapped. I was falling through it. I could feel my body covered with beetles. They were the seconds passing. I even saw all of you, standing by my bed, banging on cymbals."

There was an awkward silence.

"That was us, actually," I said. "We did stand by your bed, banging cymbals."

"It was scientific," said Menalcus. "We were frightening away the fever-spooks."

"They ran away," I said, "with their beards in their hands."

iii

Pyrrho held his hand close to the flame and burned himself.

He would not grimace or move. We fought with him, pulling him back. We scrabbled in the cinders, holding him by the arms and shoulders.

He was yelling, "We do not know . . . whether the fire . . . is hot! Only . . . that I feel like . . . I'm burning!"

iv

His sister, Philista, came to see me the next day. I was playing my pan-pipes for the goats. It made them docile.

When she stepped around the ruins of a wall, I stopped playing. "The beautiful Philista," I said.

She sat next to me and took my arm. She said, "I am worried about Pyrrho."

"Pyrrho is better."

"He's trying to get wild dogs to bite him."

"What?" I said, rising. "Where?"

"Don't worry. They won't attack. He frightened them. He's running after them, covered with meat and goat's blood."

"What's wrong with him?"

"He says he's trying to lead a new, more beautiful life."

"Fine. Where does the meat come in?"

"He says meat is necessary for love."

"His hand—has he dressed his burned hand?"

"With marinade."

"We have to stop him," I said. "He's not himself."

She held my hand close to her neck. "That's what I told him," she said. "And he said he'd never been himself. He said none of us had ever been ourselves even once."

I found him at the foot of the cliffs, running over the flat plains, screaming at the wild dogs. His skin was ruddy with drying gore. The sky was white. Pyrrho leaped over tussocks of grass and waved his scrawny arms. All along the cliffs, men were winching up sheep on long ropes. Below them, Pyrrho chased the dogs across the plains, yelling at them, demanding that they bite him.

"This is a splendid opportunity!" he screamed, presenting them with his wrists.

Wild dogs were known to attack children. Pyrrho, however, terrified them. They loped in front of him. When a few got far enough away to pause, they looked back out of the sides of their eyes, and their muzzles dipped in embarrassment.

I ran after Pyrrho. He was going to hurt himself. Sheep were suspended in air above him. Men cranked their winches, watching us run.

Pyrrho was yelling something seductive about how being bitten by a crazy dog was true beauty. "The crescent of punctures is symmetrical! I would like to achieve that kind of symmetry all over my face, arms, and legs!"

The dogs were growing distant now, far away across the grassy plains. I was gaining on him.

He did not turn back to see I was chasing him. We both could hear the silvery cough of our knees in the grass. He yelled backward, "I don't know who you are, but you can't gag glory. I'm running across plains of grass, feeling motion, and these goddamn dogs have got to turn on me sometime."

As I got closer, he stumbled and almost twisted an ankle. I could see that his hand was red with burns.

He kept running, a slight limp in his left leg. He said, "Punctures don't matter. So I bleed. What's the difference between outside and inside?"

"Pyrrho," I said, "stop."

"It's all an illusion," he said.

I threw myself through the air and landed on him, bringing him down.

He tried to hit me, but I was stronger than he was. I held him down.

I was on top. We were stacked in the grass.

Up above us, the sheep swayed on their ropes, black against the sky, white against the black of shale.

vi

We sat near one of the cranes, watching a sheep get lifted and rotated. The winch creaked. The shepherd paid us no regard. Pyrrho shielded his eyes from the sun; the goat's blood was caking on his pale chest.

I sat next to him on a fallen bust of owl-eyed Demeter.

I said, "You were the boy who thought long and hard. You wanted to be a philosopher. Things made sense to you, and we listened to what you said. You were the first to shave. None of us would hold a knife to our throats. The knife to you was just a logical extension of the hand. It was a means, and once you described it to us, we were not afraid. You make sense. Perfect sense. That is Pyrrho."

Pyrrho lay back on the marble, his head turned away from me, his arms thrown out to the sides.

I said, "I'm trying to remind you of who you are."

Pyrrho did not stir. He was striped with gore.

I said, "When the rest of us fought in the plains, you stood to the side and told us the meaning of fists. When we lifted up cattle, you explained to us the meaning of weight. You calculated the distance to the sun. You proved to us that the gods are short. We always listen to you. We sit in a circle and listen. Pyrrho speaks wisdom. That is who Pyrrho is."

He pinched himself. "Then who is this?" he asked.

I reached for his hand to pull him up.

He offered the burned hand.

I would not take it.

He looked at me, and in his glare was the disdain reserved for friends who offer aid, and who, through their very generosity, reveal that they are nothing but sidekicks, weaklings, winking traitors, and clowns.

vii

A few days later, Pyrrho showed up on the hilltop with a new boyfriend, named Dipsus. Dipsus was thin, weak, and stupid. He had patches of fur on his face, and was covered with lumps and cuts from fights he had started and lost.

"This is Dipsus," said Pyrrho. "I'm in love with him. My heart is ravished with his charms."

Pyrrho, clearly, was making another extraordinary investigation into Beauty.

Still, I thought, it is not the outward beauty, but the inward beauty, that is of highest value. Perhaps this unassuming youth has a lyrical soul.

Pyrrho said, "Dipsus and I philosophize together."

Dipsus snorted long and hard, hawked matter onto the grass, and said, "You ever wondered how you keep blowing stuff out of your nose, but you never have to put stuff back in?"

"So true," said Pyrrho. "So very true."

Dipsus said, "I think of things like that all the time. I'm the kind of shepherd that ends up turning out to be someone else's son switched at birth, and then he rules the known world. And then I'll bash up everyone I want."

"Splendid," said Pyrrho.

No one else really knew what to say.

I held out my hand. I said, "Any friend of Pyrrho's is a friend of ours."

Dipsus sprang back. "Don't you try that on Dipsus, buttermouth! Wham! I'm as strong as three men!" He stumbled backward and fell onto a goat. He slapped the goat and scrambled upright, fists ready.

Pyrrho said, "I was thinking Dipsus could join us for an evening of bucolic tale-telling and sitting by the fire."

"Forget it," said Dipsus. "I'm going to go home and bowl with my mom."

He stalked off into the tall grasses.

"Pyrrho," said Thyonicus, "he's a somewhat unusual choice."

Pyrrho raised his hands. "What is the difference between the behavior of one animal and another? From a distance, there's little to distinguish an embrace from a throttling, a caress from a slap."

Thyonicus suggested, "Well, there is the way Dipsus smells."

"Oh, smell, smell, smell," said Pyrrho. "What is smell? When I was sick, I smelled corpses and the rich odor of feasts. But it didn't mean anything. I smelled glazed piglet."

"I like pig," said my discus-thrower, who, for all his excellent qualities, was not very bright.

Somewhat ashamed of his comment, I turned back to the leather balls we were stitching. I didn't look up when Pyrrho walked away.

We all kept stitching, but glanced at one another, frowning, over the stitches; we spoke no more of what had happened.

viii

The next day, we were walking through the swamps to go to market. We had to walk single file on planks that were balanced unsteadily on tussocks. Pyrrho was whistling a victory song for Dipsus. There were twelve of us, and several mules.

Far ahead of me, I heard a cry, and swearing.

Our friend Anaxarchus had slipped and fallen into the mire. His toga was soaked, and he struggled. He clutched at the planks and tried to draw himself up.

Pyrrho kept whistling. He kept walking.

"Pyrrho," gasped Anaxarchus, coughing up brackish water. "Hand up? . . . Pyrrho?"

Pyrrho did not look at his friend. He walked on.

"Pyrrho," I called, trying to work my way on the planks past a pack-mule. "Pyrrho—could you grab him?"

Pyrrho sang, as if to no one, "Who knows what really exists?"

I was struggling with the mule. I scrambled past it, finally slithering on my knees. I ran up to Anaxarchus and took his spattered hands.

I started to yank him from the water. He was snapping his teeth and retching.

Ahead of us, Pyrrho walked on, singing, as if idly, "All perception is a swamp."

I pulled Anaxarchus onto a mound of dried grasses. He was green with weed. He clutched at his chest and coughed. I asked him if he was all right, and he said, "Yes."

"Pyrrho!" I called. "He might have died!" And to Anaxarchus, I said, "He's unbelievable."

"I know," said Anaxarchus. His eyes were big, and he gazed after our friend. "He's amazing."

"Him?"

"Pyrrho—he's incredible."

"For leaving you in the swamp?"

"It's an act of will," said Anaxarchus. "That's what it means to be human in the full bronze flesh. Marble. Alabaster." He called after Pyrrho, "Bravo! Bravo!"

Feeling somewhat irritated, I pointed out, "I'm the one who saved you."

"Exactly," said Anaxarchus. "You gave in. He knew that it doesn't make any difference whether the sack that's Anaxarchus sinks or swims."

When we got to market, Anaxarchus bought Pyrrho some ice for licking.

Pyrrho threw it at a mule.

Two nights later, we found him cut by the river and brought him home bleeding. We wrapped his arm in cloth, tightly, to grip the blood in the body. We dragged him through the door of their hut into candlelight.

Philista, his sister, grabbed at the beads around her neck when she saw him.

"Pyrrho!" she cried, and ran to his side. "Oh—what has—"

"It is an investigation into the nature of solidity and matter."

"His forearm," I said.

"With some metal he found in the brook," said Thyonicus.

"Oh Pyrrho—This . . ." said Philista, leading him to sit. She was shaking.

He said, "I want to determine what is Pyrrho and what is not. Am I unitary or made of pieces? If I remove a hand, is it still me?"

"With metal you found in a brook?" his sister said.

She held on to him, weeping.

"I find it peculiar," said Pyrrho, "that we inhabit space."

His father was watching. His beard looked pale, and his lips, weak. He went to Pyrrho and gently unwrapped the arm.

"Pyrrho," said his father, "this is awful. This does not look good."

"It makes you wonder," said Pyrrho, "why one finds metal in a brook. The world is bountiful."

"Get him some cool wine," said the father, and we did, from a jug, and he drank.

"Here is some bread," said Philista.

"Drink more of the wine," said the father.

Pyrrho's sister was perched to one side of him. She held on to her beads. His father sat on the other side. Philista's head was on her brother's shoulder. Their father put his arm roughly around the boy. It was awkward, because they were in a line.

"Pyrrho," he said, "don't you know how much we love you?"

"I love you," said Philista. "You are my brother."

The endearments embarrassed us. We went out into the night. We could see the fires of the shepherds in distant bracken. We walked toward a hilltop.

Heat rose off the grain.

Through the wall, we could hear the father plead. "My God. Why? Never mind. We don't care, Pyrrho, boy. Pyrrho-kin. We will always love you."

We could hear Pyrrho reply, "I don't even know what that means. There is no substance in 'always.' There is no substance in love."

We walked onward so we would not have to hear more.

X

"Pyrrho will destroy himself." It was known by all. The word passed among us, that summer of our sixteenth year.

There was an inevitability to it, and yet we tried to stop it. At all times, one or another of us, his disciples, found reason to be with him. He lay in front of carts. He would not stop hassling bees. He walked into the sea and had to be dragged to the shore. "Pyrrho will destroy himself." He closed his eyes and walked across clay rooftops, daring substance to give out beneath him. We put up our hands for him to walk upon so he would not fall. "Pyrrho will destroy himself." He ate rocks and slivers of metal, even urchins. His lips were cut. The rocks went down. The metal and urchins stuck like burrs. We forced open his jaws and took out shards.

On other days, he would sit near our hut and refuse to move in from the sun. His skin empurpled as the days grew longer.

I sat by him and dribbled water on his crisping skin.

He drank other things—I don't know what—things that

made him scream and clutch his stomach and throw up blood. He said that pain was just a sensation, like light. The locusts buzzed. I sat with him in the night, after he vomited. We could hear the bleating of sheep. I said, "Pyrrho, you must stop."

He said, "The philosopher Empedocles jumped into the volcano at Aetna to prove he was a god."

I asked, "What happened?"

"He wasn't," said Pyrrho, looking at the horizon.

So it went on. We came upon him tied to a stake, being hit by Dipsus. He was weak from the sunburn, hardly a human at all. His jaw rarely closed now. We pulled Dipsus away. We untied Pyrrho and took him home. His sister no longer wept.

When Pyrrho was out, Philista sat and wove in their stone hut. Her father lingered by the door and did not work. He touched his face with his fingertips, poking the flesh, searching for fruit-rot. He progressed across his cheeks slowly.

"Go plow," said Philista.

"I can't plow," said Pyrrho's father. "Out there, I keep looking back toward the house."

"He's not here," said Philista.

The father said, "When I'm in the field, I feel like I've left something at home. Something I need in my bag. I keep looking this way. It's just the house."

"Turn to your chores," said Philista.

"I'm waiting. That's my chore. It's a matter of time."

"His friends are with him," I said. "We'll take care of him."

In the darkness inside the hut, the father stared at me. I could not abide his glare, and so I dropped my gaze. We stood, the two of us, in the shadows, while Philista wove her cloth between us. The walls were stone and caulked with light. I scratched in the dirt with my heel.

"I marched on Thebes with the army," said Pyrrho's father. "I carried a spear and a shield. I climbed the walls. Do you understand?"

"This is not something you did to Pyrrho," soothed Philista. "You did nothing."

The father demanded of me, "Do you think he is in danger? What has he told you?"

I did not know what to answer. I said, "He told me the philosopher Empedocles jumped into Mount Aetna to prove that he was a god."

"How do they know Empedocles wasn't a god?" argued the father. "He might have been."

I said, "They found his slipper in the lava."

"How do they know it was his?"

"Empedocles," I said, "wore bronze slippers."

"Go and plow," said Philista. "I'll stay here."

Her father sagged back against the door frame. "He was a tender boy," he said. "There must be something that can heal him. He smiles. He . . ."

We did not move until Pyrrho came home.

We heard him outside, later that afternoon, playing a game with some small children of the neighborhood, something that involved stones on a track drawn in the dirt. He hunkered among the children, no taller than them, sketching with a stick while they each took their turn.

There was a shiftless feeling among us all. None of us could work.

We were all busy waiting.

xi

"Pyrrho will destroy himself." We wept in advance. He would not eat. His skin was loose and covered with wounds. He could not walk. He crawled toward cliffs as if they were not there. We dragged him back. He left furrows from the heels of his hands. When we set him down, he crawled again.

One day, he arranged for Dipsus to bury him in mud.

When nothing but his head showed, he screamed obscenities at his friend, daring him to fling dirt in the mouth and cram scum up the nose and be done with it, be done with it all. Dipsus said, "You're stupid," and walked away. "I hope you get— I hope you find some worms that will be your friends and boon-companions, because from me, you're not even getting dirt up your nose." Dipsus splashed in the shallows of the motionless river as he walked away.

I sat next to Pyrrho's head on the mudflats. The reeds blew in the summer wind.

"What is height?" said Pyrrho's head. "Do you see? How tall am I?"

"Pyrrho," I said, "for someone who doubts whether matter exists, you try to put an awful lot of it in your mouth."

"I doubt even whether everything is an illusion," he said. "I confirm or deny nothing."

"Do you see how your sister cries when you come home?"

"I confirm or deny nothing."

"Your father has stopped watching the flocks."

"Reality or vapor?"

"We are your friends."

"I doubt even whether I doubt."

"Pyrrho—"

"I confirm or deny nothing," he said, before I scrabbled down in the dirt in front of him, planting my knees by either cheek, and grabbed his proud, smirking little mouth in my hand and with my other hand gripped his nose, and I would not let him breathe; and at first, I thought, *This is a lesson,* but it was not a lesson, because though I was crying, at the same time I was telling him how much I hated him, and yanking the head back and forth until I knew it hurt. He could not move his limbs to stop me. They were buried in mud, and he was weak.

I jerked the head and spat in his hair. His neck popped. I

clamped my hands more firmly. The face fought me. It wanted air. The lips were against my hand, writhing. The head jacked back, trying to draw breath.

"Here is all of it!" I was yelling to him, without understanding. "This is it! Can you eat it all at once?"

The eyes were wide. He was trying to see my face. I would not let him. I put the face in the mud and pressed it there. When it started to rise, gagging, I crouched and kicked the back of his head with my heel, kicked it and held his head down in the mud. He was nothing then, nothing but an oval of dirty strands with a heel atop it in the midst of mudflats where the rushes blew.

That was it, then. The end of Pyrrho's philosophy. A hairy oval in the flats. And I was done, and stepped to the side.

The others came toward us and cried out.

I guess they took my arms. They led me—I don't know. I was sitting down.

They scooped at the mud. I cried, cradled in the arms of my discus-thrower, complaining of what had been done to me.

Pyrrho reached out his gaunt hand to claw at my ankle. He was watching me with wide eyes.

Things smelled like old rinds. The grass itself smelled of mildew. I withdrew my leg so Pyrrho could not reach me.

In the vivid silence of the mud plains, I scraped at my discus-player's chest with my dirty hands. There was the sensation of falling, though I sat on wet dirt.

They asked me what I was doing, who I thought I was.

I could not answer.

We do not know what a body is, except in a position. We cannot picture a body without a stance. When we think of ourselves, it is not a clean self, for we are lying or stooped or standing or weeping or gagging for breath. I do not know whether there is such a thing as a body at all, or just a procession of forms; and I do not know, once we were discovered, what I did with my hands.

That night, on our hilltop, we stared at the sky, which was full of the revolving gods. Dipsus fed Pyrrho grapes. Menalcus and my discus-thrower went down to the river to skip stones. I lay outside the circle with my hands by my sides.

"This is a strong time," said Pyrrho.

The last of the locusts called in the bushes.

I did not know how to answer him, or who would explain to me even how to start.

Fifteen Going On . . .

Megan McCafferty

fifteen

Hope will be gone in fifteen minutes.

Hope is not my best friend. She cannot possibly be my best friend. That's what my mother is saying to me in her tightest pursed-lipped tone.

"She cannot possibly be your best friend, Jessica Lynn Darling."

"Jessica Lynn Darling" always defines declarations of importance. And Hope being my best friend is a first-middle-last-name impossibility for one reason: My mother likes Bridget better.

"When did Bridget stop being your best friend?"

Bridget and I stopped being best friends around the same time she became so much more than just the prettiest towhead in the sandbox, on the swing set, at the Brownie meeting. She's now an intolerable blonde who bitches and moans about modeling for mail-order catalogs because she finds it "unsatisfying." If she thinks *that* is unsatisfying, she should try life as the Class Brainiac with a Caucasian fro and a bra that could serve better as an outie belly-button protector.

Bridget should try being me.

Bridget still lives across the street from me, as she has for all of my fifteen-going-on-sixteen-going-on-sixty years. Therefore, in my mother's mind, Bridget is still my best friend. This was true enough through sixth grade, a time when the ties that bind were indeed determined by who lived across the street from you or who sat next to you on the five-minute bus ride to school. But things changed once we hit middle school and Bridget became the type of girl guys wanted to get naked, while I remained the type of girl guys ignored unless they needed to copy geometry proofs. Things changed, whether my mother wants to believe it or not. And she definitely does not.

I'm tired of talking to her, so I decide to let my mother think that Hope's departure is yet another example of how I take things too seriously.

"You're right, Mom. Bridget is my best friend. I feel much better now."

I stomp upstairs to very self-consciously sulk. I want attention, but not from Mom.

From who, then?

fourteen

My mother assumes she knows everything about my social life. Not that there's much to tell when you've got only one friend you don't hate, and your first and last kiss was a Jell-O–tongued travesty that occurred precisely 698 days ago and is unlikely to repeat itself anytime soon. So, for a lack of anything else going on, if Hope and I were *really* that tight, my mother would certainly know all the ins and outs about it, right?

But the building of a friendship isn't something one chronicles like a documentarian narrating the assimilation with local natives: *The potential best friend and I are interacting in a comfortable social atmosphere for approximately 2.5 hours daily. We will increase it to three hours next week. By mid-November the transmutation from acquaintances to best friends will be complete.*

No. It didn't work like that. Hope and I didn't even

acknowledge our friendship to each other. We would never write a big fat *BFF!!!* on any of the bizillion notes we exchanged detailing all the many things that were wrong with everyone who wasn't us.

The notes came after the eye-rolling, the mutual, synchronized eye-rolling at the lunch table whenever Bridget and my other so-called friends, Manda and Sara, discussed their version of current events, i.e., how many calories were in a mouthful of ejaculate, or whether a toothbrush or an index finger was the most effective binge-and-purge method, to be used, presumably, if the answer to the former was more than could be found in a shot of peppermint schnapps.

It was our mutual, synchronized eye-rolling that said, "I hate them, too."

Hope is the type of person who instantly makes everyone comfortable. Even with all the eye-rolling and notes, I doubted she felt as strongly about the friendship as I did.

That is, until one summer sleepover before freshman year when the Clueless Crew was at cheerleading camp and it was just the two of us at her kitchen table. This didn't happen often. Her older brother, Heath, was often grounded, and therefore a semi-permanent fixture in the Weaver household. But on this night he was out with his friends, a pack of heavy-lidded boys in musty flannel and trampled jeans who smelled like tobacco juice and stood too close on purpose and made me sweat with nervousness and something else, something I definitely hadn't felt during that one and only kiss.

Together, alone, we could be ourselves. And so Hope and I ate canned pineapple rings covered in whipped cream and rainbow sprinkles because we were starving and really wanted ice cream sundaes but Mrs. Weaver hadn't gone food shopping in ages.

"You know what I'm afraid of even though I know it's stupid and irrational?"

Hope's question made me contemplate the source of what, at the time, were my most recent stupid, irrational fears: the huge underground zit on my chin. My blood pulsed through the bulge so it had a heartbeat—it had taken on a life of its own. Part of me thought that it wasn't acne related, but indisputable evidence that a species of intergalactic pod people had chosen to colonize right on my face.

Or, I thought, it could be the humble beginnings of a three-hundred-pound, Jabba the Hutt–looking tumor, like the one I'd watched a woman have surgically removed on the Learning Channel.

Or, as a third, even more stupid and irrational variation of the same fear, it could be a buba. I learned in history class that bubas were the red, bulbous cysts that marked the first stage of the bubonic plague. Oozing always followed the throbbing. When the bubas dried up and turned black—the third stage—your medieval ass was doomed. You were dead within thirty-six hours, and not even the lowliest peasant would dare come close. No one so much as covered you with a sheet. No respect for the departed. You just rotted and stank. Alone for eternity.

There was no way that Hope's fears could be as bizarre as my pimple paranoias, but I was eager to find out for sure.

"What?" I asked.

She stuck the spoon into the center of a pineapple ring, then pushed her flame-colored corkscrews out of her face.

"I'm afraid that if I use a tampon, it will somehow free itself from my vaginal canal and float around my body until I die of Toxic Shock Syndrome."

I laughed so hard that I fell smack on the linoleum. When I quieted down, Hope said something that let me know that our friendship was not one-sided, as I had feared.

"Now you know what you're getting into, being best friends with me."

thirteen

I look up at the Sophomore Friendship Shrine that borders my bed. The pictures are all relatively recent, of Hope and me from spur-of-the-moment sleepover photo sessions. Me, red in the face, doing a headstand. Hope, eyes shut, in mid-gyration, doing her best booty-shaking Britney imitation. These pictures often make us wonder what possessed us to pose in all our pajamaed splendor in the first place. They are both hideous and hilarious, and for that reason, I love them. They make me feel like I fit in at Pineville High even when I don't and never will because the size of my brain and my boobs are in inverse proportion to what's required for popularity.

I'll want to look at the pictures later. But not now. I don't want to be forced to look at me and Hope and all the fun we've had together. The Sophomore Friendship Shrine doesn't create the proper moping atmosphere, and that's precisely what I need right now. I look at my watch, and sigh loud and deep for no one's benefit but my own.

I don't want to ask for a ride. This is not a time to ask my mother for favors. Years from now, I don't want her saying, "Remember that day I drove you to that girl's house for your final farewell? What was her name again?" I don't want her becoming part of this moment that should be between only Hope and me.

Even though it's sub-zero, I decide to run because right now Hope is the closest she'll be to me for, well, *ever,* and I'll never be able to run to her house again. It's only five-tenths of a mile away. We measured it on the odometer in my mom's Volvo when we were trying to persuade her that it wasn't too far for me to walk or run by myself in the post-dinnertime darkness. Half a mile is close enough for me to get there in about three minutes, but far enough for the Pineville zoning

Nazis to have put us into two different elementary schools, keeping us apart for the first twelve years of our lives for no good reason at all.

I lace up my sneakers and dart out the door before my mother tries to make me feel better by reminding me that when I'm older I will look back on all of this and laugh, laugh, laugh as hard as I did that day on the cool linoleum floor.

twelve

I am running. My lungs seize with each freezy breath, but I like the sharpness of the pain.

It's a very melodramatic touch.

Though I can usually tune out everything around me, today it seems that whichever way my head turns, my eyes settle on something that somehow relates back to the thing I don't want to think about. As I pass the kiddie park, for example, I see the bench where Manda went down on a senior third-stringer on the football team before this year's Homecoming dance. It was a bet. The guy got a case of beer and Manda got a new private nickname from Hope and me: the Bench-warmer.

Manda revealed her sin to Hope during a drunken confessional through the stall walls of the girls' bathroom. Manda would tell things to Hope that she wouldn't even share with the other members of the Clueless Crew. To her credit, Hope kept her secret, which is to say, she only told me. We both decided that if we couldn't dodge Manda—and we couldn't, though we tried—the least we could do was avoid sitting on that bench. I was still pissed at Manda for ruining my park for me.

"If she's going to be a skank—"

"And she will," Hope interrupted, but not in the annoying

way that Sara does. Sara interrupts because she thinks whatever she has to say is more important than anything I could possibly say. Hope interrupts because what she has to say is the same as what I would say, that is, if Hope hasn't already said it.

"Then why does she have to do it in the place that holds so many happy childhood memories for me?"

Hope was quiet for a moment, and in the silence she doodled a cuter, caricaturized version of me, with smoother hair and a way-too-wide smile on my face. Then she put down her pen and said, "Your memories are your own."

"So?"

She shook her head, as if it were a no-brainer.

"Only *you* can wreck them," she explained. "Or not."

eleven

I'm running faster now, but still slow enough to notice a blur of Milwaukee's Best beer cans precariously piled in a curbside recycling bin. It reminds me that tonight is New Year's Eve. Tonight, the Clueless Crew and everyone else will get trashed to celebrate surviving the turn of the new century. Everyone else, that is, except the Weavers, who have chosen this monumental night of all nights to embark on the first leg of their journey toward a new life. If this doesn't tell you everything you need to know about Hope's parents, nothing does.

I doubt that Y2K will bring the apocalypse in the form of earthquakes and locusts, but my world is definitely coming to an end, albeit in a more subtle but no less devastating way.

High-school students get drunk. Even the ones in the honors classes, like me. I try not to feel bad about it every time I do it, which isn't often. But even with my participation in planned bouts of drunkenness, I still don't feel like I'm having the time of my life that is promised to me in all the teen sex comedies of the eighties golden era.

Tonight will bring many bonding moments thanks to Beast and Boone's Farm. I am expected to do the chugalug love thing, too, especially now that I have a reason to drown my sorrows. Parties always depress me, and I have no reason to think that tonight's will be any different. I hate watching piss-drunk Prince Charmings hit on girls less aesthetically attractive than I am, but dumber, thereby making them somehow more *overall* attractive than I am. These guys think they're being funny and clever when they use ironic pickup lines that not so deep down, they really mean.

That's a nice sweater, but it will look even better on my floor tomorrow morning. . . . Are you tired? Because you've been running through my mind all night. . . . What's your favorite letter of the alphabet? Mine's U, baby. . . . Are those space pants? Because your ass is out of this world. . . . Your father must be a thief because he stole the stars from heaven and put them in your eyes. . . .

Hope made me realize that I wasn't the only one who hated parties. But she had different reasons, ones I wouldn't understand until later, until it was too late.

ten

I glance at the watch again. Ten minutes left. *Tentententen.* The number sounds in my head with the pound of each foot on the pavement. *Tentententen.*

I think of the Top 10 lists Hope and I compiled to make our boring Pineville afternoons less so: The Top 10 Things That Went Wrong with Jessica's First Kiss (#1: Squeegee!); The Top 10 Reasons Why Pineville Sucks That Don't Seem to Bother Anyone Else (#1: Six liquor emporiums and zero bookstores); The Top 10 Advantages of Being a Virgin (#1: You can buy a VW Beetle with all the money saved on abortions).

I remember our last list: The Top 10 People We Ranked On

in Our Last Phone Conversation Even Though We Know It's Really Bad for Our Karma but We Can't Help Doing It Anyway Because They Annoy Us So Goddamn Much.

"Shouldn't the Clueless Crew be designated as numbers one through three?" I had asked, ever the follower of rules and regulations.

"No," Hope replied. "They get the top spot because they're one person with three heads."

"Like one-third of a Hydra," I said.

"Right," she said. "The Sara head shuts guys up."

"The Bridget head turns guys on," I said.

"And the Manda head sucks guys off!"

This last line was said simultaneously, which would have been miraculous if it didn't happen all the time. We had elevated the concept of Us vs. Them to an art form. An admittedly immature one, but an art form nonetheless.

nine

I'm not running anymore. I'm sitting, sweaty and sad, on the curb outside Hope's house. In nine minutes, it will be forever referred to as the House That Used to Be Hope's House. I'm shivering because it's cold, but for other reasons, too.

I want a passerby to notice me and ask why I am sitting there looking so pathetic.

I want to talk to someone about Hope.

I want to talk about why she's my best friend.

I want to talk about how she's the only person at Pineville High, in the world even, who understands what I say and why I say it and how Hope would appreciate my pursuit of the proper moping atmosphere and how it *is* possible to create a lifelong bond in less than four years and how I'm afraid that calls and e-mails will start out strong and slowly fade away because she will be much better at moving on than I will and how I hate us having to call and e-mail each other at all, instead of being able to just pop by each other's houses unannounced and how Hope would totally understand why I might get drunk with the Clueless Crew tonight and not hold it against me even though she has more than one reason to and how unfair it is that Hope's parents are moving to Tennessee because her brother died of a heroin overdose in New Jersey and how they think that she will be spared the same fate if they take her away from here, from me.

I want to talk about how this idiotic parental logic proves that I know their daughter better than they do.

eight

But no one passes by.

seven

I imagine Hope in her room, still packing even though her parents have warned her to be ready to go. She is totally unaware that I am sitting on her curb, fewer than fifty yards away, but senses I am nearby.

We spent our last night at Helga's Diner, a hole-in-the-strip-mall kind of place that is still undiscovered by the rest of our class. It's our favorite getaway, where we escape to Patsy Cline, coffee, strawberry pancakes, and tales of love gone wrong from our favorite waitress, Thelma. At one A.M., after six hours and enough caffeine to guarantee that both of us are hyper-awake until the *next* millennium, my mom dragged us out of our booth and drove us back to our respective homes. Thelma was relieved when we left, saying she couldn't take any more crying and carrying on from her two favorite customers.

Before she got out of the car, Hope reminded me to stop by her room before she left. And that's when I told her that I might not be able to make it because I had, uh . . . *something* to do with my mom. Hope accepted this, the lamest of excuses, knowing it was a lie, knowing like best friends know things. And so she got out of the car quickly, before my mother could embarrass both of us by loudly announcing that she had no idea what I was talking about.

Hope understood why I needed to lie, and why I'd spend our last moments avoiding the one person I wanted to be with. She knew I was afraid of showing up at her house early and just sitting there, silently watching her pack, getting all emotional over a Jane's Addiction T-shirt or a half-empty box of Tampax.

And I know this now: that if I'd had the nerve to tell her what I was thinking, Hope would've laughed—a loud, nasal, spitty laugh—before pointing out the obvious.

"Jessica," she would've said. "The box is half full."

six

"Jessie?"

Hope's mom calls out to me from the front porch. Mrs. Weaver is a shorter, faded version of Hope. She's wearing a pair of too-blue jeans and a too-new sweatshirt revealed beneath an unbuttoned too-puffy coat. Her husband is wearing the masculine version of the same outfit. These are moving clothes bought especially for the occasion.

"Why are you sitting out here, dear?"

Her words hang in the air as icy puff-puff-puffs.

Mr. Weaver also sees me but gives only a halfhearted kind of wave. He knows I blame them for this.

"I'm . . ."

I can't think of anything logical to say, so I just stand up and walk toward them.

"We were expecting you here earlier," she says.

Mrs. Weaver looks nervous, as if she knows the move could

save Hope in a way she couldn't save her only son, yet, at the same time, could contribute to the shocking chain of events that will eventually turn me into a Jersey Shore crack whore.

"Uh . . ." I say, glancing at the U-Haul parked in the driveway.

"We're supposed to be leaving in a few minutes, but you know Hope. . . ."

Yes, I know Hope. Better than anyone. Better than *you*.

"You should go on up there now," she says. "See if you can get her moving. . . ."

You're moving just fine without my help. One thousand miles away . . .

"We still want to leave on time. . . ."

I look at my watch. *Tick tick tick.*

Now I have to see Hope, but not because Mrs. Weaver told me to. I have to see her because *not* seeing her doesn't make any sense anymore. Not that it ever did.

five

When I walk in her room, Hope is lying on top of a pile of clothes she has yet to shove in her suitcase. A floral granny dress. A beaded cashmere sweater. A patchwork denim jacket. She's on her back with her legs flipped up and over her head, so the toes of her beat-up Chuck Taylors are touching the carpet in back of her. She speaks to me through her knees.

"Hey," Hope says.

"Hey," I say.

"I'm distracted," Hope says.

This doesn't surprise me. Hope can focus about as well as an ADD-addled zygote. Whenever Hope and I studied together, she was astonished that I could be silent for more than two minutes without sharing a random observation like:

"Frosted Pop-Tarts have ten fewer calories than regular Pop-Tarts."

Or:

"There's a town in Arkansas called Toad Suck and people actually live there."

Or:

"I only have hair on my big toe."

And so on.

All non sequiturs were followed by, "What's up with *that*?!" And no matter how many times I'd shrug in ignorance, she'd still look at me expectantly, thinking I might have an explanation for all these things that made no sense at all.

"I'm distracted, too," I reply long enough after her initial comment to illustrate my point.

And then it gets too quiet.

"I have to go," I say, though I just got there and I'm not the one who has to go anywhere. I just can't be there, knowing that she will soon be gone.

Hope rolls her legs forward and looks almost surprised for a second.

"Most people would want to take a picture right now," she says.

"With plastered-on, toothpaste-commercial grins."

"When we don't feel like smiling at all."

"Exactly."

I would never add a fake momento like that to the Sophomore Friendship Shrine.

four

I hug Hope. Her arms hang long and limp at her sides as if they have—independent from the rest of her body—fallen into a deep slumber. A few seconds into the hug she wakes them up and clumsily returns the gesture. I've caught her off guard. I've never hugged her before, not even after Heath died.

I regret the hug immediately. We've never been touchy-feely friends, unlike the Clueless Crew, who make a huge production out of kissing one another hello with a wet MWAH! smacking sound just to show everyone how tight they really are. Hugging Hope at that moment, to me, is the first of many changes that will occur between us with her there and me here, changes we won't seek out but that will happen anyway, whether we want them to or not.

"I'm sorry we're moving right before your sweet sixteen," she says after dropping her arms out of our bungled embrace.

My birthday is in nineteen days.

"Bitter," I correct.

"Bitter sixteen," she repeats, but quieter.

Neither of us laugh at the joke.

"I have your present," she says, handing me a flat, rectangular package wrapped in white tissue paper. "But don't open it until your birthday."

"Sure," I croak. "Now I have something to look forward to."

This comes out sounding more loserish than I had intended. Hope's face caves in on itself.

"Don't worry about my birthday," I say, steadying my voice as I look around the room for the last time. "Because I really don't care."

Hope is trying very hard to put her face back together.

"Really," I say.

Then I turn and walk out the door, letting it close by itself.

We make a point not to say good-bye because this isn't really good-bye. Or so we silently promise ourselves, anyway.

three

I pause outside Hope's door, thinking about the words "I don't care."

Hope more than anyone knows that I *do* care about my

sixteenth birthday, as I always have since seeing the Molly Ringwald movie that promised the fulfillment of my most important blow-out-the-candles wishes on that day. I care about turning sixteen because I have a tendency to care too much about everything. But I claimed not to care because I had to say *something* and it was the first thing that came to mind. If I had taken the time to dig deeper, I would've started to cry. And I don't have time to cry. I don't have time to be sad. I have to get psyched up for a New Year's Eve party I don't want to go to.

Even though I really need something to look forward to, I stop in her driveway and tear the tissue paper off the package she's just given me. In my hands, I see Hope and me rendered in bits and pieces of magazine pages. Hope carefully cut and glued each scrap in a mosaic recreation of a toothy, goofy photo taken at that pineapple-and-whipped-cream sleepover. Browns, reds, greens, blues, and too many colors to count, tiny like the confetti that will be thrown all wild and *WHOO-HOO!* into the air when the clock strikes midnight.

I don't know what else to say about it but this: It is the coolest thing I've ever seen and will permanently replace all the photos on the Sophomore Friendship Shrine.

I am stunned to tears. I look up through watery eyes to see Hope laughing at me in the window. She mouths the words, "I knew you'd open it."

And I knew she'd watch me.

two

I walk, slowly and alone, staring down at the bricks beneath my feet. I watch them turn to gravel, the gravel turn to grass, and concentrate on each step. I enjoy the quiet and wonder how long it will last. How long *I* will last.

A shrill blond voice shouts hello from a distance, but I don't acknowledge it. She's too late. I don't feel like talking

about Hope anymore. The moment has passed. So I won't
vent to Mom when I get home, or to the Clueless Crew at the
party, or to anyone else, ever.

one

I've just left behind the only person who would know exactly
what to say.

acknowledgments

Many thanks go out to:

My agent and dear friend, Joanna Pulcini, who has my deepest respect for helping me keep it together when everything was falling apart.

My editor, Kristin Kiser, for being so cool about my ever-changing book ideas. And her assistant, Ellen Rubinstein, for helping execute said ideas with marvelous, miraculous aplomb.

All the incredibly talented contributors, whose passionate responses to my proposal made this book what it is.

My peeps—especially Monica, Jeannie, and Erika—for reminding me of who I was and who I still am.

The Fitzmorris and McCafferty families, for their continued unconditional support.

Collin James, whose unparalleled exuberance made me reevaluate my career plans for the first year of motherhood so it included this book.

Christopher Joseph, for giving me love, encouragement, and—most important—sleep when I needed it most.

about the contributors

Steve Almond's story collection, *My Life in Heavy Metal* (Grove, 2002), is out in paperback. His stories have been anthologized in the *Pushcart Prize 2003, Best New Stories from the South, Best of Zoetrope, Best American Erotica,* and elsewhere. His new book, *Candyfreak: A Journey Through the Chocolate Underbelly of America*, is just out from Algonquin. It's a non-fiction project about obscure candy bars. He cowrote *Which Brings Me to You: A Novel in Confessions* with Julianna Baggott, also to be published by Algonquin. For more information, check out www.stevenalmond.com.

The inspiration for "The Day I Turned Chickenhearted": "Everything you are in life, you are at sixteen. Only more."

M. T. Anderson is the author of three novels for teens and several books for children. His most recent novel, *Feed* (Candlewick Press, 2002), won the Los Angeles Times Book Award and was a finalist for both the National Book Award and the Boston Globe/Horn Book Award.

The inspiration for "The Mud and Fever Dialogues": "Pyrrho, Empedocles, and Anaxarchus were all real philosophers; this story is based loosely on stories of their lives and teachings. Though Pyrrho could never be convinced that the universe actually existed, he lived to the ripe old age of ninety."

Julianna Baggott is the author of the national bestselling novel *Girl Talk* (Pocket Books, 2001), *The Miss America Family* (Pocket Books, 2002), and *The Madam* (Atria Books, 2003), as well as a book of poems entitled *This Country of Mothers* (Southern Illinois University Press, 2001). She has also contributed dozens of short stories and poems to such publications as *Ms.*, *Poetry*, and *Best American Poetry 2000*, and has read her work on NPR's *Talk of the Nation*. Her next book, *Which Brings Me to You: A Novel in Confessions* was cowritten with Steve Almond and will be published by Algonquin. She is currently working on her first novel for young adults, *The Anybodies*.

The inspiration for "The Future Lives of Emily Milty": "My own life didn't inspire my short story. I don't find my own life very inspiring, which in some ways is a lot like my character, Emily Milty, which makes the first statement ironic. My memories of sixteen are blurry, but that's probably because I was partially blinded by eyeliner and my nauseous infatuation with Paul 'Augie' Augustine."

Cat Bauer's first novel, *Harley, Like a Person* (Winslow, 2000), was an American Library Association Best Book for Young Adults, a Quick Pick for Reluctant Readers, and a Popular Paperback. It was also selected as a Booklist Top Ten Youth First Novel, a Bookreporter Top Ten Teen First Novel, and a BookSense 76 Pick. In Europe, *Harley* is published in Danish, as *Harlekindukken*, and in Dutch, as *Harley, Niet de Motor*. A former actress, Cat now lives in Venice, Italy, where she contributes regularly to the *International Herald Tribune*'s Italian supplement. She is also working on her next novel, which spans two continents. Visit her website, www.catbauer.com. "Venetian Fan" is dedicated to Spencer Davis.

The inspiration for "Venetian Fan": "Cold cuts catered by Uncle Phil straight from the meat department at the A&P— that's what I remember about my sixteenth birthday. I was born in July, so I had a pool party. Sunglasses and bathing suits. Girlfriends. Some relatives. Probably my boyfriend showed up. A typical suburban New Jersey scene, nothing like my story. 'Venetian Fan' was inspired by the Titian fresco of St. Christopher in the Palazzo Ducale in Venice, where I now live. I imagined what it would feel like to be alone in a foreign country on your sixteenth birthday—a thrilling, awkward crossroad between childhood and adult."

Tanuja Desai Hidier's first novel, *Born Confused* (Scholastic, 2002), is both a Larry King and a *Sunday Times* (London) book of the week, and an American Library Association Best Book for Young Adults. She has been a recipient of the London Writers Award for fiction as well as the James Jones Fellowship; in 2003 her short story "Tiger, Tiger" was included in the Desilicious anthology (Arsenal Pulp Press). She has also worked as a filmmaker and is the lead singer/songwriter in two bands, one in New York, the other in London. Their CD of original pop/rock/folk songs based on *Born Confused* (including the track that led to this story) is now available. Please visit www.ABCreativeD.com for more information.

The inspiration for "Cowgirls & Indie Boys": "As for Sulekha, sixteen for me was a borderline: neither here nor there yet everywhere. I was so delighted when Megan asked me to contribute to this anthology, as it allowed me to re-explore that epic moment. I'm deeply interested in the idea of borders—physical, mental, sexual—and of home, possibly because as a child of parents who immigrated from South Africa and India (though probably for a lot of people, regardless of where they're from), the idea of home was and is such a complex one. At sixteen add in the fact that your body and mind are in the midst of such massive changes, your very tools to navigate the world need to be mapped anew as well. Sweet? Bitter? All of that, and everything in between."

Sarah Dessen is the author of five novels, including *This Lullaby* (Viking, 2002), a Los Angeles Times Book Prize finalist, and *That Summer* (Orchard, 1996) and *Someone Like You* (Viking, 1998), which were adapted into the 2003 film *How to Deal*. Her latest novel is *The Truth About Forever* (Viking, 2004). She lives in North Carolina. Visit her at www.sarahdessen.com.

The inspiration for "Infinity": "My family has a summer house in Massachusetts, where I first experienced my own rotary panic. Even now, when I approach one, I still have a moment when the whole thing just seems entirely too daunting. So I'd always wanted to write about it. I think getting your license is like a lot of things in adolescence: incredibly liberating and really scary at the same time. New responsibilities always bring new dangers. What really matters, in the end, is how you learn to face them. That's what growing up is all about."

Emma Forrest, a Brit living in Manhattan, began her writing career at age sixteen as a journalist at the *Sunday Times of London*. In the intervening decade she has contributed to numerous publications, from *The Guardian* to *Vogue*, specializing in no-holds-barred interviews with celebrities like Kate Winslet (whom she made cry) and Brad Pitt (who commissioned her to write a script). She is the author of the novels *Namedropper* (Scribner, 2000) and *Thin Skin* (MTV/Pocket, 2003), and her latest novel, *Cherries in the Snow,* to be published by Three Rivers Press.

The inspiration for "The Grief Diet": "'The Grief Diet' was inspired by the dark places you can wander into if you only ever listen to your music through headphones."

David Levithan is the author of *Boy Meets Boy* (Knopf, 2003) and *The Realm of Possibility*, which will be published by Knopf in 2004. He grew up in New Jersey, lives in New Jersey, and just might spend the rest of his life in New Jersey if he's not careful. At age sixteen, he was involved in the fencing team, Junior

Statesmen, Quiz Bowl, and took AP Physics. All of which is pretty funny now. Especially the AP Physics. Visit him at www.davidlevithan.com.

The inspiration for "The Alumni Interview": "I think sixteen is that year when it finally sinks in that you're growing up, that life is changing quickly, that home isn't going to always be home, and that love has a deeper meaning than you ever imagined. For whatever reason, this made me think of alumni interviews—that first nervous step toward college and the future. Intersect that with love and identity, and you have the crossroads of sixteen."

Carolyn Mackler is the author of the acclaimed *The Earth, My Butt, and Other Big Round Things*, a Michael L. Printz Honor Book and an American Library Association Best Book for Young Adults. Her first novel, *Love and Other Four-Letter Words*, was an ALA Quick Pick and an International Reading Association Young Adults' Choice. Her third novel, *Vegan Virgin Valentine*, will be published by Candlewick Press. Carolyn lives with her husband in New York City. Visit her online at www.carolynmackler.com.

The inspiration for "Mona Lisa, Jesus, Chad, and Me": One of the things about growing up for which I was least prepared was that some friends slipped away. There wasn't even a falling-out. It was usually just a drifting apart, developing different views on sex, guys, life, religion, and love. But it didn't hurt any less. And it always took me a while to sort through what it meant to let friends go and accept that they may never come back."

Sarah Mlynowski is the international bestselling author of *Milkrun*, *Fishbowl*, and *As Seen on TV* (all from Red Dress Ink). Her first teen novel, *Bras & Broomsticks* (Delacorte, 2005), is being translated into ten languages. Check out her website and say hello at www.sarahmlynowski.com.

The inspiration for "The Perfect Kiss": "Growing up, I expected my sixteenth birthday to be a magical moment of metamorphosis. My breasts would blossom into C-cups, I'd develop a profound understanding of both politics and my parents, and a devastatingly handsome man, possibly answering to the name of Matt Dillon, would materialize by my side. My story was inspired by the juxtaposition between these lofty expectations and how I actually spent my sixteenth birthday: bedridden (still flat-chested and unprofound) with mono instead of Matt."

Sonya Sones is the author of *Stop Pretending: What Happened When My Big Sister Went Crazy* (HarperCollins, 1999), a novel-in-verse for teens, which has received a Christopher Award, the Myra Cohn Livingston Award for Poetry, the Claudia Lewis Poetry Award, and the Gradiva Poetry Award, and was a finalist for the Los Angeles Times Book Prize. Her second novel-in-verse, *What My Mother Doesn't Know* (Simon and Schuster, 2001), was named an International Reading Association Young Adult Choice, a Booklist Editor's Choice, and a New York Public Library Book for the Teen Age, and was placed on the Texas Lone Star Reading List, as well as being nominated for ten state awards. Both novels were chosen by the American Library Association as Best Books for Young Adults and Top Ten Quick Picks for Reluctant Young Adult Readers. Her newest novel-in-verse is *One of Those Hideous Books Where the Mother Dies* (Simon and Schuster, 2004). Find out more at www.sonyasones.com.

The inspiration for "Cat Got Your Tongue?": "For me, turning sixteen meant finally, *finally* getting my driver's license! "Cat Got Your Tongue?" was inspired by something that actually happened to me when I was much older than sixteen, but it was fun to imagine how I might have reacted if the same thing had happened on the very day that I had first gotten my license."

Zoe Trope is the pseudonym for a seventeen-year-old writer in Oregon. She is the author of *Please Don't Kill the Freshman* (HarperTempest, 2003), a memoir of her high-school years. For her sixteenth birthday, she ate a gyro, went bowling, and read magazines with a friend. You can reach her via e-mail at zoe_trope@hotmail.com or read her blog at www.zoe-trope.com.

The inspiration for "Relent/Persist": "You will never love anyone like you loved at sixteen. Nothing can ever compare."

Ned Vizzini began his writing career in high school in the late nineties. He is the author of *Teen Angst? Naaah* (Free Spirit, 2000) and the forthcoming novel *Be More Chill* (Hyperion/Miramax Books, 2004). *Teen Angst? Naaah* . . . was honored by New York Is Book Country, BookSense, the American Library Association, and the New York Public Library. Ned maintains nedvizzini.com and does his best to keep up with the loving contingent of dorks and rejects who e-mail him through the site (you can, too). He lives in Park Slope, New York.

The inspiration for "Rutford Becomes a Man": "When I was about sixteen, I had very elaborate conspiracy theories about how the Cool (with a capital C) people ran the world and made a concerted effort to baffle and shame the Uncool people. I told my dad about this, and he told me I needed to get to a shrink; furthermore, if I were in the Wild West, he said, he would just send me to the whorehouse and I'd turn out fine.

Joseph Weisberg's *10th Grade* (Random House, 2002) was named one of the Top Ten Novels of 2002 by *Entertainment Weekly*. It was also a New York Times Notable Book and won the Young Adult Library Association's Alex Award for adult novels that appeal to teenage readers. Joseph's work has also appeared in *Slate, Glamour,* and a Chinese magazine with an untranslatable name.

The inspiration for "Kissing Lessons": "Sixteen was a big year for me because it was slightly less bad than all the years that came before it."

Jacqueline Woodson is the author of a number of novels for children and young adults. She has received numerous awards, including a National Book Award, a Boston Globe/Horn Book Award, and the Coretta Scott King Award. She lives in Brooklyn with her partner and young daughter.

The inspiration for "Nebraska 99": "When I was growing up in Brooklyn, sixteen was about becoming a real girl—and all that that implied. I knew at sixteen that I would never be this femmie girlie-girl that the world thought I should be. It was a year of struggle, compromise, and, eventually, a year where I came to accept who I was becoming."

about the editor

Megan McCafferty is the author of *Sloppy Firsts* (Crown, 2001), an American Library Association Top Ten Quick Pick for Reluctant Readers, an ALA Popular Paperback, and a New York Public Library Book for the Teen Age. Its sequel, *Second Helpings* (Three Rivers Press, 2003), was a *Booklist* Editors' Pick for one of the best novels of 2003. A former magazine editor and writer, Megan lives with her husband and young son in New Jersey. She is currently writing the third Jessica Darling novel, to be published by Three Rivers Press in 2005.

The inspiration behind "Fifteen Going On . . .": "I was devastated when I found out that my best friend was moving midway through my freshman year of high school, not long before my birthday. I stayed home with a vague, phlegmy illness throughout her last week in school. Even at the time, I was aware that my sickness was probably more psychosomatic than viral in nature. Like Jessica in the story, I just didn't want to go through the motions of best friendship, knowing that she would soon be gone. So instead of savoring our last moments, I avoided them altogether. Unfortunately, this is how I handled most of my problems when I was in high school."

Also by Megan McCafferty

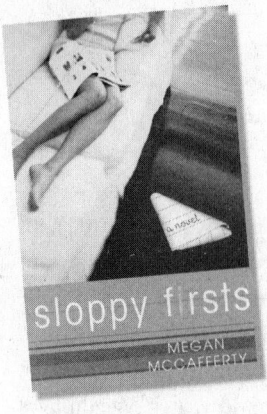

Megan McCafferty's fresh, funny, utterly compelling fiction debut tells the story of sixteen-year-old Jessica Darling as she embarks on another year of teenage torment at home and at school. A poignant and hilarious novel that's sure to appeal to readers who are still going through it, as well as those who are grateful that they don't have to go back and grow up all over again.

0-609-80790-0
$11.95 paperback

In the uproarious, much-anticipated sequel to *Sloppy Firsts*, hyperobservant, angst-ridden teenager Jessica Darling faces the social and emotional ordeal of her senior year at Pineville High. With keen intelligence, sardonic wit, and ingenious comic timing, Megan McCafferty again re-creates the tumultuous world of today's fast-moving and sophisticated teens.

0-609-80791-9
$10.95 paperback

THREE RIVERS PRESS
NEW YORK